Bloom Where You're Planted

Kari Joyner

To Beverly —
I hope you enjoy it! ♡

— Kari Joyner

For all those little girls out there who will go to bed tonight
without their mammas
For all those mammas out there who try again, even after
they fail
For all those sisters out there who fight for each other, who
believe in each other, who hold each other up in the bad
times and celebrate each other in the good times
For Shari Scott, the best baby sister on God's green Earth.

The Front Porch

2016

She usually slept in on Saturday mornings, but she had to finish her book this weekend, so she'd set her alarm clock for six, which meant she drug herself out of bed a little after seven. She put on a pot of coffee and decided to risk sneaking into the kids' rooms to gather their dirty laundry and get an early start on her most dreaded weekend chore.

"Hey," she whispered to her twelve-year-old daughter as she opened the door, surprised to find her awake at such an hour.

"Hey," croaked her daughter.

"You don't have to get up, baby. It's still early. I'm just gathering up the laundry. Hey, don't forget I'm writing today--"

The girl interrupted her mother, rolling her hazel eyes to add emphasis as she spoke. "I know, I know. We are not to bother you while you are writing unless there is *actual* fire or *actual* blood," she recited, as she rolled from her stomach to her back in order to better see her mother's face. "You think you'll finish it today?" she asked, sleep still thickly coating her voice.

"God, I hope so, little girl," she answered as she poked around her daughter's room. "If I don't, I think I'm gonna start a bonfire in the front yard tonight 'n' burn the damn thing," she laughed. "You and your brother can roast marshmallows over its fiery corpse."

"God, you're so morbid, Mom," she said as she propped herself up on her elbow, watching her mother bend to pick up dirty socks. "Anyway, you're not burning anything until you let me read it first. You know you promised me I could read it forever ago."

"Yeah, yeah," she sighed, satisfied that all the casually discarded items of clothing had been located. *Oh, to be a young girl again,* she thought, *ignorant about how laundry gets from the floor to the drawer...Oh well, I'll let her enjoy the oblivion while she still can.* "I'm gonna venture into your brother's room for his laundry. Wish me luck," she said, rolling her eyes and smirking. Y'all are on your own for breakfast."

"Got it."

"You know where to find me if you need me." She stepped over a pile of books and papers, heading for the door.

"Good luck finishing it. Come get me if you want me to just do it for you," the daughter muttered into her pillow as she snuggled into her still-warm bed, readying herself for a few more hours of delicious Saturday morning sleep.

She was still smiling at her daughter's humor as she shut one bedroom door and headed down the hallway to open another. She crept over to her son's bed and stared down at him sleeping peacefully. His cheeks were still just a little chubby, but the tell-tale features of adolescence were rapidly encroaching on the few remaining remnants of that sweet baby face. She knew she should leave him alone, but she couldn't help herself. She reached down to feel what was left of the squishy part of his cheek. She hadn't meant to wake him, but he stirred and opened his sleepy blue eyes.

"Hey, mister. Good morning."

"Mamma, nooo," he whined, closing his eyes tight against the morning sunshine streaking in through the curtains. He covered his head with his blanket.

"You don't have to get up, baby. I'm just starting laundry. Oh, and don't forget I'm writing today--"

Again, she was interrupted. "I know, Mamma. When you're writing we have to leave you alone. You didn't have to wake me up just to tell me that," he complained, head still under cover. "What's for breakfast?"

He sounds like a tiny, grumpy old man. Little brat, she thought with affection. "Whatever you make, kiddo. You're on your own today. I'll be on the porch 'til around four. That's when that man's supposed to be here."

"Aw man, that's gonna be so weird, Mamma," he said, sitting up in his bed. "Does he *have* to come here?"

"Oh, don't be so dramatic, little grandpa. He's probably just gonna be here for a little bit. You don't even have to meet him if you don't want to."

"Do you promise?"

"Yes, I promise," she answered, as she gathered his dirty laundry.

"What about my sleepover, huh? If you're with *him* all night, who's gonna take me?"

"I told you it probably won't take that long."

"Fine," he acquiesced.

"Fine, punk."

"Fine, punk," he repeated as he plopped backwards in his bed with all the force he could muster at such an early hour.

Finally got a little giggle out of the cranky ol' thing, she mused. "Don't forget I'm super busy today!" she called, as she exited his room and headed for her least favorite place in the house: the laundry room.

"*You* don't forget!" he called.

"No, *you* don't forget!"

They kept this up as she walked away until they couldn't hear each other anymore. Play-arguing was how they showed their affection for each other these days. His choice, not hers. She would've rather had a hug or a snuggle. But good luck getting very many of those from an eleven-year-old boy. *I'll take what I can get,* she mused, shrugging her shoulders and smiling.

After she got the laundry going, she made herself a cup of coffee and headed out to the porch with the mug, her phone, and a cigarette. She wondered if it was too early to call her sister. She thought for a moment and remembered there was a craft fair this weekend. Her sister would have just finished the night shift at the local hospital where she worked as a nurse and would soon be packing up her homemade soaps and bath salts to sell at the fair.

She lit her cigarette and scrolled through her calls until she saw her sister's face, thinking what a shame it was that her little sister, one of the people she loved most in the world, was so far down on the recently called list. They talked every day, but mostly through text messages because they were both so busy with work and kids.

"Yesss?" her sister answered, impersonating a deep, manly voice.

"What's up, chicken butt?"

"Just got off work, gettin' ready for that craft show in the city. You comin' today?" she asked, now using her normal voice.

"Hmmm, let's see….uhhh… nope. No, I'm not," she joked as she took a puff of her cigarette and sipped coffee.

"You're smoking, aren't you?" her little sister asked.

"Yep," she managed as she exhaled a large plume of smoke.

"I thought we were quitting! I'm gonna be the only organic bath product salesman in the world who tells people about how healthy it is to use all this shit while puffin' away on a stogie! We *have* to quit!"

"I know. We will. Just let me get finished with this stupid book first. Then I won't be so stressed out, and we can quit together."

"Right," little sister countered sarcastically. "I forgot you were *unplugging* today to try to write your ending. Have you started yet?"

"Uh, what do *you* think? It's not even eight o'clock on Saturday morning. I haven't even had a whole cup of coffee yet." They both laughed.

"You better get started. You know how fast a day can go. Oh! And the *mystery man's* supposed to be there today! Are you *so* excited?"

She sighed. "Yes. No. I don't know. Nervous, I guess. That's the reason I called. What do you think I should wear?"

"Hmm - good question. What were you thinking? Give me some choices and I'll pick."

"I was thinking maybe just jeans, y'know? Like, maybe it won't be so awkward if I'm just dressed comfortable."

"Ehh - I guess - but don't you think you want to be a *little* dressed up? Like, so he knows you think this is important to you?"

"Yeah, maybe. I hadn't thought about it that way. I could just wear what I have on now," she teased.

"Which is…?"

"A gross, old, holey t-shirt that comes down to my knees, no bra, and flannel pajama pants with Christmas trees all over them, complete with my lovely plastic Crocs, of course."

"Niiice...goin' for the homeless look, I see. Good choice, good choice."

They both laughed and talked for a few more minutes, finally deciding that she should wear the jeans, but nice ones with a nice, dressy shirt, which was what she would have worn anyway, but it made her less nervous after discussing it with her sister.

"Okay, I'm going."

"I was gonna say it before you!" Her sister pretended to be incensed.

"Well, I'm busier than you. Plus, I was done talkin' to you. You're so boring."

"Ha. Ha. You're soooo hilarious. I love you."

"I love you more."

"I don't think so. Hey! Before you go, just remember that you met this guy online. He could be a freak. Or a murderer or something. Be careful. And promise you'll answer the phone if I call to check on you."

"I know. I'm not getting my hopes up, and I'll keep the phone right next to me. Good luck peddlin' your soap today."

"Okay, thanks. Love you!"

"Love you too!" They hung up, and she felt better about everything.

Alright. Enough stalling. Time to finish this book, she told herself. She took one last puff of the cigarette she wasn't supposed to be smoking and crushed the butt into the cool grass beside the porch steps.

She had always loved old, sprawling farmhouses. As a child, she had romanticized them in her head. Now that she had one of her own, the reality of owning an older home - leaky roof, old pipes, rotting wood - was not so idealistic. But the porch made up for any and all inconvenience. It served as her outdoor office whenever possible because of the view of the wide, blue Oklahoma sky and the gnarled, towering, hundred year-old, papershell pecan trees that grew wild throughout the property. The porch was big enough for a swing and two nice, comfortable Adirondack chairs set far enough back that some semblance of privacy could be obtained, despite the fact that a newly asphalted neighborhood street had recently replaced the old, mostly deserted bumpy dirt road that used to curve around in front of the house. Someone had bought up all the land around the old farm and started building a community of sprawling country homes. But she didn't mind. It was nice to see people every now and then out and about, enjoying the outdoors.

Several hours remained before she even had to think about her meeting, and she had already decided she would not let the thought of it distract her. For her own sanity, she had to finish this book. The ending had been weighing on her for weeks now. Hearing from her estranged mother hadn't helped. *Crap, I'm letting my mind wander again!* she thought. *Focus! If you start thinking about her, you'll never get anything done! You need to finish this!*

She opened her laptop, logged in and set the computer aside to let the book load. After taking a sip of coffee and realizing it was now lukewarm, she got up to refill her cup. Out in the road, she noticed an older gentleman was standing, staring at the house. She waved, and, seemingly caught off guard, the man waved back. *Maybe he's looking for a lost dog or something,* she shrugged. It wasn't uncommon for people to lose track of their animals around her house. She figured it was the wooded area just behind the back property-line calling to their wild instincts. *Oh, well,* she thought, turning her attention back to the task at hand: *coffee.*

Returning with a fresh cup, an ink pen and a battered, marked up hard copy of her unfinished manuscript in tow, she settled in. She was glad she'd decided to throw on a sweater while she'd been inside. Springtime could be a deceiving season for a less experienced Oklahoman. With luxurious sunrays warming a pristinely cloudless sky, a person who hadn't lived there all her life might assume she could get away with wearing shorts, maybe even going barefoot. But the lifers knew better. The temperature might be comfortable one minute, then, with one soft breeze, it would become frigid. *Not quite warm enough for bare arms yet,* she thought as she shook off a small shivery wind that stirred the loose hair at the back of her neck.

Gently tossing the manuscript onto the brightly flowered cushion in the empty chair beside her, she pushed clunky, plastic rimmed glasses up on her nose, tucked behind her ears several strands of fine blonde hair that had escaped from a still damp bun, picked up her laptop, and started reading.

Not five minutes later, the words, "Excuse me, young lady," startled her.

She looked up to find the older gentleman, who had been standing in the road, now stood at the foot of the porch steps. She'd been lost in thought and hadn't even noticed him walk up.

"Hi," she said, trying to hide the fact that she was annoyed and embarrassed -- annoyed at the interruption and embarrassed by the fact that she was in her pajamas. And braless. She forgot about all that though, when she noticed the man's face was red and sweaty. He seemed as if he might be struggling to breathe. "Are you okay?"

"Well," the man said in a shaky voice, "I - to be honest with you, I don't think I am."

The innate courtesy most midwestern girls are raised to cultivate kicked in, and, without hesitation, she said, "Here, please, sit down." She set her laptop aside and hastily stood to clear off the chair beside her so the man could sit. "Can I get you anything? Is there anyone I could call for you?" she asked, slightly alarmed.

"I could really use a glass of water if it's not too much trouble," the man managed as he looked up at her and attempted a smile.

"Sure. Yeah, of course. You just rest. I'll be right back." She rushed into the kitchen and grabbed a clean glass from the dishwasher. She let the water run from the tap for a few seconds until it felt cold to the touch, and then she filled the glass. As she rushed back outside, she had two thoughts: One, *Should I call my sister? She's a nurse; she'd know what to do.* And two, *Do I have time to run and put on a bra?* She decided *not yet* was the right answer to both questions and continued on her course.

Maybe he was just winded. No sense overreacting. After a few minutes, if he still seemed like he was having a hard time, she'd either call her sister or call 9-1-1, depending on how serious the situation was.

"Oh, thank you, young lady. I'm so sorry about this," the man apologized. When he switched her manuscript to his left hand in order to accept the glass of water, she realized, half mortified, that he had been reading it! The shock must have registered on her face because he said, "Oh, I'm sorry. I just saw it sitting there and picked it up. Thought it might take my mind off the way I was feelin'. I didn't mean to impose. Is it yours? Did you write it?" he asked.

"Oh, it's fine, really. It's just something I've been toying with." *And never let anyone read - not even my sister*, she thought, annoyed. "It's not ready for people to read yet. You seem like you're feeling a little better," she said, attempting to steer the conversation away from her book. His face was still sweaty, but not as ruddy as it had been. He still seemed a little out of breath.

"I am feeling a little better, and I thank you for the water. If it's no trouble, I'd like to sit here for a few minutes and get my breath back though. He set the glass of water down on the old cable spool that served as a table, still maintaining eye contact and showing no sign of setting her manuscript aside.

"Sure," she said, making her way back to the chair she'd been sitting in before the man's arrival. "I was just sitting out here trying to write an ending to that thing." She gestured toward the manuscript. "You're welcome to join me."

"That sure is nice of you, but I don't want to bother you if you're trying to get your work done. Are you a writer?" he asked, genuinely interested.

"No, not really," she said as she looked down at her lap. "I *wish* I was a writer. I'm actually a schoolteacher. High school English," she said, smiling politely. *Wonder how old he is,* she thought to herself. If she had to guess, she'd say he was in his early sixties. He still had most of his light brown hair and was a bit weathered around the forehead and temples, but the eyes were still a vibrant blue. His clothes, faded Levis, a plain navy sweatshirt, and Nike tennis shoes could easily have been those of a sixty-year-old man's. *He seems healthy,* she mused, wondering still if she should call someone. *I'd rather not have my Saturday morning ruined by this complete stranger having some sort of attack out here on my front porch,* she reasoned, then immediately chided herself for thinking such selfish thoughts.

"But you want to be a writer?"

"Oh, most definitely!" she replied, a little too emphatically.

"Well, if you don't mind my asking, why hasn't anybody ever read this thing?" he asked, lifting the manuscript slightly.

"Uh, well, I guess I've never let anyone read it because I'm afraid of what they'll say." She was appalled at herself. Why was she telling this stranger things she'd never even admitted to *herself?*

"I could read it for you."

She fake laughed, a nervous habit she'd picked up at a very young age and used unconsciously whenever she felt uncomfortable. "What? You mean - *now?* Oh, I don't think so."

"Sure. If not now, then when? I was out for a walk before I came up to your porch, not because I enjoy walking, but because it's such a beautiful day." He looked out at the clear blue sky. "I wanted to spend it doing something outside. Why not this?" He smiled.

It was a tempting offer. She didn't know this person, so she didn't have to care what he thought. He could be her guinea pig. "Why not?" she laughed again, but more genuinely this time, giddy at the prospect of an actual, real-life person reading her manuscript. "Sure, why not?"

He smiled back at her. "Well, alright then. He settled into the cushioned Adirondack chair, looked down at the manuscript, and began to read.

Joyce

Chapter One

1969

God, it's been so long since I've seen her happy, thought Kate. Mom was standing in the front yard under the Arizona sun, looking up at Dad. They were laughing at each other. Mom wore white shorts that fanned out mid-thigh and narrowed up to the waist where three navy-blue buttons on each side fastened vertically from just below the hip bones up to the smallest part of her waist. They were stiff cotton, and freshly ironed creases, razor sharp perfection, ran down the center of each leg. A sliver of Mom's slim, sun-tanned abdomen was exposed, and the fitted white cotton top, displaying a neat, perfectly symmetrical line of matching navy buttons, was held in place by thin, white straps that crisscrossed in the back. Kate remembered watching Mom make the outfit. She had ripped a picture of a Hollywood starlet wearing the same shorts suit from a magazine, hung it on the wall above her old Singer sewing machine, and worked feverishly through the night to produce a perfect replica the very next morning.

As she watched her parents running around in the front yard like a couple of kids, Kate allowed her thoughts to wander back to the morning Mom had finished making the shorts suit. Sparks of excitement, so real that Kate thought she might be able to reach out and catch them if she had been just a little faster, seemed to dance from

Mom's eyes and out into their living room like fireflies at dusk. Mom stripped down to her underwear and bra right in front of Kate and her sisters. She slipped one long, slender, tanned leg into the shorts, then the other. She hurriedly shimmied into the top and motioned to Kate.

"Katie Rhea!" (Mom was the only one who called her by her given name - and Mom's family, people Kate had spoken to only a few times in her life, mostly through letters, sometimes on the telephone, as they lived in Oklahoma, which was several states away from their home.) "Katie Rhea!" Mom yelled again over the blaring country music that perpetually played on the radio. This time it was "Stand by Your Man," sung by a woman Mom adored, Tammy Wynette. "Come 'ere 'n' help Mamma! Hurry up," she yelled, smiling, laughing, dancing.

Feeling special because Mom had trusted her over her sisters, Beverly and Birdie, to do the honors, Kate tripped over to Mom and fumbled for the hidden zipper in the right side of the crisp, white shorts, silently praying her hands were clean. Then she slid the smooth, white zipper tab from the middle of Mom's slender hip all the way up to the tiniest part of her copper colored waist. They fit perfectly. Mom, pleased with her accomplishment, hopped up and down, clapping her long, graceful, neatly manicured hands. As if on cue, Beverly, Birdie and Kate imitated her, all admiring their mother's talent and beauty, laughing and dancing freely.

Kate's thoughts jerked back to watching her parents in the front yard when she heard Dad yell through fits of laughter, "Joyce! Stop it!" He peered through his hands, spread wide in front of his face, palms out, as he ducked and ran around the yard, gulping and giggling breathlessly. His black-as-coal hair was cut close to his scalp, a military haircut, even though Dad had finished his service before Beverly, the oldest of the three girls, had been born. His light blue shirt was streaked with dark blue wetness.

Mom's bare, brown feet seemed to float above the crisp, dying grass in the yard, and Kate thought, *She is beautiful. I want to be just like her when I grow up.*

By this time, Kate had figured out that she must be dreaming. Mom's skin was too shimmery to be anything but imaginary, Dad's teeth too white. The water from the hose, too cold and too clean to be real, glittered in the sunlight. Kate refused to let herself fully acknowledge that this was only happening in her mind. She pushed reality aside and willed herself to concentrate on one thing and one thing only: the dream. She knew it was going to end all too quickly, and she wanted to enjoy every second of it before the harsh reality of what her life had become would demand all her energy and attention.

Mom cornered Dad between their old, silver Chevrolet and the front porch of their neat, tidy house. She had him trapped. She held the garden hose folded in her hands, fingers twitching with mischievous impatience. Through involuntary start-stop chuckles, Dad begged Mom not to spray him, knowing all the while, as they all did, that there was no hope for him. Mom straightened the grass-green plastic hose, softened and faded by the never-ending sun and laughed maniacally as she annihilated Dad.

The dream was so real, Kate could feel the heat of the day on her back even as the reality that none of this was actually happening asserted itself and became too obvious to be ignored for much longer. She felt the mist of water bouncing off Dad, but it was not cold as she had expected. It was warm, and her clothes were stuck uncomfortably to her itchy back. Reluctantly, regretfully, she opened her eyes and let the dream slip from her grasp.

"Goddammit, Beverly!" Kate yelled. How can you piss the bed and sleep right through it?"

She reached to her right over her body and whipped the damp sheet and blanket off all three of them. Beverly was awake, but barely. She was still groggy. Her bright, red hair stood up all over her head like a tangled mass of copper electrical wire.

"Birdie! Get up! Beverly's pissed the bed again!"

Birdie lay on her right side, facing the wall. Kate shook her, but it did no good. She ended up standing at the foot of the bed and dragging Birdie by her ankles until her feet were far enough down that when Kate released them, they fell with a thud to the dingy, cheaply-tiled floor. Finally, Birdie was awake.

Soaked in her own urine, Beverly stood watching her sisters.

"How can you be almost ten years old, almost *two* whole years older than me and still be peeing the goddamn bed? What the hell is *wrong* with you?"

Birdie began to whimper and let her body slump to the floor. "I'm telling Mom, Kate! You're not our boss," she spat through sleepy, angry sobs, chunks of her tangled, wavy chestnut hair stuck by her tears to her reddened cheeks. Her nose was beginning to run.

Kate eyed Birdie. "Shut your ass up, you big ol' silly! Do you want to lay in a puddle of your big sister's piss all night and wake up in the morning smelling like you peed your pants when you go to school? If you *do*, I'm not taking you with me! And tomorrow's show-and-tell day. So, you just lay there on the floor, ya big ol' baby, and bawl like a stupid idiot. I don't give a shit!"

Kate turned her attention from Birdie to Beverly: "Beverly! *Bev-er-ly*! Wake *up* and help me strip the *bed*!"

Beverly had crawled into a corner of the room and gone back to sleep already, wet clothes and all.

Damn, thought Kate.

Seething, she stripped the tattered mattress and hauled the urine-soaked bedding to the bathroom, where she threw it into the rusting ceramic tub. As she tramped through the living room on her way to the kitchen, flipping on the lights, Kate surprised the cockroaches, who scattered so quickly it would make someone who didn't know better wonder if they'd really seen anything at all. She prayed there would be dish soap. She already knew not to even check for laundry soap; it had been used up days ago. *Please, please, please. Let there be dish soap* she prayed. Kate was in luck. What was left of the thick, yellow dishwashing liquid had oozed to the top of the bottle, which was resting upside down, propped up between the wall and the back of the faucet on its lid so that not even a drop would go to waste.

Tiptoeing to reach it on the ledge behind the sink, Kate stretched her fingers as far as she could to knock the bottle off balance and let it fall into the basin where she could reach it.

After retrieving the bottle from the sink, she made her way back to the bathroom. Kate ran hot, steaming water into the tub, plugged it, and used as little soap as possible to scrub the soiled sheets, wishing for some bleach, even just a capful. At first, bending over the side of the tub, Kate scrubbed furiously, taking her anger out on the white, threadbare sheets, heavy with water. But, eventually, her arms and back fatigued, and the warm, soapy water began to wash away her anger. Left in its place was that old, familiar feeling again. *I want my mom.* The thought of Mom reminded Kate of her dream. She caught herself wishing they were back there in that world, a world that meant clean laundry and routines and full bellies. And Dad. But most of all, it meant Mom. Kate felt hot tears sting her eyes, and she didn't fight them. She let them roll down her cheeks and drop into the sudsy, lemon-scented water.

As she rinsed the sheets and wrung them out as well as she could, her small body struggling to twist the material tightly enough to expel the water, she began to wonder where she was going to sleep and what she'd use to cover up with to stay warm. They had long since discarded all the spare blankets and sheets they had ever possessed. Though she was sweaty with exertion now, she knew that once she was able to find dry clothes and lie down, she would quickly cool down.

Once she had managed to wring them out, Kate, carefully balancing on the side of the tub, gripped each of the bulky, wet sheets, and, one at a time, she looped them over the rusty shower curtain rod to dry. She had to be especially cautious when she attempted this maneuver. The only way she was ever able to get the sheets onto the rod was to stand on the edge of the tub on her tippy toes, lean to one side, and (with all her might) sling the bedclothes as forcefully as she could. She had lost her balance once or twice when she had first started washing their sheets in the bathtub, and it had taught her some valuable lessons about taking her time when performing such a task.

After changing into dry clothes and draping the wet ones over the side of the tub, she slipped silently through the house to put the dish soap bottle back in its place. *Don't know why I'm bothering to be quiet*, she thought, as she passed by her sisters. *They sleep like the dead. Nothing could wake them up.* She turned off the light and headed through the door.

Kate was tempted, as she walked through the living room, to just sleep on the couch. The small ticking alarm clock on the rickety, wooden coffee table announced that it was well past one o'clock in the morning. It was highly unlikely that Mom would come home tonight. This couch wasn't as pretty or as comfortable as the one they'd had at the good house, but it sure beat the floor. Mom's old, tattered wedding ring quilt (off-limits to the kids), made by her mother and given to her on her wedding day, perched, neatly folded, on the back of the couch. But, even as Kate entertained the idea, she knew she wouldn't do it. It would mean she had given up hope.

Dish soap balanced upside down behind the sink again, Kate rummaged through the only closet in the tiny apartment hoping to find something to make the floor a little more comfortable. She skimmed over the sparse collection of the remnants of their past. Three matching white little girls' church dresses, each one size bigger than the last; two of Mom's old dresses, one black linen, one red satin, too fancy for her to wear in her new life; and several shirts and pairs of pants, long outgrown by Beverly and Kate, barely even fitting Birdie anymore, sagged on old, bent, twisted wire hangers. Again, Kate felt that familiar pang in her chest. Memories of a better life assaulted her as she stepped back to slide the thin, hollow closet door between her and what used to be. But she stopped short when something toward the back of the closet caught her eye. *Mom's white coat.* Not white exactly, more of a cream. Mom had always called it "winter white." Kate slipped her arm between the coat and the other clothes and pushed them away from it. Too small to reach the top of the hanger, she unbuttoned the coat's top button and yanked it down. It was wool, and it smelled like Mom. Not like stale beer and cheap whiskey, the way she smelled now, but like she used to smell. Kate breathed in deeply, taking in all at once the perfume Mom used to wear, her soap, and the faint scents of a mixture of tobacco, Dad, and home. Kate wrapped herself in the coat, lay on the floor in front of the closet, and let the memories come, along with the tears. As she cried herself to sleep, it wasn't the loss of their house or their friends or their furniture that she mourned. It wasn't even Dad, not really. She knew she could handle his absence because he was coming back someday. Dad had not chosen to leave them; he'd been forced to go. Kate knew that, as soon as humanly possible, Dad would run back to them. The thing Kate really missed, the thing she longed for, was her mom.

Kate remembered how she used to get irritated with Mom sometimes for never letting her alone to play. She seemed like she always wanted Kate with her, always wanted to teach her something. If Mom was sewing, she wanted Kate beside her so she could teach her the cross stitch, or a blanket stitch. If Mom was cooking, she wanted Kate in the kitchen with her so she could teach her how to bake a cake or prepare a chicken. She used to listen carefully to Kate's questions and seemed like she always had the perfect answer for everything. Now, even when Mom was home, she seemed like, even though her body was there, in her head, she was somewhere else. When Kate would try to talk to Mom about something that had happened at school, or tell her a story about Beverly or Birdie, Mom would only reply with words like, "Yeah?" Or, "Uh-huh?" Or, "Oh," which meant she wasn't really listening at all. Eventually, Kate stopped trying to talk to Mom because it was the loneliest feeling in the world to know that her mother didn't care. She would rather Mom yell at her when she was drunk and mad at the world than ignore her the way she did sometimes.

Kate ached for her real mom, not the mean, miserable drunk who had taken her place. The last thing that occurred to the little girl before she fell asleep was that her birthday was coming up. Surely Mom would remember.

Chapter Two

Joyce did not return the next day; Beverly, Kate and Birdie woke themselves up, got dressed, and walked themselves to school. Though it was only the beginning of October, this was their third school so far this year. None of them had made a single friend at this new school. Why should they? They all knew the routine by now: start a new school, make friends, settle in. Then Mom would start to drink, a little at first, but more and more as the days went by. Soon, she'd start staying out until the wee hours of the morning, eventually not bothering to come home at all. The girls would worry, wonder where she was, and pray she wasn't hurt or worse. Then she'd show up and announce they were moving. They'd load the beat-up Cadillac with as much as it could hold and leave everything else behind to start anew somewhere else. It seemed like things got a little worse with each move. The houses or apartments they rented got a little more run-down, the food and money seemed to run out a little faster, and Mom seemed to disappear earlier and stay gone for longer periods of time. The only thing that seemed more plentiful was the roaches.

They were becoming three lonely little vagabonds. Their clothes were dirty, worn, and ill-fitting. All three girls were acutely aware of how they looked, but they did not dare miss school. When Joyce had first started disappearing, leaving the girls to fend for themselves for days at a time, they had been giddy at the thought of not having to go to school. That is, until they got hungry. Very quickly all three realized that school, for them, meant food. So, even though they had no money, no clothes, no friends, they dragged themselves to school every single morning. The other kids were mean to them, calling them names, telling them they smelled bad. But, for two meals a day, they would endure the teasing.

"Kate," asked Birdie, "do I get to go to the big kid class with you today?"

"If you're good you do. The teacher said at the end of the day any kid with a little brother or sister could come to our class for show-and-tell."

"But we don't have anything to show for show-and-tell!"

"That's okay. We can just watch the other kids."

Kate felt guilty for the way she had talked to Birdie last night when Beverly had peed the bed. She was the youngest one, barely starting the first grade. She didn't understand why Mom had become so erratic. She didn't understand that their father had been sent to prison and wouldn't be coming home any time soon, or that there was no home for him to come back to. All she knew was that her life had been turned upside down. At least some of Kate's and Beverly's clothes could still be handed down to Birdie; she didn't look quite as much like a little beggar as the older sisters did. *I'm gonna try to make life a little easier on Birdie Kay*, Kate thought as they walked to school that morning. *She's the one who got to know Mom and Dad at their best for the least amount of time out of us three girls. My dad would want me to look after my little sister. But I'm not doin' shit for Beverly.*

The school day dragged by for Kate. She hadn't gotten much sleep the night before because of Beverly, and, even when she finally *had* laid down to rest, she'd slept fitfully, waking with every little noise, thinking maybe Mom had come home after all. After lunch, with her belly full, the restless night caught up with her and she began to nod off during silent reading time. It was all she could do to keep her eyes open.

Finally, the first graders who had older siblings in the third grade were escorted in for third grade show-and-tell day. Birdie put her little chin in the air and proudly marched to her big sister's desk.

"Hey, I know you!" She grinned at Kate. "Candice! Candice!" Birdie called to another first grader with yellow pigtails and snaggle teeth. "This is my big sister Kate!" Birdie bounced on her tiptoes with excitement. Kate waved at Candice who waved back enthusiastically and then went to find her big brother Joshua. The classroom was all abuzz.

"Third graders, remember, we are on our best behavior today. We are going to be what?" The teacher held her hand to her ear, a signal for her students to repeat what she had practiced with them earlier in the day.

"Good examples," the third graders repeated in unison.

"Very good, class! Now, make sure that if you have a little brother or sister visiting you today that you find him or her a nice, comfy place to sit."

Once all the children were finally settled, Birdie sitting cross-legged on the floor alongside Kate and the other children, show-and-tell began. The first boy had brought a real live turtle to show. He passed the turtle around and told the class that he had found it in his backyard. So far, Kate was not impressed, but Birdie sat mesmerized. The next student was Vi, a little girl Kate loathed. She was always dressed to the nines, her hair perfectly coiffed, and Kate thought she was the meanest little bitch she had ever met in all the schools she had ever attended. Vi made Kate's school days a living hell. She was always leading the pack whenever the kids got bored and decided to pick on her. Kate secretly hoped that Vi would trip and fall as she was going up to give her presentation. Of course, the little brat had the neatest show-and-tell item. It was a real-life parasol she'd gotten when her family had taken a trip to China that summer. All the other kids were rapt with curiosity; Birdie was in awe. Kate was disgusted. She put the gold necklace her dad had given her in her mouth and leaned back on her hands trying to seem as uninterested as possible in Vi's stupid parasol. The necklace was one of the few possessions Kate still had that she took pride in. Dad had given it to her for her seventh birthday. It was real gold, and a dainty little K hung from the chain. She had gotten into the habit of putting the K in her mouth whenever she was bored or tired or fidgety. Leaning back on her hands with the K in her mouth, Kate dozed off before she could stop herself.

She was shaken awake by the red-headed boy sitting next to her. She had been dreaming of Mom and Arizona again.

"Mom, I don't want to plant yellow flowers," Kate whined. "I want pink or red!"

"Well look who got all high and mighty, little Miss Priss! We always plant golden Lantana! It's sa pretty, sweetheart!"

"Well I don't like it," harrumphed the little girl. Mom lifted herself out of the cool dirt in the newly dug flower garden in front of the house and walked over to meet her daughter. "Come 'ere, Katie Rhea. Help Mamma get these in the ground," she coaxed. "It'll be fun. Y'know why we always plant golden Lantana? Huh?" asked Mom, handing Kate a small shovel and guiding her hand to show her how deep the hole should be dug. "Well, all flowers are pretty, but some are stronger than others. We plant this because it gets hot in Arizona. If a flower's gonna have a chance at livin' around here, it's gotta be tough. Gotta be able ta handle the heat 'n the bugs too." Mom patiently aided Kate in shaking one of the Lantanas out of its plastic container and watched as her middle daughter slid the flowering plant into the freshly dug earth. "Ain't a lotta water here neither. These flowers gotta go a long time sometimes without even a little drink. And me 'n' yer daddy get busy. We got a diner ta run and three mean little girls ta raise," she teased. Kate looked up from her planting quickly when she heard the part about the three mean little girls, but instantly recognized the look on her mother's face as one of mirthful teasing and so went back to her planting project as her mother continued to speak.

"Hey, baby. Look at Mamma." Kate raised her head again and gave her mother her full attention. "We choose these flowers over all the others because they're strong. They're survivors. They grow no matter what tries ta stop 'em. Every time I plant these yellow flowers, I learn a lesson from 'em."

"You learn lessons from flowers, Mom?"

"Yep. I sure do. I wish I could tell you life's always gonna be pink 'n red flowers for you, baby. I do. But that just ain't the truth. Sometimes things are gonna be just plain hard. But you gotta keep on growin', like this flower, little girl. No matter what. You hear me?"

"Yes. But I still want pink and red flowers, Mom." Mom patted Kate's small, blonde head and smiled. "Sometimes we just gotta learn to be happy with what we got, kiddo. Lord knows sometimes it ain't much." She sighed and bent to help little Katie Rhea finish planting the flowers. They worked side by side in silence, helping each other when they needed to, content to be in each other's presence.

***

"Wake up, stupid!" The red-headed kid beside her had ahold of Kate's shoulder, violently shaking her with one hand while trying to hand off what looked like a wadded-up tissue with the other. The necklace fell from Kate's mouth during all the shaking and a long, slimy string of drool ran down her chin. Everyone in the room, including Birdie, was staring at Kate. Attempting to salvage what dignity she had left, she wiped her chin with her left hand and reached for the tissue with her right. She must have squeezed too tightly because she heard a small crushing noise and an audible gasp from everyone in the room as she took the tissue in her hand. Silence followed. As she opened her hand and looked into the tissue, she saw a tiny, blue speckled robin's egg. It had been crushed; runny, yellow yolk spilled from the ruined shell. Staring at the palm of her hand, Kate heard a child begin to wail, and she figured show-and-tell was over.

Chapter Three

For once, Kate was relieved the next time they moved. The robin's egg incident had been particularly mortifying with her baby sister there to witness it, and she was glad to put it behind her. Birdie had been very understanding, and, thankfully, she did not feel the need to share it with Beverly or Mom. All the girls had quickly figured out that naiveté was not a luxury any of them could afford in their new life; neither was telling everything you knew, especially to adults. That only brought unwanted trouble.

Beverly was the only one who was ever truly naive to the ways of the world, which was strange because she was the oldest of the three girls. When Dad had gone away and Mom had first begun drinking heavily, Beverly was the one who took it the hardest. She had started wetting the bed at night and washing her hands obsessively throughout the day. Kate, however, seemed to adapt to this new kind of life as if she'd been preparing for it since the day she was born. She also excelled at the other previously unneeded skills necessary for the survival of children of alcoholics: lying and fighting.

All the girls learned to lie at an early age, though. It helped them to avoid getting into trouble. When the girls still lived in Arizona and Mom and Dad were still running the diner, the girls would meet up after school outside Birdie's classroom and walk the six blocks together to the family diner. There, they would finish any homework they had been given and busy themselves in the back as not to get in the waitresses' and cooks' way when they served the early dinner crowd.

Kate, the orneriest of the three, one day decided it was time they all learned to smoke cigarettes. It was easy to sneak behind the counter and swipe a pack of smokes. The girls were a common fixture back there and, when the dinner rush was on, with all the hustle and bustle around them, no one even noticed Kate slipping the Camel cigarettes into the waistband of her skirt.

"Come on, Beverly! Stop bein' a chicken-shit! Go get us some matches!" The girls were in the bathroom reserved for employees, which was conveniently located in the back of the building. This was where they always went when maximum privacy was required.

"Kate, I'll get caught! I'm not as slick as you are! You just go do it."

"No way! I already got the cigarettes. You do it!" Kate, even at the ripe old age of seven, knew instinctively never to be the only one to blame. Sisters were less likely to cave and confess under duress when they couldn't pin the entire crime on another sister without also implicating themselves and the roles they had played in the perpetration. Therefore, if they were going to do this, each girl had to do her part. Equal culpability meant shared punishment, which was much easier to take, especially since Birdie was still a baby, as far as parents were concerned. Most older kids are innately jealous of younger siblings; they take all the attention. But Kate learned early on that this fact could be used to her advantage. When Mom was considering their punishment she was forced to consider that her precious Birdie was still a little bitty thing; she couldn't be too harsh on her; therefore, if Mom wanted to be fair, she had to dole out an easier punishment to all involved.

As the two older girls were arguing, Birdie walked away. She skipped up to the counter and said hello to Mr. Aires, a regular fixture at the diner. He was there almost every day. He never ate though. He just sat at the counter drinking black coffee and smoking cigarettes.

"What are you up to, young lady?"

"Nothin'. Just playin'."

"Well, you'd better stay out of your mamma and daddy's way. It's busy in here today."

"I will, Mr. Aires. I'm just gettin' us some candy. Don't tell Mom, 'kay?" Birdie, with her shiny brown, curly hair and big hazel eyes, could charm just about any adult, including Mr. Aires. Easy prey for an adorable five-year-old girl. She had learned early in life that the Oklahoma accent she'd picked up from Mom upped the cuteness factor several octaves because Arizona people had no accent to speak of. She used this to her advantage. Like Mom always said, "Girls, you gotta use all the tools the good lord gave ya if you're gonna make it in this world."

"I won't say a word if you promise to eat all your supper," Mr. Aires whispered. He winked at Birdie and went back to his coffee. Best not to witness the crime.

"Promise," smiled Birdie, knowing she had Mr. Aires right where she wanted him.

She was so short that, if she stood right next to the counter, no one sitting at the shiny red stools on the other side could even see the top of her head. She reached for three chocolate bars. And a pack of matches.

Kate and Beverly were still arguing when Birdie returned, matches in hand. She could see on her big sister's face that she was impressed. This made Birdie proud. Beverly only looked mad.

"I was gonna do it!" huffed Beverly, arms crossed.

"Yeah, yeah," grinned Kate. "Good work, Birdie Kay. What else did you get?"

"Nothin'," Birdie lied. Neither girl questioned their precious baby sister.

"Beverly, you think you could go lock the bathroom door, or are ya too chicken to even do that?"

"God, I hate you, Kate! You're so damn mean!"

"You better quit cussin' or I'm tellin' Mom, Beverly," chided Kate. This was a sister joke between all three girls. Mom had cussed fluently all their lives, but she refused to let the girls do it. She'd tell them they weren't old enough yet. She'd say that she'd let them know when they were. But whenever Mom wasn't within hearing distance, they practiced. They all knew from listening to Mom that there were unspoken gender rules associated with using such attractive words. Men were free to let any cuss word fly, but a lady, a real lady, was only to use certain cuss words: hell, damn (or any variation of damn, such as goddam, goddammit, and, Beverly's favorite, dammit-all-to-hell), and sonofabitch. A lady used shit sparingly, and a *real* lady never uttered the word fuck unless provoked to near uncontrollable rage. Even then it was to be used sparingly so that the word always retained its maximum warning value for whomever's benefit it was uttered. All three girls wanted to grow up to be ladies, just like Mom. So far, none of them had ever worked up the courage yet to use the "F" word.

Beverly laughed at Kate's inside joke, but only mildly so that Kate would know her older sister hadn't completely forgiven her for the chicken-shit remark. She locked the door and returned to her sisters to smoke her first cigarette.

The sharp smell of the sulfur dioxide from the match when first struck against the box was glorious. Kate lit her cigarette fist. She had watched every adult she ever knew do this a thousand times and had lately been paying close attention. She didn't even cough after her first puff. Birdie, impressed and eager to win the admiration of her sisters, went next. It took a few tries, but she finally got hers lit and only coughed a little. Of course, Beverly took forever. It was like she wasn't even really trying. Once she did take her first puff, she not only coughed, but she started choking. Her face turned red, then she ran to the toilet and threw up. *What a baby*. Both of her younger sisters looked on as Beverly splashed cold water on her face from the sink. When she studied her red, puffy face in the mirror, she could see both of her sisters' reflections. They wore expressions of utter disappointment.

The doorknob jiggled and panic took over. The girls began gathering up the evidence as whoever it was began knocking on the door. Then, "Anybody in there? Girls? Is that you? What are you doin' in there?"

"Nothin', Mom! We're just talkin' to Beverly while she poops," yelled Kate as she hurriedly wiped up cigarette ashes with a piece of wadded-up toilet paper.

"Well, hurry up and come outta there. The crowd's dyin' down, and I want y'all to eat your supper while it's slow."

"Alright! She's almost done! Can we have hamburgers tonight?"

"We'll see. Hurry up now. Y'all *better* not be in there playin' in the sink again! If I see one wad of toilet paper stuck up on the ceilin' ever' one a you girls is getting a spankin'! Y'hear me?"

"Yes, Mom," sang all three in unison, rolling their eyes and stifling giggles.

Finally, she went away. The girls flushed all the evidence down the toilet, and Kate stuck the pack of remaining cigarettes and the matches in the waistband of her skirt. They ran out of the bathroom after the color had returned to normal in Beverly's face.

Every day after school for the next several weeks the girls smoked cigarettes. They became quite good at it, even Beverly. The new routine was that they would meet up as usual after school and walk to the diner, but instead of going straight inside, they would head around to the back of the building and light up. They were very stealthy, and it took a whole month and a half for them to finally get busted. Thankfully, it was Dad who caught them. He was such an easy, loving man when it came to his girls, he just couldn't see them doing any wrong, ever. When he came around the corner, carrying a bag of trash, he ran right into Birdie, who was puffing away.

"Birdie Kay?" Dad using Birdie's first and middle names like that (the family's term of endearment for the baby of the house) made all the girls feel immediately guilty. He just stood there staring at his three girls, all smoking cigarettes, shock registering on his face. They all stared back, cigarettes poised in mid-air. Silence.

Finally, Dad spoke. "Girls, what in the world are y'all doin out here? You know what your mamma would do if she caught you all?" Even though Dad was from Arizona, he had picked up a little of Mom's midwestern dialect.

Kate pushed Birdie out in front toward Dad as if to say, "Do that cute thing you do and get us out of this!" Birdie took the hint and, discarding her cigarette, ran to Dad and hugged him around the tops of his thighs. "Daddy, we were just pretending we were grown-up ladies, fancy like Mom. Please don't tell, Daddy! Please! We promise to never ever do it again!"

Kate picked up where Birdie left off. She ran up and hugged Dad too, also promising never to smoke another cigarette as long as she lived (while silently lamenting that she had just wasted a perfectly good, half-smoked cigarette). Beverly, slow as usual, was the last to catch on.

"Well, now, girls, you know your mamma wouldn't like me keeping this from her."

All three girls stared up at their daddy, eyes wide, mouths open in shock at his betrayal. They looked innocent, and they knew it. They were all adorable on their own, but, when all three of them stood beside each other, they were irresistible. Dad always bragged that he had the prettiest girls in the world; Beverly was the prettiest red-head, Kate was the prettiest blonde, and Birdie was the prettiest brunette. All three girls had Mom's hazel eyes, though Kate's were the only ones shaped like Mom's too. Dad called them cat eyes and liked to tease Kate by saying that when a person had cat eyes, it meant they were always up to no good. He'd grab her cheeks playfully and look deep into her eyes and say, "This is my ornery one! She's just like her mamma!"

Of course, Don Bloom could not resist all three of his babies staring up at him, and he reluctantly agreed to keep his daughters' secret.

The girls walked around on pins and needles for days afterward, anxious and nervous that Dad would tell Mom. But he kept their secret. The day it happened they all swore off cigarettes. This pact lasted perhaps two weeks, but Kate, addicted to the glamorous allure of smoking, soon faltered and was back at it again, only much more careful about hiding her newfound habit. Birdie soon followed in her sister's footsteps. But Beverly seldom ever joined her sisters after their close call with Dad. She did, however, keep her sisters' secret.

***

The lies the girls told in their new life, with Dad gone and Mom often absent, were a little more complicated. At their next new school there was a young counselor who hadn't yet realized she couldn't save the world through public school counseling services. She was still doing her damndest to make a difference when she spotted Kate. She was always calling her out of class asking her questions. Kate liked Miss Bailey. She was pretty and young, and she always smelled like flowers. She wore high heels and lipstick. She seemed genuinely concerned with Kate's well-being. She smiled a lot, and when she laughed, it made Kate feel like laughing with her, something she rarely did anymore. Kate felt like she could talk to Miss Bailey.

"Hello, Kate. How are you today?"

"Hi, Miss Bailey. I'm good. How are you?"

"I'm fine. How are your sisters doing?"

"They're good. Why?"

"Well, Kate, I've noticed some things about you and your sisters, and I'm a little worried that you're not being taken care of the way you should be. Is everything okay at home?"

"What do you mean?"

"Well, I mean, sometimes you girls seem like you're tired in class. Some of your teachers have mentioned that you even sometimes fall asleep. One of your teachers told me that she isn't sure you're getting enough food at home. Are you getting enough to eat?"

Alarm bells went off in Kate's head. Mom had told them all they should never trust the people at the school. She had said if people knew about their life they wouldn't understand and that they might try to take the girls away to live somewhere else. And that no one would ever want to take on three new children, so they would most likely separate the girls, send them to live in separate homes. They might never see each other again. Kate could never let this happen. She had already lost so much. She would not lose Mom and her sisters as well. Who would take care of them? None of them could survive a day without Kate.

"We are fine, Miss Bailey," Kate said as icily as she could, trying to mimic the tone she had often heard Mom use. We get lotsa rest, and our Mom cooks us supper every night. We're just fine."

Silence.

"Can I go back to class now?"

"Of course, Kate."

On her walk home from school, Kate prayed her mother would be there. She would know what to do. But what if she wasn't home? What if she didn't come home? Mom had been gone for several days. Going by the amount of time she usually stayed gone, Kate tried to calculate when she might be home, but gave up after a few tries. There were too many questions floating around in her head for her to concentrate on math. Would the counselor call the welfare people? Would they come to their house and see that Mom wasn't there? Would they see that there was no food in the house and take them away? Kate's stomach was in knots.

But, by some miracle, when she got home, Mom *was* there. Kate told her about what had happened at school.

"Mom, we should leave. We should go tonight."

"Those sonsabitches! Who does that little floozy think she is? Askin' you all those questions! She sure thinks she's hot shit, don't she?"

"Mom, what are we gonna do?"

"Katie Rhea, look at me. Nobody is gonna take you girls away from me. You're my girls, and you're stayin' right here with your mamma, where you belong."

Kate didn't sleep that night. All sorts of horrid scenarios kept running through her head. What would Mom do? How would she keep them from being separated? She couldn't even keep them fed. How would Birdie and Beverly survive without her? How would *Mom* survive without her?

The next day, Kate was having a terrible time concentrating. The teacher was talking about the pyramids in Egypt, which Kate couldn't have cared less about. It was an hour before lunch, and she was starving. Her gnawing stomach pains were the only thing keeping her awake. She was keeping her mind occupied with all the things she hoped the cafeteria would be serving that day when there was a knock at the classroom door. The teacher, irritated at the interruption, went to answer. Kate's shock was immediate and all-encompassing. Standing at the door was Mom - dressed to the nines. She wore her old, black linen dress and matching black high heels. The dress still fit her very nicely and she looked like her old self again. Kate had forgotten what a strikingly beautiful woman her mother was. Her black, shoulder-length hair had been carefully styled into a chic bob, and the woman's make-up was flawless. All the children began to whisper and ask, "Who's that lady?" Kate, bursting with pride, got up and ran to her mother, but stopped short before hugging her around the waist. Mom would be mad if she messed up her dress.

"I'm Joyce Bloom, Katie Rhea's mamma," she said. "I just need her for a few minutes."

"Of course, Mrs. Bloom," stammered Kate's teacher. She, too, was obviously affected by the sudden appearance of Kate's beautiful mother. "Take all the time you need."

"Mom, you look so pretty!" Kate said as they walked together down the elementary school hallway, Joyce's heels clicking elegantly. "What are you doing at my school?"

Smiling and very lady-like, Joyce bent down and said so low, Kate had to strain to hear her, "I'm here to set that nosy little bitch counselor of yours straight. Show me where her office is."

If Kate had been alarmed the day before when the counselor was asking all those questions, it was nothing compared to what she felt at that moment, which was pure, unadulterated panic. But what could she do? If she told Mom no, things would just get ugly. People didn't tell Joyce Bloom no. *At least she doesn't smell like liquor. Maybe she'll take it easy on Miss Bailey once she sees how young and nice she is. After all, she was only trying to help me*, Kate told herself.

Kate showed Mom where the counselor's office was. Mom introduced herself very formally, and she said, "Could we speak privately in your office?"

"Of course," said Miss Bailey, smiling nervously. She glanced at Kate just before she showed Joyce into her office, and, as their eyes met, Kate suddenly felt very sorry for Miss Bailey.

As soon as the door was shut behind them, Kate heard Joyce's voice: "How *dare* you insinuate that my girls are not being taken care of? You have no business scarin' my daughter like that. She came home a mess and said you threatened to take them away from their home and separate them!"

"I-I...n-never...." stammered Miss Bailey. But Mom didn't give her a chance to finish.

Kate and the secretary locked eyes for a moment, and the secretary whispered, "It's okay, sweetheart."

Kate surmised from the secretary's attempt at comforting her that she must have looked as terrified as she felt.

The yelling went on for what seemed like an eternity. Amongst other things, Kate heard Joyce threaten Miss Bailey's job and imply that she must be very lonely at home and jealous-hearted to be threatening to take away other people's children. The last thing Joyce said before the door opened to reveal Miss Bailey sufficiently reduced to tears was the cruelest. Kate and the secretary heard Joyce say, "And wipe off that lipstick. You look like a cheap whore." With that, Joyce made her exit, slamming the office door behind her. She smiled sweetly at the secretary, who smiled back as if she hadn't heard a word, and said, "Come on, Katie Rhea. Let's get your sisters out early and go for ice cream."

Although Kate did feel sorry for Miss Bailey, she also felt very proud of her mother as they held hands and walked back down the hall. She really was a beautiful woman. But she was more than that. She was confident and smart and tough. And nobody messed with Joyce's girls.

As they went to Beverly and Birdie's classrooms to pull them out of school for the rest of the day, Kate, for the first time in what seemed like a very long time, wanted to be just like her mother again. Maybe this was a wake-up call for Mom. Maybe this was what she needed to get their lives back on track.

Grinning from ear to ear, Kate crowded into the front seat with Mom and her sisters. Her chest was swollen with pride, and she felt like maybe everything was going to be okay after all.

Chapter Four

Things were better after the day Mom showed up at the school and chewed out Miss Bailey. She got a job waitressing at a restaurant downtown and kept it. She came home in the evenings with leftover food and tip money. The girls ate hamburgers and french fries mostly, but some nights Mom even brought home steaks and baked potatoes. Most of the time Mom drank her dinner, but the girls didn't mind; at least she was home. For the first time in a long time, there was money for cleaning supplies. The house was kept up. There was even money for clothes after a few months. Mom took all three girls downtown to a second-hand clothing store, and she bought everyone outfits, complete with shoes that fit. Mom even got her old guitar out and started playing songs again.

She was never very good at playing the guitar, but she loved music and had fun playing silly songs with the girls. Back home, she and Dad would laugh and sing and dance several evenings a week. Their favorite funny song was a little racy, but they didn't care. Mom had refused to sing it with them on all their long car rides. The girls never pressed the issue because they knew it probably brought back painful memories of Dad. But one night when she brought out her guitar, it was the first song she suggested. So, they all sang it together to the tune of Jerry Lee Lewis's "Great Balls of Fire."

You keep a-knockin', but you can't come in
I'm in my nightie, and it's mighty thin
I need the money, but I know it's a sin
So quit your knockin and come on in!

The girls collapsed in giggles after singing several verses of the song, but Mom got quiet. It took the girls a few minutes to realize she wasn't laughing with them.

"Mom, it's okay," Birdie tried. "He'll be back, and everything will be good again."

"No, he won't," Mom replied, no inflection in her voice. She stared off into space for several minutes, then got up, grabbed her keys, and walked out the front door.

Chapter Five

School had been out for several weeks, and it was starting to get hot. By the next morning, it was apparent that Mom would not be home anytime soon. Luckily, there were a few groceries in the house. Kate's birthday was coming up, and she was sure Mom would return before then, so the girls made do with what they had and waited for her.

On the morning of her ninth birthday, Kate got out of bed and went to sit on the porch to wait for Mom, sure she would be pulling up in her old green Cadillac any second. But, by two o'clock in the afternoon, she had not returned, and the heat was stifling, so Kate went inside.

Birdie walked out of the kitchen as Kate came in the front door. Kate could tell by the startled look on her little sister's face that she was up to something.

"What's wrong with you? Why are you looking at me like that?"

"Nothin'. Why are you in here? I thought you were waitin' on Mom on the porch."

"I got hot. Where's Bev?"

Birdie again looked guilty and tried to evade Kate's question.

"Birdie Kay! Why do you have that shit eatin' grin on your face? And where's Bev?"

Knowing she couldn't fool her big sister, Birdie gave in. "We're doin' somethin' in the kitchen. For you." She said this last part shyly, almost embarrassed.

Hope rose up in Kate. *Has Mom snuck home? Is she trying to surprise me for my birthday? She could have snuck in the back door, and I wouldn't have even known it because I've been out on the front porch all morning.*

"What are y'all doin'?" Kate asked, a grin spreading across her face. "Who's in there?"

"Just Bev. Now, you go back out on the porch and promise you'll stay there 'til we call you. Promise?" Birdie asked, mischief dancing in her eyes. She gripped Kate's shoulders, spun her around, and all but shoved her out the front door. Kate went good-naturedly, even though it was hot as hell on the porch.

Once Birdie had gone back to the kitchen, Kate sat on the front steps fantasizing about what was in store for her. *Has Mom really come back? Has she brought a gift? Is she in the kitchen right now baking The Birthday Cake?* She hadn't made that since before Dad left.

Mom only made The Birthday Cake four times a year, once for each of the girls' birthdays and, of course, for Dad's birthday. She never made it for her own, though, because she said it'd be like a bus driver's holiday. The first time Kate heard this analogy she'd had to have Mom explain it to her.

"Well, the last thing a bus driver wants on his vacation is to take a trip because that's all he ever does every day is drive. On my birthday, it wouldn't be a treat for me to have The Birthday Cake if I was the one who had to make it because I cook every day."

"Well, Mom, why don't you tell Dad how to make it and we can help him bake it on your birthday?" Kate had asked.

"Because it's a secret recipe, baby. Did you know I don't even have it written down anywhere? I got it all locked away right here," she had said, pointing at her own head.

"Will you show me how to make it someday?"

"I'll sure think about it." Mom laughed. And Kate had laughed with her.

Sweat beads were beginning to form on Kate's upper lip. She was becoming impatient. *I wish they'd hurry.*

She could already taste the rich, sweet, chocolate frosting of The Birthday Cake. She didn't know how much longer she could wait.

Finally, after what seemed like ten forevers, Birdie burst through the screen door onto the porch.

"Are you ready for your surprise?"

"Yes!" Kate yelled as she ran past Birdie, straight to the kitchen. She burst into the room with her little sister at her heels, and all she saw was Beverly, tired, sweaty, and red in the face. *No Mom. She must be hiding,* thought Kate. She ran around the kitchen, but Mom wasn't there. She ran to the back door and slung it open. *She must be on the back porch,* thought Kate. But still no Mom.

"Where is she?"

"Where's *who*?" asked Beverly."

"*Mom!*" screamed Kate. "Isn't that my surprise?"

From behind, Kate felt Birdie's skinny, sweaty little arms go around her.

"No, silly! We made you a cake!"

"Happy birthday!" Both sisters yelled in unison.

Birdie ran over to Beverly's side, and together, they grabbed the corners of an old, faded cup towel and lifted it to reveal a dripping, soggy mound of instant mashed potatoes piled high on a chipped ceramic plate. The potatoes were runny and dripping onto the counter. There were three toothpicks stuck into the top of the hill of whitish mush.

"Ta-dah! We made it all by ourselves," chirped Birdie.

This was more than Kate could bear. *She didn't come home for my birthday. She didn't come home for my birthday.* The thought ran through her head over and over. *She didn't come home for my birthday.* Beverly and Birdie's proud expressions slowly changed to disappointment and concern for their sister.

"It was all we could find, Kate. We're sorry," Beverly explained.

"You don't like it?" Birdie asked.

Kate could not think of a single thing to say. She could only stare. *She didn't come home for my birthday.* An overwhelming impulse to run possessed her. She could not stand here in this kitchen, this house that wasn't a home, this house that did not contain a mother, for a single second longer. As she turned to go, she heard her sisters begging her to stay, then to come back. But she physically could not stop herself from running away.

Kate raced down the sidewalk, tears blinding her. *How could she? How could she not come home on her daughter's ninth birthday? Does she even remember? Did we even cross her mind today? What if she's hurt and can't come home? That's gotta be it! She's hurt. Or worse.* Terrible thoughts tumbled around in Kate's mind, blurring together.

Finally, out of breath and sweating, she slowed to a walk. As Kate calmed down, something strange happened to her. She began to laugh. She thought of her sisters working tirelessly in their empty kitchen trying to come up with something they could use to make a birthday cake for their sister. *And they came up with mashed potatoes?* Suddenly, things didn't seem quite so bad. Maybe Mom forgot her birthday, but her sisters remembered. And they had tried so hard to give their sister a cake. The urge to be with her sisters turned her around and sent Kate in the direction of home.

As she neared the house, she noticed a strange car in the driveway. It was too nice to belong to one of Mom's shady friends who dropped by every once in a while to borrow money or sleep on the couch for a while. It occurred to Kate that it could be the welfare people, and she started to run again.

Beverly stood at the door speaking with a nicely dressed older-looking man when Kate finally jumped up the steps of the front porch.

"Er...hello. I'm Michael Davis. Your mother Joyce works at my restaurant. She was supposed to work last night, and she didn't show up. I got worried about her and thought I'd better come check on her. Your sister here was just telling me that she hasn't been home in a few days? Is that right?"

"Uh, well, she's supposed to come home tonight. She's... (*Think, Kate, think!*) visiting a sick friend." The way she said it, it sounded more like a question than a statement. So, Kate quickly followed with, "She must have forgotten to tell you. It happened really fast." *That sounds good*, thought Kate, as she used every bit of self-control she possessed to push down the panic rising within her. She hoped this excuse sounded halfway believable. *How could Beverly have been so stupid? Is she trying to get us taken away?* "Do you want us to have her come see you when she gets back?"

"Uh, okay. That'll be fine. I hope her friend gets better."

"Thank you. We'll tell her you stopped by."

"Okay, thanks. Bye."

"Bye."

Relief flooded through Kate as Michael Davis stepped down from the porch. But then the man stopped and turned around, his brow furrowed in thought.

"Are you sure everything's okay here? Do you girls need some help?"

"No, no. We're fine."

"Have you been staying here by yourselves this whole time?"

Kate forced a laugh. "Of course not. We're just little kids, mister. Our aunt's taking care of us. She's just gone to the store." *Good one,* thought Kate.

"Oh. Okay. Well, if you're sure you don't need any help…" his voice trailed off.

Kate had to think of something fast to get this guy out of here and to keep him from calling someone. She would have to get him on her side.

"Hey, mister."

"Yes?"

"I wasn't supposed to leave the house while my aunt's gone to the store." She hoped and prayed she sounded like a normal kid. "You won't tell on me, will you?" She tried her damndest to widen her eyes and muster up some tears.

It must've worked because Mr. Davis, after a moment's indecision, smiled and said, "Your secret's safe with me, young lady." This time, burden lifted, Mr. Davis was able to leave with a clear conscience. That was the first time Kate figured out that nobody really ever wants to step in and help another person, not if it means inconveniencing himself, not really. They feel obligated, sure. But give them one tiny sliver of a chance to get out of it, and they will take it and run every time.

The man walking away from them probably hadn't believed one word of what Kate told him, but it was enough. It was enough of a reason to walk away from three children who were in trouble, three children who did need help, three children who were all alone in the world.

As soon as Mr. Davis was safely gone, Kate told Beverly to go get Birdie.

"What are we gonna do? We *have* to find her," pleaded Beverly. "This is bad. Real bad. She's never been gone this long. We have to find her, Kate."

"I know. Where could we look for her? I don't even know where she goes when she leaves. Do you?"

"No," answered Birdie and Beverly.

"What about her friends who come over here sometimes? Do you think she ever does the same thing? Goes to their houses to sleep or hide or borrow money?"

"What about the time she left us in the car and went into her friend's house over on Stein Street? Remember that? She was in there for a long time. We could walk there. It's not that far from here," said Birdie.

Kate contemplated this. "I guess that's a start."

"Come on, we'd better get to walkin'. It's gonna be dark here in a little bit," said Beverly.

It took them a few tries to find Stein Street, and when they did, it took even longer for the girls to find the right house. Most of the white, shotgun-style homes looked almost exactly alike. The sidewalks were so hot, they scorched the bottoms of the girls' bare feet. They had to alternate between walking on the dried grass, which was littered with sharp, stinging stickers, and the burning sidewalk. Beverly and Kate had to stop several times along the way to help Birdie dig the painful, poking stickers out of her little feet. Finally, Birdie spotted the house. The older sisters silently thanked heaven for their little sister's ironclad memory.

As the girls neared the small, run-down house, they heard loud music thumping inside. It was so deafening the windows appeared to vibrate. Kate was the only one brave enough to knock on the door. Her heart beat so violently in her chest that, for a minute, she thought she might vomit on her own feet. But Kate reached down deep inside and found the courage she needed.

A small boy finally came to the door after the third time Kate knocked. In truth, at this point, it was more like she was pounding on the door. It was obvious someone was home, but less apparent whether the people inside could hear the knocking because the music was so loud. The little boy who answered was even younger than Birdie. Four, maybe five years old at the most.

"What do you want?" the little boy asked, scowling.

"We're looking for our mom. Is your mom or dad home? We just want to ask if they've seen her," Kate stated, less intimidated now that she was speaking to a child who was younger than her, rather than the scary adult she had imagined would answer the door.

The wiry, towheaded little boy stared at Kate for an uncomfortable moment and then retreated, leaving the door wide open. She wasn't sure what this meant. *Does he want me to follow him inside? Am I supposed to wait here?* Kate wasn't sure, but when faced with the choice between going inside or waiting on the porch, she chose the latter.

Three or four minutes later, a bearded, shirtless man appeared in the doorway. He wore cut-off jean shorts and tall, white socks pulled up just below his knees. The socks had red stripes at the tops.

"Who the fuck are you, and what the hell do you want?" was his greeting. Before Kate could answer, the man used his fist to pound hard on his chest once, which released what sounded like a growl at first, but as it rose from his sternum, morphed into a monstrous burp. Then he raised his arm, revealing a matted tangle of dark underarm hair, and rested his hand on the top of the door frame. He adjusted his feet so that he could lean his hip against the door jamb, and he looked down at Kate, bored.

A brutal combination of the odors of half-digested cheap beer and oniony body odor enveloped Kate, causing her to involuntarily take a step backward, desperately seeking unscented oxygen. "I'm sorry, sir," Kate said, terrified and disgusted. No matter how hard she tried, she could not bring herself to say anything else to the large, smelly, sinister man before her. This is when Birdie stepped in front of Kate and smiled her bewitching little smile to which no man, young or old, seemed immune.

"Hello."

"Well, hello, little lady," the not-so-grumpy-anymore man replied. "What are you doin' at my front door? You sellin' cookies or something?" He smiled. His body language went from unwelcoming, even borderline threatening, to friendly and intrigued in an instant.

What is it with Birdie Kay and adults, men especially? Kate made a mental note to address this freakish talent of her little sister's later when they had time to talk about it. For the time being, she was simply grateful for her Birdie's strange ability.

"I'm lookin' for my mom. We came to your house one time, but we didn't go in. Just our mom did. We were in the car. We can't find her. Do you know where she is? Her name's Joyce."

"Well, I knew you looked familiar, little lady! Y'know you look just like yer mamma, don'tcha? Just like her!"

The man was beginning to give Kate a strange vibe. She suddenly felt an overwhelming urge to protect her little sister, even though she was in no obvious danger.

"Do you girls want to come inside? I bet we could figure out where she is if we put our heads together. I got some cold pop. Y'all thirsty?"

The man's sudden change in demeanor put Kate on edge. He must have been scaring Beverly too because she stepped in front of Birdie protectively and said, "We just wondered if she was here, sir. We won't take up any more of your time."

Instinctively, all three girls began cautiously inching away from the man and down his porch steps. Kate thought he must have been drunk or on drugs because it took him a moment too long to realize the girls were retreating. Beverly was the last to reach the bottom porch step, and right before she got there, the man reached out with a giant paw and swiped at her, as if he were trying to grab her. This sent all three girls shrieking and running with everything they had in them.

"Aw, y'all come back, now! I didn't mean to scare ya! I was *just* playin'!" yelled the man as he laughed. "Go check down on Main Street! Your mamma's a regular ol' barfly down at Oscar's almost every night of the week!" the man yelled after them.

"That sonofabitch! Don't you listen to him, Birdie Kay! He's just a mean ol' drunk, that's all. Mom's not a barfly." Beverly defended Mom passionately. But Kate stayed silent.

They finally felt far enough away that they were safe again. Birdie sobbed uncontrollably.

"Huh, Kate? Isn't that right?"

Still, Kate walked on silently.

"Kate!" Beverly yelled. "*Tell* her, Kate! She don't listen to me the way she listens to you. Tell her!"

Kate eyed her distraught little sister and lied, "She's not an ol' barfly, Birdie Kay. That man's so drunk he don't even know what state he's in!"

Kate's reassurance seemed to comfort Birdie. Her uncontrollable sobs gradually became pathetic little hiccups until they ceased altogether.

As the girls walked back toward home, the conversation again turned to what they should do. Should they go home? Should they look for Mom at Oscar's Bar downtown?

Kate winked at Beverly over Birdie's head as they walked side by side, Birdie in the middle. "Let's go home."

Beverly, for once not the slowest brain on the block, nodded with understanding. They walked home in silence.

Once they were home, neither of the older girls spoke of their experience that evening. Instead, they laughed about Kate's birthday cake. This seemed to placate Birdie enough that soon she was fast asleep.

Kate pulled Beverly aside, and they spoke in whispers. "I'm goin' to look for her. You stay here and watch her," Kate whispered.

"No, you're not, Kate!"

"Oh, shut up, Bev! Nothin's gonna happen."

"Oh, really? Are you tellin' me you weren't scared to death today at that man's house? He wanted to hurt Birdie Kay. I *know* you know that. I saw the look on your face when he started lookin' at her like that!"

"Okay. You're right. It *was* scary. That's why we need to find Mom!"

"Okay, fine. But what are you gonna do if you don't find her? What are you gonna do if you *do* find her, Kate? You can't drag her home. You know how mean she gets when she's been drinkin'. Plus, I'm a little scared that man might show up here now that he knows Mom's not with us. Aren't you?"

"Hell yeah, I'm scared! Why do you think I want to find her so bad?"

After this, Beverly grew silent. She understood Kate was right. They had to do something.

Kate knew how to get downtown. It was just down the street. She didn't even have to turn left or right, just walk straight ahead. She was sure that once she got there, with every other business closed, she could just look for all the cars, and she'd find Oscar's Bar easily enough.

***

It was dark out, and Kate made Beverly lock the doors. They made sure all the windows were locked, and Kate promised she'd come back as soon as she possibly could.

Downtown was about a mile away. With nighttime, it had finally cooled off some, which somehow made the day's events seem less scary. As she walked, Kate let her mind wander. Every time she thought of home, she thought of Bloom Street. It struck her as funny that they were still technically *in* Arizona, just really far from home.

Grandma Bloom and Dad had always assured the girls it was simply a coincidence that the street they lived on was called Bloom Street, but Kate had always liked to daydream that it had been named after her family because they were special. She didn't feel very special now. She wondered to herself as she walked why Mom hadn't accepted Grandma and Grandpa Bloom's help after Dad was sent away to prison. They had offered. Mom had never told the girls this, but Kate had gotten out of bed to go to the bathroom one night right after Dad had gotten into trouble and was surprised to find that Grandma and Grandpa Bloom were in the living room with Mom. Her grandparents were usually in bed before dark, and it had to be late at night. She wondered what they were doing up so late, so she stood quietly in the hall and listened.

"Joyce, we want you to stay here. Where will you go? You've got three little girls to think of." This from Grandma Bloom.

"I have family in Oklahoma, Beth. We'll go back there. I've been meaning to take the girls back home for a visit anyway. They haven't seen my parents since they were small. A change of scenery will do us all some good."

"What about the diner?" Grandpa Bloom asked.

"You know we've been in trouble for a while. With Don in jail, I don't think I can keep it afloat."

"Joyce, you know we'll do everything we can to help you and those girls," said Grandma Bloom.

"You know I love you both. You've been so good to us. You gave us this house to live in, you gave us the money to start the diner, you paid for Don's attorney. But I just can't stay in this house and run that diner without him." Here Joyce began to cry.

"Oh, honey, please don't give that a second thought. You're family. We would do anything in the world to help you and those girls. Please don't cry. We'll get through this together."

"Beth, I just can't stay here. I can't live in the home we made together and run the business we started without him. I'm barely holding on by a string as it is. I can't handle all these memories. And what am I supposed to tell his girls? That their daddy is coming back? *When?"*

"It might not be too long. His lawyer said he could get out on good behavior in as few as three years. Don't you want to be here in case he comes back? Don't you want him to have something to come back *to*?" Grandma Bloom pleaded.

"I just can't do it, Beth. I just can't do it. If I don't get out of here, I think I might lose my mind. I can't even look those girls in the eye for fear I might go off the deep end any minute. I just don't know what else to do."

"Well, I can understand you wanting your parents at a time like this, and I don't blame you. But, to be honest, I'm going to miss those girls! I can't imagine not being able to see them every day. It breaks my heart."

"I know it does, Beth. And I don't want to hurt either of you. You've been so good to us. But this isn't forever. It's just for right now."

"Well, at least let us help you, Joyce. Let us give you some money."

"No. You two have done more than enough for us. I'm going to sell the diner and pay you back the money you gave us as a down payment. I'll use the rest to get us to Oklahoma and get settled."

"Oh, no, honey. We wouldn't dream of taking that money. That was a gift to you. We never expected to get it back," said Beth reassuringly.

"Well, how 'bout you keep it for us? Then when we get ready to head back this way, we'll have a little money?"

"I guess we could do that," said Grandpa Bloom.

"I can't believe he's really gone," said Mom, tearing up again.

"I can't either." Now both Bloom women were crying.

"Well, girls, our boy *is* gone. For the time bein', anyway. We gotta accept it and move on. Last thing he did before they took 'im away was ask me to make sure his girls were taken care of. If you need anything, Joyce, you call. Be it day or night. Day or night. You hear me? And take care of those girls. They're my boy's whole world."

"I will."

As far as Kate knew, Mom had never once even sent her grandparents a postcard to let them know they were all still living, let alone called them. As she walked toward Main Street, she grew increasingly angry with Mom. *Grandma and Grandpa Bloom are good people. They care about us. Why did Mom refuse to accept their help? We could have stayed home and waited for Dad. We could have stayed at our school. Grandma and Grandpa would have helped Mom.* Kate didn't understand how she could tear them away from everything they knew. *To go to Oklahoma? We don't know those people. I can barely remember her family. I haven't even seen them since I was a tiny little girl. And I know Birdie has no memories of them. What is wrong with our mother?*

As she neared the downtown area, Kate was forced to bring her mind back to the task at hand: *Find Mom and bring her ass home!* She could see a group of vehicles parked all in one area, and she knew it was Oscar's Bar. Beverly's questions echoed in her mind: "What will you do if you don't find her? What will you do if you *do* find her?"

She did find her. Joyce was perched at the bar, and Kate spotted her as soon as she walked in the door. There she sat, smoking, drinking a beer, laughing and having a good ol' time. Anger swelled in Kate's chest. *Here I am dragging my drunk mom out of a goddamn bar on my birthday!* As soon as she opened the door, the stench of stale beer assaulted her. It only added to her anger that at the ripe old age of nine, she knew this smell all too well. She approached the bar cautiously, having already caught the suspicious eyes of several of the bar's patrons.

"What are you doing in here, little girl? You're not near old enough to be here," was her greeting.

"I know, sir. I'm just here to get my mom," was her reply.

Oddly, the man who'd said it turned his attention back to his drink and said nothing more.

"Mom!"

Joyce looked around at the sound of her daughter's voice. "Oh, hey, baby! What are you doing here?" Joyce asked, obviously drunk.

"You need to come home," was all Kate could say. She was seething with anger. She wanted to say so much more. She wanted to shame her mother for being here instead of being at home. But, as she looked at her mother's smeared eye makeup and her pathetically tangled hair, she could not bring herself to say anything else. She could only stare at her mother, at the mess before her. She could only feel pity for this woman who was merely a shell of her former self. She couldn't help but remember how upset Mom had been with Dad when she first heard that he'd been arrested. Kate had wondered how he could do that to Mom when she worked so hard to give them a good life.

He had been out with his buddies for a drink. They'd had a high time, drinking until they were way past drunk. They'd been walking home together when one of them had the bright idea to try to break into a parking meter and steal the quarters inside, such a juvenile thing for a grown man to do. They somehow succeeded in getting the quarters out of the meter, but the fun didn't stop there.

They decided to have a drink with their newfound riches, but all the bars were closed. So, they thought it would be a great idea to break into their favorite bar and have a few drinks. They would leave money on the bar. Surely the owner wouldn't mind.

Dad and his friends succeeded in breaking into the bar and then decided that they'd like a little music to go along with their drinks. They played songs on the jukebox with their stolen quarters so loudly that a passerby called the police and said that someone had broken into a local business. The police came. Dad's friends had the good sense to run and get away, but not Dad. He got so tickled that he couldn't do anything but stand there bent over in a laughing fit. He was arrested, of course. And, of course, he refused to give up his accomplices, so he got the maximum sentence for robbing a parking meter, which belonged to the state, and for breaking and entering. Ten years in prison. *Poor Mom.*

She was left to run a business and raise three little girls with no father. Kate's anger melted away, and she could only feel sorry for her mother. Even though Kate and her sisters had lost a lot, their mother had lost more. And she was expected to move on, to pick up the pieces and keep going. For the first time, Kate was able to put herself in someone else's shoes. She walked over to her mother and said, more gently this time, "Mom, you need to come home."

"Oh, Katie Rhea! You silly little thang. Mamma'll be home in a little while, baby. I promise."

"No, Mom. You need to come home now."

The bartender looked from Kate to Mom and back again. He must have felt some pity for Kate because he said, "Joyce, I was about to cutcha off anyway, honey. Go home with your girl now. We'll be right back here tomorrow."

But Joyce was not to be swayed. "Uh, *Jerry,* I am a paying customer, *sir.* And the customer is always *right!*" She looked from Jerry to Kate and, when she got no response from either, she said, *"Right?"* No response. "Right?" This time she yelled it.

"Right, Joyce. You're right, honey. But I think your little girl needs you at home."

"Jerry, did you know I used to own and run my very own diner? And it was a successful diner too, not like *this* dump bein' run by a damn Yankee!" She was slurring her words.

"Well, you sure don't seem to mind it too much, Joyce," Jerry replied.

"Hey, *mister*! You watch your mouth in front of my little girl! Y'hear? She's a little lady, and I won't have you sassin' me in front of 'er!" Mom was getting loud and attracting a lot of attention. Kate felt increasingly anxious.

Jerry seemed to notice this and take pity on the little girl. He came around to the other side of the bar and spoke to Kate, ignoring Joyce's ongoing verbal assault. "How 'bout you and me help her out to the car?"

"Okay," was all Kate could say.

Joyce protested all the way out the door, but at least she didn't fight them. Kate half expected her mother to start flailing wildly any second. Once they got to the car it was quite apparent that Joyce could not operate a motor vehicle in her impaired state. After Jerry guided her into the back seat, she slumped over and was silent. She seemed almost grateful to be able to close her eyes.

"You ever drove a car before, kid?"

Feeling more comfortable around Jerry now, Kate was honest with him. "Once. With my dad, but it was only in a parking lot. And he was there with me, telling me what to do. And I had to sit on his lap. I couldn't even see over the steering wheel. There's no way I can drive a car," she screeched, bile rising in her throat at the thought of doing something so insane.

"Alright, alright. Calm down, kid." He looked Kate up and down, sizing her up. "I'll bet it was quite a while ago that you drove with your dad. You've grown since then, right?" Jerry didn't wait for Kate's answer. "Well, I'd like for tonight to just stay between you and me, but I can't leave the bar to drive you and your mom home, kid," Jerry said as he looked Kate in the eye. "Listen, I used to steal cars and take 'em for a ride all the time back when I was a kid. I couldn't a been much older than you are now when I first started. It ain't that hard, kid. You remember what your dad taught you? Where the gas is? The brake?"

Kate shook her head yes, but she wasn't sure if she remembered or not.

"Well that's all you gotta know. That and the gear shift. Hell, a monkey could drive a car. Nothin' to it, especially in this dead ass town. There's no traffic here. You could weave all over the road and never hit another car." Oddly, Jerry's gruff demeanor and his off-handed attitude about a child driving home her inebriated mother made Kate feel a little more confident.

"Do you really think I can do it?" Kate asked.

Jerry leaned back a little to get a better look at Kate's eyes. "You're a lot older than you really are, ain'tcha, kid?"

Jerry's insightful comment made perfect sense to Kate. She bobbed her head up and down.

"Good luck, kid," Jerry said. He slapped the roof of the car twice and walked back into the bar.

Once again Kate realized that the only thing most people need is a flimsy excuse to walk away. Then she turned her attention to the car. *Shit.*

She thought for a moment and tried to remember what Dad had told her about the R and the D. But it was such a long time ago. She wished she had paid more attention. *It's not that far. I can do this,* she thought. *And it sure is a helluva lot faster than walking.*

As soon as she got into the car, Kate realized she had a big problem. She couldn't figure out how to move the seat forward. She used every ounce of strength she had. Jerry must have been watching her from the window. After a few minutes of her struggling, he exited the bar again.

"You havin' trouble, kid?"

"I can't get the seat to move."

"Hop out for a minute. Let me help you." Jerry got into the car. He told her to step out of the way, started the engine, and backed the car out of its parking spot and into the road. There he left the car sitting with the motor running and the door wide open. Without a word, he ran inside and came back out with a thick telephone book. Kate looked on in fascination. Kneeling outside the driver's seat, Jerry scooted the seat up as far as it would go and placed the telephone book in the seat. "Come 'ere, kid. Sit down on the phone book 'n' make sure you can see over the steering wheel."

Kate did as she was told.

"Looka there. Works like a charm. Make sure you can reach the pedals."

Kate again did as she was told and was surprised to find that she could see over the steering wheel and reach the pedals.

"All right, kid. The rest is up to you. You're all set. Now, you're gonna keep your foot on the brake while you slide the gear shift into D. Then you'll let off the brake. You're not in any hurry, y'hear me? It's a straight shot to your house. You go as slow as you need to. If you never even *touch* the gas pedal that's *fine*. Just watch for other cars and take your time. You probably won't even see another car on the road, but if you do, you just slow way down and let 'em go by, ya hear me?"

"Okay," Kate said, shaking her head, trying to remember everything Jerry was telling her.

"Now, when you get close to your house, don't try to turn into the driveway. You just pull as close as you can to the curb and put it in park and turn off the engine. You hear me? Your mom can worry about parking it in the driveway tomorrow."

"Okay," said Kate.

"Good luck."

Kate looked at Jerry through the driver's side window and thanked him. She hoped he knew how grateful she was.

She slowly let off the brake and started to roll forward. The enormity of what she was about to do hit her. She slammed her foot down on the brake, throwing herself and Joyce forward. She looked back at Jerry, frightened, and he was laughing, shaking his head from side to side.

"You'll be fine, kid!" Jerry yelled, waving his hand for her to go on. Kate couldn't figure out if this man was kind or crazy. Either way, she didn't have much of a choice. So, she concentrated on the road ahead of her and did the best she could.

Once she got herself situated, the hardest part was keeping Mom in line. When Kate had first gotten into the car, Mom had appeared to be passed out. But once they were moving, she popped up in the back seat. She wanted to know who had told Kate she was old enough to drive. Kate tried to pacify Mom by telling her the truth, but there was no reasoning with Joyce.

"Yerrr in so much trouble, little girl," Mom slurred.

"Mom, I'm just trying to get you home. You're too drunk to drive."

"*What*? I will slap your little face, young lady! How dare you speak to yerrr mother thataway?"

Kate could see the top of Mom's head when she glanced up into the rear-view mirror, and her hair looked like several birds had taken up residence in it. It was knotted up on the top of her head so severely that Kate had to laugh. This just got Joyce even more agitated.

"Jist what do you think yer laughin' at, young lady?" Her accent was so strong when she was drunk. It was almost ridiculous. Kate thought she sounded like a hick; this only made her laugh harder, which infuriated Joyce, but luckily they were almost home.

Kate composed herself. "I'm sorry, Mom. I'm not laughing at you. I was laughing at something else," she said, trying to pay attention to the road in front of her as they inched toward home. She looked at the speedometer. It was fluctuating between 10 and 15 miles per hour. *Almost there*, she kept telling herself. *Just a little farther.*

Finally, *finally* they made it home. It was the longest mile of Kate's young life, especially with Mom critiquing her driving skills the entire time. But she finally did it; she got them home. She even remembered to turn off the headlights. Beverly burst through the door. Relief relaxed her face and flushed her cheeks. She ran out to meet Kate and to help her walk Mom into the house. It felt like it took longer to get her inside than it did to drive her home. For such a thin woman, she sure weighed a lot. But, together, they finally managed to get Mom inside and on the couch. She immediately passed out, to the girls' relief.

The next morning Mom was awake before the girls. Birdie had slept through the whole ordeal, thank goodness. And the scary man never came around, so they had dodged a bullet once again. Kate and Beverly were a little afraid to leave their bedroom. They weren't sure how Mom would feel about Kate having come to get her from the bar, so they sent Birdie in to test the waters. When they heard no screaming, they decided it was safe to enter. And there was Mom in the kitchen making pancakes like nothing had ever happened.

"Mornin', sleepy heads," she said to them.

Both girls were still cautious. This could be a trick to lure them closer so that she could pounce. But Birdie was seated at the table, and Mom was serving her breakfast. The temptation was worth the risk. They each took a seat at the table, and Mom set plates piled high with pancakes in front of them both. Then she took a seat at the table and lit a cigarette, contentedly sipping coffee and watching the girls eat. Kate realized that, with all the excitement yesterday, she had not eaten anything and was ravenous. They ate for a while in silence, and then Mom spoke.

"Girls, I'm sorry I left again. You know I've been havin' a hard time lately. But things are gonna get better around here. Mamma's gonna take care of her girls. I promise."

No response seemed necessary. The girls continued to eat, relieved that Mom was finally home. They sat at the table for a while afterward telling Mom about the previous day's adventure. She seemed genuinely upset that she had missed Kate's birthday and promised to make it up to her. Mom was appalled to hear the girls had gone to her friend's house unattended, and she made them promise they would never do anything like that ever again. They promised. Happily. All was right with the world for the time being, and that was enough for Joyce's girls.

Chapter Six

1970

Miraculously, Mr. Davis forgave Mom and let her keep working at his restaurant, no questions asked. Mom worked harder than she ever had before. She made it up to Kate for missing her birthday. She took the girls out to dinner at her restaurant on her night off, and Mr. Davis treated them to cheeseburgers, french fries and milkshakes. Kate noticed the way the man looked at Mom, and she felt very possessive suddenly. But Mom did not reciprocate Mr. Davis's looks. Kate wondered if the real reason he had come by the house that day had more to do with his admiration for Mom than he had let on. It occurred to Kate for the first time that maybe being a beautiful woman wasn't such a good thing after all.

School started again. This year was different, however. Mom took the girls to another second-hand store and bought them all new outfits for the first day. She even made sure they each had their own paper and pencils. She hadn't done that since Dad had been with them.

The first few weeks of school went well. Birdie had always been outgoing and somehow managed to make friends at every school they had ever attended, but this had proven a lot harder for Beverly and Kate. This year, however, both girls managed to make a friend. They hadn't been this settled in a long time, and all three girls relished the idea of being "normal kids" again. Kate had even gone to visit a new friend, Angie, at her house a few times.

One day Mom asked Kate out of the blue if she'd like to go see Angie. This was a bit odd because usually

Angie invited her first. But Mom had become irritable over the past few days, so she didn't question her. When they pulled up in front of Angie's house, she told Kate that her sisters would have to go too because she needed to run to the store. Again, Kate found this odd (and a little embarrassing), but she didn't want to upset Mom; things had been going so well.

Angie Lopez was in Kate's class, and the two had hit it off immediately and became fast friends. One of the things Kate liked about going to Angie's house was that she had such a large, happy family. Angie had two older brothers, an older sister, and three younger siblings. Angie's father worked, but her mother stayed home. Every time Kate saw Angie's mother she was in the kitchen. Their house always smelled heavenly. It was a tiny house, and it barely accommodated such a large family, but somehow they always made it work.

Another reason Kate liked to play at Angie's house was the food; there was always something good to eat. Kate was pretty sure Angie's mother baked every day. She was a large, dark-skinned woman with thick, black hair. She always wore very colorful, long dresses, and Kate never saw Angie's mother when she wasn't wearing red lipstick. Mrs. Lopez was always smiling, even when her husband had too much to drink and told loud, funny stories, gesticulating wildly as he spoke.

Mr. Lopez never seemed mean, but every time Kate saw him he was either about to start drinking after a long day at work, had already started drinking, or he was being told by Mrs. Lopez or one of their older sons that he'd had enough and should stop for the night. Kate always enjoyed the man drunk or sober.

When the girls walked up to the door, Kate knocked. One of Angie's older brothers answered, smiled, and invited all three girls into the house. After a few moments, Angie came into the room and was pleasantly surprised to see not only her friend, but an additional two playmates. The girls were welcomed by Mrs. Lopez as well. There was a confused expression on her face, but she was too polite to do anything other than invite the girls into her home.

"Do you want to play house with my dolls?" Angie asked Kate, Beverly and Birdie once they had all gone into the bedroom Angie shared with two sisters.

"Okay," said Kate.

"I don't really like to play dolls," said Birdie. "Let's go play outside."

"But I was playing house before you got here. I want to keep playing," explained Angie.

"I'll take her outside," a shy little girl in the corner said. It was Angie's little sister Sarah. Sarah had a long, black ponytail. She smiled to reveal that her two front teeth were missing. Birdie assessed this new little girl and, even though she looked to be at least a year younger than Birdie, she was deemed a sufficient playmate, and the two girls scampered happily out of the room to entertain themselves outdoors.

Beverly found herself engrossed in one of the many books on a bookshelf on the opposite side of the room, and this left Kate and Angie to play house, which they did for over an hour. Then Mrs. Lopez asked the girls if they would like to stay for dinner. Mom had not said when she'd be back to pick them up, so Kate happily accepted the invitation. Room was made for the girls at the family table, and Mrs. Lopez scooped heaping piles of steaming pinto beans into each girl's bowl. Then she handed out warm, freshly made flour tortillas. The meal was delicious.

"So, what have you girls been playing at this afternoon?" asked Mrs. Lopez as she served her other children, her husband, and then herself.

"We were playing house," Angie responded.

"We played outside!" Sarah sang. "Some mean boys rode by on their bicycles and called us names, so we threw rocks at them!" Sarah and Birdie's cheeks were pink from exertion, their upper lips still sweaty as they entertained the family with the story of their afternoon war with the mean boys.

"Why were the boys so mean to you?" asked Mr. Lopez.

Both little girls shrugged their shoulders, eyes wide and innocent. "I don't know," they said in unison.

After dinner, the girls helped clear the table. Kate was beginning to feel that old, familiar nervous knot in her stomach, and she wasn't sure why. It had been such a lovely day.

Kate liked to listen to the way they all spoke to each other, genuinely interested in what their family members had done and seen throughout the day. She wished her family could be a little more like the Lopezes.

"Would you girls like to watch some television until your mother gets here?" asked Mrs. Lopez.

"Yes!" exclaimed Birdie.

"Yes!" giggled Sarah.

The older girls looked at each other knowingly, smiled, and followed their little sisters into the living room. There was a television show already playing on the television. Kate did not recognize it, but all the girls were soon completely engrossed in the story line. The children were so interested they did not notice it was getting dark outside. Finally, when it was time to turn off the television, Mrs. Lopez turned to Beverly, Kate and Birdie and asked, "Girls, did your mother tell you what time she was going to pick you up tonight?"

"No," all three girls replied, the realization slowly dawning on them that Mom might not come back for them at all if she had gone off to drink. So, Kate thought, this is *why I've been so nervous all night. Shit. What are we gonna do if she doesn't come back for us?*

"I'm sorry, girls. I don't mean to be rude. It's just that tonight is a school night, and you should all be going off to bed soon."

"Oh, it's okay, Mrs. Lopez," Kate spoke up, hot embarrassment making its way across her cheeks and down her neck. "We can walk home."

"Well, Kate, it's probably three miles to your house, and it's dark outside. Do you think your mother could have forgotten about you?"

"Yeah, that's all it is. She just forgot about us is all. We can walk home. We do it all the time. Come on, Birdie; come on, Beverly. Let's get goin'."

"How about I give you all a ride home since it's dark out?" asked Mr. Lopez.

"Oh, no, sir. That's okay. We walk it all the time. We got each other. We'll be fine."

"Well, I can't let you all walk that far in the dark. Come on. I'll take you home."

All three girls looked at each other. What else could they do? Mom wasn't there to get them. These people were obviously ready for them to go home.

"Okay, Mr. Lopez. Thank you. I'm sure she just forgot. She does that sometimes," Kate said, praying Mom would be there when this man dropped them at home. *What will we do if she's not there?* This was the silent question each girl was asking the others with her eyes.

The ride home was agony. The girls were in the backseat of Mr. Lopez's old blue Ford, so they couldn't exactly discuss their options. Kate tried to come up with a good lie about where Mom could possibly be and why she had neglected to pick up her children, but nothing was coming to her. Mr. Lopez was a smart man and a good father. He wouldn't just walk away and leave the girls home alone. Kate silently wished Mr. Lopez had drank a little more that evening. But he seemed sober as a church mouse tonight.

Of course, when they stopped in front of their house it was as Kate had suspected it would be. Mom's old, beat-up Cadillac was nowhere to be seen. Silence filled the inside of Mr. Lopez's car. Finally, "Thank you, Mr. Lopez!" shouted Kate, and she began to exit the vehicle. Beverly and Birdie followed quickly, but Mr. Lopez stopped them.

"Just a minute, girls. I think we should all wait here together until your mother returns. You are too young to be home alone. Something bad could happen to you, and if it did, I would never forgive myself."

"Aw, Mr. Lopez, we stay by ourselves all the time," whined Birdie, desperate to get out of the car and escape this uncomfortable situation.

"Well, you're not staying home alone tonight. Get back in and shut the door," Mr. Lopez commanded in his "dad" voice. The girls climbed back in and shut the doors. *He's gonna take us to the police station! Then they're gonna take us away from Mom! They'll separate us!* These thoughts rushed through Kate's head, and she was on the verge of panic when Mr. Lopez spoke again: "How would you girls like to come sleep at our house tonight? You could ride the bus to school in the morning with Angie and Sarah." Kate had not considered this scenario. Mr. Lopez's offer helped her to relax a little.

When they returned to the Lopez house, Mr. Lopez locked eyes with Mrs. Lopez who was sitting in the living room reading a book. He almost imperceptibly shook his head from side to side, and this seemed to be some sort of signal to Mrs. Lopez. She immediately put her book away, smiled, got up from her seat on the couch, and began making sleeping arrangements for the three girls. Within moments, it seemed, pajamas were procured for each girl, pallets were made on the living room floor, the lights were out, and the girls were alone at last.

"Where do you think she's at, Kate?" whispered Beverly.

Kate sighed. She hadn't really had time to think about that. Where was Mom? Was she hurt? Was she unable to get to the girls? Even before the last question had run all the way through Kate's head, she knew the answers.

"We all know where she's at," replied Kate, also whispering. "The real question is when she's coming back. We can't just stay here. We need to come up with a plan."

"Well, I say we just leave right now. Just wait 'til they're all asleep and get up and walk home," suggested Birdie.

"Hey, yeah!" agreed Beverly. "That's a good idea. Maybe they'll just think Mom came and got us in the middle of the night."

"Yeah, but then what would happen if she really did come to get us in the middle of the night and we weren't here? Then what, huh? We'd be in big trouble, y'all. And what if we left and she didn't come after us? You know Mr. and Mrs. Lopez'd be worried about us in the mornin'. You know they wouldn't just let it go. One of 'em'd be up at the school askin' questions. No, we gotta think this through and be real careful. Last thing we need is for the welfare people to come around and start askin' questions, 'specially when Mom's been doin' so good lately. We gotta come up with something good. She won't be gone long this time. I know she won't."

"Yeah, I guess you're right, Kate. You got any ideas?" asked Birdie.

"Not yet. I'm thinkin' though. You go to sleep now. You got school in the mornin. Me 'n' Bev'll figure somethin' out."

Birdie sighed and stretched. "Alright. You can wake me up if you need me though."

Kate smiled at the dark. "Okay. Thanks."

After a few moments of silent contemplation, Kate was ready to compare notes with Beverly. "So, I'm thinkin' that if we just go ahead and go to school tomorrow that by the time school lets out we'll be alright. Mr. Lopez will have worked all day. By the time he gets home he probably won't even remember we were here tonight. And Mrs. Lopez has all them dang babies to take care of and all that cookin' to do. She ain't gonna want us back here another night. So, if we just walk home like normal, I bet they'll just sorta forget about us. What do you think?"

No answer.

"Bev?" Kate shook her older sister's shoulder, perhaps a bit more roughly than necessary. *How in the hell could she fall asleep at a time like this*? Kate asked herself, incredulous at her sister's blatant disregard for their well-being. *Oh well, it'll give me more time to think if I don't have to listen to her stupid ideas.*

The dawn snuck up as Kate lay on her pallet plotting and planning throughout the night. At one point she almost dozed off, but then she was startled to full alertness when the possibility that Beverly might pee on these people's floor entered her mind. This really caused Kate's gut to squeeze tightly on itself, and it burned so badly that she knew she would not sleep that night. Every hour or so she would shake Beverly awake and ask her if she needed to go to the bathroom. After one pee-check Beverly confirmed that yes, she did need to go. "I'm scared though, Kate. It's dark and I don't remember where anything is."

"Come on. I'll go with you," Kate offered, knowing she sounded like a much better sister than she really was.

The girls found the bathroom together. It was the first door on the right down the hallway just outside the living room. Beverly peed for what seemed like forever. But the sound of that urine hitting the toilet was music to

Kate's ears. *There's no way she'll pee on their floor now,* thought Kate.

Once the girls felt their way back to the pallet, Beverly immediately fell back into her deep, dreamless slumber. It occurred to Kate that Beverly hadn't even bothered to ask if her sister had come up with a plan for tomorrow. *As usual, they just know I'll take care of it,* thought Kate. And, as usual, she did.

With the dawn Mrs. Lopez came. She padded into the living room past the girls as quietly as possible and into the kitchen. Kate pretended to be asleep. Soon, she smelled all the smells of morning time. Coffee brewing, eggs cooking, bacon frying. It smelled heavenly. It reminded Kate of the days of the diner. These were the things she had smelled every morning of her life that she could remember up to about a year and a half ago. Kate's stomach began to growl. To get her mind off her hunger, she decided to go over the plan in her head one last time. But Mrs. Lopez was way ahead of her. She and her husband must have discussed their own plan because once everybody was up, dressed, and sitting around the breakfast table, Mrs. Lopez announced that she wanted all three girls to ride the bus home with Angie and Sarah after school that day. She declared in her authoritative way that it was dangerous for children to be left at home alone and that she would have no way of knowing whether Mom had gotten safely home or if the girls were home alone and fending for themselves. Therefore, the girls were to ride the bus back to the Lopez house after school, and when Mom got ready to come get them, she would know exactly where they were. Kate attempted a protest, but it was only half-hearted. The prospect of caring for herself and her sisters for several days with no food and no money was not particularly attractive to her, if she was being honest with herself. Yes, it was embarrassing, but at least they would have something to eat 'til Mom decided to come get them. And it didn't sound like Mrs. Lopez had any intentions of calling the welfare people on them, so it didn't seem like a half bad solution.

The girls did as they were told after school and rode home with Angie and Sarah. Mrs. Lopez greeted them all when they arrived and had a snack waiting for them. Then there was homework, which all the children finished quickly and with no major problems. Next, Mrs. Lopez informed the girls that, as long as they were staying with them, they would be expected to help with the daily chores. The girls didn't mind. Birdie actually seemed to be enjoying herself. Everyone in the Lopez family had a job to do, even the girls, for the time being. Birdie swept the floor, Kate dusted the wood furniture, and Beverly took out the trash.

After chores, the children had some time to themselves before it was time to start getting ready for bed. All the girls played house again. The evening passed peacefully, and Kate began to wonder if Mom was planning on leaving her and her sisters with the Lopezes forever. It was nice living with a normal family. The routine was comforting. *I wish she would just leave us here and never come back.* Kate was so shocked by her own thought that she was afraid to think anything for a few seconds. *Did I really just wish my mom would never come back? Did I really just wish to never see her again?* Kate felt appalled by the thoughts she was having. She was ashamed of herself. *Yeah, maybe Mom isn't perfect, maybe she's not as good of a parent as Mr. and Mrs. Lopez, but she's my mom! I oughta be grateful! Instead, here I am wishin' my own mom away.* She tried not to think about it anymore, but no matter what she tried to concentrate on her thoughts kept circling back around to the idea that Mom should just leave the girls with the Lopez family.

Chapter Seven

A loud banging on the front door announced Joyce's return. The girls had been playing in Angie and Sarah's room. It was evening time, and everyone had already bathed and was ready for bed. Mr. Lopez, well into his second six pack of beer had been sitting in the living room, so he was the first to see Joyce had returned for her children. He swung the door open mid-knock.

"Where are my girls? I want my girls," Joyce, obviously drunk, yelled in Mr. Lopez's face.

"Well, they're already in their night clothes. Why don't you go on home and sober up, Joyce? You can come get them tomorrow." He gave her a knowing look. "When you're in better shape to handle them," he said, lifting his eyebrows.

Eyes narrowed to mere slits, Joyce responded in a slow, menacing tone, "How dare you talk to me like that, *Mexico*? Who in the hell do you think you are?" She poked Mr. Lopez in the chest with a long, bony finger. "So, I've had a few drinks tonight? Looks like you're doin' the same, Mr. High 'n' Mighty."

"Joyce, I'm not gonna argue with you. You are drunk. Your girls are settled for the night. Go *home*. You can have them in the morning."

"Why, you Mexican sonofabitch!" Joyce screamed as she reared back one long, bare arm preparing to slap Mr. Lopez's face. By this time, all the girls had run from the bedroom and were hiding in the hallway listening.

Mr. Lopez easily caught Joyce's arm mid-swing and held it for a moment. Their eyes locked, Joyce said, "Give me my girls."

Calmly, Mr. Lopez answered, "Tomorrow."

Equally as calmly, Joyce made a sound like she was clearing her throat and spit in Mr. Lopez's face. Kate could not stand to see such a kind man treated so poorly in his own home for another second. Straightening her shoulders, attempting to act casual, she left their hiding spot in the hallway.

"Hey, Mom!" She feigned excitement. "I'm so glad you're back! I was ready to go home. I missed you so much!" She hugged her mother around the waist.

This eased some of the tension between Mom and Mr. Lopez. He let go of Mom's arm and pulled a handkerchief from his pants pocket. After wiping his face, Mr. Lopez peered down at Kate. "I thought you girls were all ready for bed, Kate."

"We were, Mr. Lopez. We were just playin' and waitin' on y'all to tell us when it was time."

"Hi, Katie Rae," Mom finally managed. "You ready to go home? Where's your sisters? Why don't you run get 'em for me real quick so we can get outta here?"

Feeling that the situation had deescalated, Kate ran back to the girls.

"You aren't leavin' with her tonight, are you?" asked Angie, concerned.

"We *got* to, Angie," Kate replied. "She won't leave y'all alone if we don't just go with her."

Angie nodded, put her hand on Kate's shoulder, and said no more.

When the girls had changed back into their own clothes and given back Angie and Sarah's pajamas, they headed for the living room, but stopped short when they heard Mrs. Lopez's voice. "Where in the world have you been, Joyce? Those little girls have been worried sick about you! What would happen to them if something had happened to you?"

Kate, Beverly and Birdie watched their mother, who just stared back at Mrs. Lopez, seemingly uncomprehending.

"They are your girls, Joyce! They are all you have left in this world! And you just run off and leave them with people who are strangers to you! What is wrong with you?"

"Nothin's wrong with me, Maria! I'm just - just - I get sad sometimes 'n' I just gotta get outta there."

"Well, it's not right, Joyce. It's not right the way you're doing those girls. I almost called the welfare people on you. If I had, they would have taken those girls. You know that, don't you? They would have taken them away from you."

"I know," was all Mom said. Kate had never seen Mom speechless before.

Now Mr. Lopez spoke up: "We're going to be keeping an eye on you and those girls, Joyce. And if you leave them like that again I won't care what my wife says. No matter how much she begs me, I will call the welfare people next time. You hear me?"

"There won't be a next time." Mom searched the room until her eyes found the girls. "Are my babies ready to go home?" Mom yelled.

"Yes!" her girls sang in unison. As they ran to their mother, the woman who had abandoned them, left them with people they barely knew for days, Kate couldn't help but wonder if her sisters wanted to stay right where they were as badly as she did.

Chapter Eight

After the Lopez incident, the girls decided they would try to help Mom, especially since the Lopez parents had threatened to involve child services. They tiptoed around Mom, trying not to stress her out. They cooked dinner, cleaned the house, and rolled Mom's cigarettes for her. They did everything they could think of to make Mom's life easier. And it worked. For a while, anyway. Mom went a whole three months without running off and leaving the girls. This hadn't happened in at least a year. Then Birdie got into some trouble at school.

Gangs were a big part of the youth culture in eastern Arizona. At school, Birdie had begun to feel the pressure of joining one. She had always been popular at school and had few problems making friends, but at their new school the kids were a little rougher than usual.

As they were walking home from school one day, Kate noticed there was dried, crusted blood around Birdie's right ear.

"Birdie Kay, what happened to your ear?" Kate asked.

"Nothin'." She stared straight ahead.

"There's blood all over it. What did you do to it?"

"Nothin', Kate."

Kate wanted to believe her little sister because things had been so peaceful lately at home, but she knew when Birdie was lying.

"Birdie Kay, what happened?" she asked, more seriously this time.

"I said nothing happened, Kate! God, why can't you just shut up about it?"

"Because I know you're lyin', that's why! Why can't you just tell me what happened? Why is it even a big deal? Just tell me what happened. Is somebody picking on you?"

"No! God, you're so nosy!"

"Birdie, just tell her. You know she's not gonna let it go 'til you tell her what happened," Beverly, who had been a silent observer up until now, chimed in.

Birdie sighed and said, "It's just some girls who want me to join their gang. It's not a big deal."

Kate laughed. "Their gang?" she asked, incredulous. "You're in the second grade!"

"I know! They're so dumb," Birdie chuckled, trying to make light of the situation.

"So, what happened?" asked Kate.

Resignedly, Birdie sighed. "I told them I didn't want to, but they just kept bugging me about it all day. Then, at lunch, on the playground, a bunch of them made a big circle around me and started hollering at me. They were so mean! They made me cry! It was *so* loud, Kate!" Here Birdie couldn't hold back her tears. "One of them got right up next to me like she was gonna tell me a secret and started screaming right in my ear! I put my hands over my ears, but she just kep' screaming. Then they were all screaming in my ear! I squatted down real low, so it'd stop hurtin', but they just got down beside me and kep' screaming. I felt something wet, and I thought one of them had spit on me, but when I looked, there was blood on my hand. When they saw the blood, they all ran off. It was hurtin' really bad, but you woulda been proud of me, Kate. I remembered not to tell my teacher because I didn't want 'em to bother Mom. I did good, didn't I? It still hurts, but it'll be okay. I'm tough. We don't have to say anything to Mom, do we?"

Kate and Beverly walked toward home silently, stealing glances at each other over Birdie's head. They were both thinking the same thing: *What should we do? What would be more stressful to Mom? To find out what those kids did to Birdie Kay? Or to find out that we knew and didn't tell her?*

The girls didn't need to decide. When they got home, Birdie tried to go straight to the bathroom to clean her ear off, but Mom noticed it right away.

"Birdie Kay, come 'ere, sweet girl. What'd you do to your baby ear?" Mom had been sitting on the couch smoking a cigarette when they walked in the front door. She held the cigarette expertly in her mouth and grabbed Birdie's head with both hands, unaware that her daughter was in agonizing pain. Birdie tried to bear Mom's examination with nonchalance, but she was only a little girl, and when Mom started to pull on the ear to try to look inside it, Birdie let out a howl.

Mom surprised everyone when she announced they were going to the hospital. Stunned, all three girls loaded themselves into the car. Mom didn't say a word on the drive. When they pulled into the parking lot, she turned to face Birdie, who sat in the front seat holding her ear. "Baby girl, you gonna tell Mamma what happened?"

Silence.

Beverly spoke up and told Mom everything. To her credit, Mom held herself together. All three girls knew she was getting bad. The shaky hands and Mom's sweat-covered brow over the last few days hadn't failed to escape their attention. They knew she was on edge and that beer was not going to do the trick for very much longer. They'd seen a vodka bottle in her possession, and they all knew that it wouldn't be long 'til she disappeared again.

Eerily calm, Mom spoke. "I want you girls to tell the doctor exactly what you told me when we get in there. You understand?" They did.

***

That night, after Birdie had been diagnosed with a busted eardrum and sent home with instructions for rest and a prescription for pain medication, Birdie asked Mom, "Are you mad?" Tears brimmed her eyes.

"Oh, baby, I'm mad, but I'm not mad at you," Mom answered as she stroked Birdie's head and held her close on the couch. Mom sat looking into the distance for several minutes. All three girls stared at her, silent. They half expected her to get up, grab her keys, and disappear into the night. Instead, Mom spoke: "You know what? That filthy school's fulla lice and dirty Mexicans anyway! Joyce Bloom's girls are too good for that goddamn school! How would y'all like to go to Oklahoma and see Mamma's family? Huh? How would y'all like that?"

All three girls liked Mom's idea very much. Kate and Beverly hopped around the living room clapping their hands and giggling together. Birdie watched them enviously, wishing she felt well enough to join in her sisters' celebration.

Though they celebrated on the outside, the girls worried on the inside. Could they really go back to Oklahoma? Just like that? What about money? Would their old jalopy car make it that far? All these thoughts threatened to ruin the family's celebration, but none of them dared let those thoughts in. They, instead, chose to enjoy the moment.

Chapter Nine

As it turned out, Mom had been thinking about taking the girls back to Oklahoma ever since the Lopez parents had threatened to call child services. She had continued to work as a waitress and socked money away for several weeks. They couldn't leave the very next day. There was packing to do. There was money to borrow from Mom's boss. She knew he was partial toward her and promised that she just wanted to visit her parents and would be back inside of two weeks, knowing she had no intention of ever returning to Arizona. Of course, her boss fell for it.

Sure enough, within the week, Mom had scraped together enough money for them to travel from Arizona to Oklahoma. "I just have to make one stop first," Mom announced as the last of their belongings were loaded into the old Cadillac. When they pulled into the parking lot of the girls' old school, all three girls gasped and immediately began to protest, though they knew it would do no good.

"Now listen! Hold your horses, girls!" Mom raised her voice above theirs. "I just want to run in real quick and talk to the principal about what happened to Birdie Kay. I'll be right back!"

The girls sat helpless inside the sweltering car, dreading what their imaginations (and experience) insisted was going to happen. Kate kept looking over her shoulder expecting the police or the welfare people to pull up any minute and foil their escape plan. As the minutes ticked by, the silence and the heat grew. Little wisps of dust floated through the air. Kate felt salty beads of sweat forming on her upper lip. Her bare legs stuck to the seat. None of the girls spoke. They all stared at the door, collectively willing

Mom to appear. After nearly twenty minutes, a beautiful woman came sashaying out of the schoolhouse, practically skipping down the sidewalk. Because of the carefree lilt in her step, it took the girls a beat longer than usual to realize it was Joyce.

Mom slung the car door open, and a gust of hot, dry air swept across their faces. She plopped herself down in the driver's seat, grinning from ear to ear. All the girls stared at their mother, who they had rarely seen in such a good mood.

"What?" asked Mom, still with a shit-eating grin plastered on her face.

"You just seem so happy," Kate finally managed. "What happened?"

"Oh, nothing much. Just gave those bastards a piece of my mind, that's all! Do my little girl like that and think they're not gonna hear from Joyce Bloom? I don't think so!" Mom cackled. "Y'all ready? Mamma's gotta make one more stop and then we're Oklahoma-bound!"

The girls didn't find out until years later that Joyce had marched into the principal's office like she owned the place, cussed the principal up one side and down the other, threatened to sue the school, and somehow walked out with a personal check from the principal for a hundred dollars.

They stopped at a grocery store on their way out of town where Mom told the girls to wait in the car. She came prancing out fifteen minutes later carrying a grocery bag full of travelling snacks and a six-pack of beer. Once she was in the car, she flashed a wad of cash. It looked to Kate like more than enough money to get them where they needed to go. Maybe this was what Mom needed to get her back to her old self. Maybe she just needed to be around her family, around people who loved her and knew how to help her. Maybe this was their chance to start over. Maybe everything would be alright, and these past few terrible years would someday be a distant memory that they looked back on and laughed about. Suddenly, Kate felt like everything was possible, like they could start their lives over again. An unfamiliar feeling rose from the pit of her stomach and seemed to catch in Kate's throat. *What is this? Hope maybe?* she asked herself as Mom started the car and backed out of the parking lot.

Oklahoma

Chapter Ten

Three hot, dusty days later, they crossed the border into Oklahoma. Everyone was tired of being in the car, but the girls were happy to leave Arizona behind, so they didn't much mind that two days earlier Mom had switched from beer to vodka. Mom was actually kind of funny when she had been drinking. They had listened to stories about her home for the past few days and all felt a little closer to Mom after hearing about the farm, Mother and Papaw, and her brothers, John and Buddy. Some stories they had heard many times, but there were several new ones. All the girls felt like they knew Mom better than they had ever known her before. When Mom got tired of talking, she would turn up the radio. They sang every song they had ever heard together. And sometimes they would turn off the radio and sing songs from happier times. Everyone in the car was thinking of Dad, but no one mentioned him.

Gradually, the landscape went from flat and brown to hilly and green. The closer Mom got to home, the more sentimental she got. And the more she drank. Finally, the highway speed slowed to country road speeds. Then, suddenly, it seemed everywhere the girls looked, there were barbed wire fences - and cows. Black cows, brown cows, black and white cows. *So, this is Oklahoma*, thought Kate, unimpressed. Then, at last, Mom pulled into a sort of driveway, but instead of cement or gravel, the driveway was made of hard-packed red dirt. Barbed wire surrounded the land. The house was short and squat and sprawling. There were several big, red barns dotting the property as far as the girls could see. An old tractor rested in the front yard, and the largest man the girls had ever seen climbed down from the cab carrying a toolbox. Clad in denim, he wore a large, whitish cowboy hat. Mom stopped the car and began to do something none of the girls could have ever imagined their mother doing: *squealing*. Like a little *girl*. Before the girls could process this, however, Mom sprang from the car and sprinted toward the large, menacing man. She jumped into his arms and, switching the cowboy hat from head to hand, he swiftly caught her and swung her in circles as if she were a toddler! All three girls sat in stunned silence staring at their mother in disbelief. None of them could remember ever seeing Mom so happy. Then the man put Mom down and started toward the car, toward *them*. They were terrified. But, as the man drew closer to the car and they could make out his features, they felt less threatened. He had thick, yellow-blonde hair (not unlike Kate's) and, as he drew closer, they were able to make out bright, crystal blue, kind eyes, made even more striking by the man's dark, suntanned skin. He was smiling at them.

The man slung open the driver's side door and hollered in a raspy, baritone voice with a thick redneck accent, "Joyce! Who are these grown women you brought with you? They're sa perty! Any of 'em single?" Then he laughed, loud and genuine, exposing large, healthy, white teeth. If the girls hadn't already been disarmed by his appearance, the laugh did the trick. They liked the man immediately, even though he was a stranger to them. "Y'all get outta that ol' hot car 'n come on in the house 'n meet Bobbie! I know she's got somethin' ta eat in there! She's always cookin' somethin'! I think I mighta seen a chocolate cake in there this mornin'!"

If the girls thought they liked Uncle John, they knew they loved Aunt Bobbie from the very first time they laid eyes on her. She was a tall, slender woman with a bouffant hairdo. She wore lots of makeup: blue eyeshadow, frosted pink lipstick, and drawn-on eyebrows. All three girls thought she appeared very sophisticated. Aunt Bobbie wore blue jeans that were snug but fit her well. She wore a blue button-up men's collared shirt tucked in and a skinny, silver belt with tan cowboy boots. They had never seen anything like her. Aunt Bobbie smiled a lot. And she made the best chocolate cake! It was almost as good as Mom's birthday cakes.

Mom and the giant man, Uncle John, talked, laughed, and drank late into the night. Aunt Bobbie couldn't have been happier to have three little girls in her home. She fed them, and then she gave them free reign of her humongous bathroom. The girls bathed (at Aunt Bobbie's urging) with Avon products: pink and purple bubble baths, thick liquid body soaps, rich, pearly shampoos, creamy hair conditioners, and warm, thick, luxurious towels to dry themselves. After all those days of travelling in the hot, cramped car, a full belly and a long soak in the bath were just what the girls needed to feel like themselves again, or even better!

Even though Kate was immensely enjoying herself, she couldn't help but feel apprehensive. She kept waiting for the other shoe to drop. It had been so long since someone had been kind to them. It had been even longer since the girls could think about themselves instead of always worrying about Mom: was she about to leave? When would she be back? Was she okay? To Kate, the sensation of thinking about herself for once was unfamiliar and overwhelming. For some reason, she fought the urge to cry.

Aunt Bobbie seemed to somehow sense Kate's trepidation. After the girls had donned night clothes, clean and full of good food, Bobbie, who had put fresh sheets on the pull-out couch-bed in the living room, tucked in Birdie and Beverly. Then she came and sat beside Kate. She didn't say anything at first. She just looked her in the eye, held her hand, and smiled down at her. Kate could not look away from this stranger who she referred to as "Aunt Bobbie." *Why does she look like she knows what I'm thinking right now?* Kate wondered.

"I'm so glad you're here, sweetheart."

Kate smiled, but haltingly. She still wrestled with the urge to cry, and, for some reason, it embarrassed her. "I'm glad we're here, too," she managed to whisper.

"I've always heard your family talk about what a pretty little girl you are, but I had no idea you were so gorgeous!" Aunt Bobbie smiled conspiratorially. Kate couldn't help but giggle. She and Aunt Bobbie laughed and talked like old friends about nothing, about everything. She was surprised at one point when she looked over and saw that Birdie and Beverly were both fast asleep.

"She pees the bed, you know," Kate said as she nodded toward Beverly.

Aunt Bobbie laughed, "Well, I appreciate the warning. You know what you want for breakfast in the mornin'?"

"You're cookin' us breakfast in the mornin'?" Kate asked, surprised.

"Course I am, gal! Yer all three sa skinny I can see right through ya to yer bones!"

Kate laughed. She felt she needed to say something monumentally grateful to this kind, kind woman, but she couldn't think of anything except, "Thank you, Aunt Bobbie."

Aunt Bobbie smiled, and Kate returned her smile, realizing the urge to cry had left her.

As she drifted off, Kate thought to herself that if Beverly did pee the bed she would happily get up and wash the sheets in the bathtub so that Aunt Bobbie wouldn't have to. *I hope there's dish soap in the kitchen. Shoot, this place is so fancy they might even have bleach.* Kate slept better that night than any night in her recent memories.

***

When she woke late the next morning, she was relieved to find that Beverly had not wet the bed. As a matter of fact, Beverly was altogether gone. And so was Mom, along with the gold K necklace Dad had given her.

Chapter Eleven

"I am so sorry, Aunt Bobbie. I know she'll be back here pretty soon to get us. We won't be any trouble. I swear. We won't be any trouble. I promise, you won't even know we're here. I'm really sorry," Kate implored.

"Oh, honey. I don't want you to worry yourself one little bit about that. To be completely honest, sweetheart, your Uncle John and me, we were sorta hopin' you girls'd come stay with us for a while. We even talked to your mamma about it a little last night. She did leave a note for ya. You feel like readin' it right now, or do you wanna wait 'til after you get some food in yer belly?"

Kate didn't quite know how to take this news. First, Mom had never left a note before. Second, why did she choose to take Beverly with her instead of Kate, who had always been her favorite? And, more important, was Mom's favorite daughter happy about this decision? Finally, most important, why did Aunt Bobbie seem so happy? Didn't she know that it would more than likely be weeks before Mom came back for them? She thought back to the Lopez family. Yes, they had been kind to the girls after Mom had left them in their care, but they were obviously bothered by the prospect of three more mouths to feed for an undetermined length of time. And Kate couldn't blame them. Hadn't she been the one left to feed and care for her sisters many times when Mom had decided to go off on one of her escapades? She knew what it was like to have other people's welfare depend on her, and it was never anything to smile about. So, why was Aunt Bobbie so happy?

"I think I'd like to read it now," Kate said. Aunt Bobbie rose from her seat in the living room and went into the kitchen. She returned with a folded piece of paper and handed it to Kate. She gingerly unfolded the stiff, white paper and braced herself for the worst:

> *Dear Katie Rhea,*
>
> *Mamma has not been herself since your daddy had to go away. We both know my drinking has gotten out of hand. Your Uncle John and Aunt Bobbie have offered to keep you girls for a little bit while I try to get better. I don't know where I'll go or what I'll do, but I hope that the next time I see you I will be able to be the mother to you and your sisters that you deserve.*
>
> *Be a good girl. Your Uncle John and your Aunt Bobbie are good people, but it has been a long time since they have had kids around. And even when they did have kids around, they had two boys. Raising girls is a lot different. Be patient with them.*
>
> *Beverly is going to stay with Mother and Papaw. She is a little harder to handle than you and Birdie Kay, so I thought it would be for the best.*
>
> *Please don't hate me and know that I am doing what I think is best for you and your sisters.*
>
> *I will always love you. Thank you for being such a good girl. I will see you soon, my sweet girl.*
>
> *Love,*
>
> *Your (not perfect) Mamma*

***

Aunt Bobbie, wearing a fluffy pink bathrobe and rollers as fat as orange juice cans in her hair, sat patiently with her legs crossed, flipping a matching pink house slipper on and off of her left foot, smoking a cigarette and drinking coffee from a thick, chipped, white ceramic mug as she watched

Kate read Joyce's letter once, twice, finally, three times. *Well, Kate, you knew this was coming. Better make yourself useful around here 'til she gets back.* "Do you need any help with breakfast, Aunt Bobbie?" was all Kate could think to say.

As she asked Bobbie this question, the little girl carefully folded the note from her mother and walked over to place it in the crinkled brown paper grocery bag that held everything she owned in the world.

"Oh, baby!" Bobbie sobbed. "Come 'ere." She held out her arms and stared at Kate, who looked back, confused. She stood stock still. "I know this is so hard for you, sweetheart! But it's okay. We'll get through it. I know you're gonna miss your mamma. Come 'ere," she beckoned, arms outstretched, wiggling her shiny, long, frosted pink fingernails.

Aunt Bobbie was so sincere that Kate felt she had to reciprocate her aunt's affections, though, if she was being honest with herself, she felt nothing. She experienced a hollowness in the pit of her stomach that was oddly comforting. This, she was prepared to deal with. *At least this time she left us with someone who might like us, someone we're kin to,* Kate thought as she uncomfortably returned Aunt Bobbie's heartfelt hug. Although she seemed sincere, Aunt Bobbie's earnest affection made Kate uneasy. *What does this woman want?* She asked herself. *We don't have anything to offer her except more work. She's a grown-up. She's gotta know all we're gonna do is make her life more inconvenient. She'll have to cook more, clean more, spend more money to feed us.* Then Kate figured it out: *Oh! Maybe she wants us to do all that stuff for her. Maybe she's thinkin' me and Birdie'll be a big help to her.* Kate looked around Aunt Bobbie and Uncle John's spacious, well-furnished living room. *We could do that,* she thought. *Shoot, if they'll feed us and let us stay here 'til Mom comes back for us, I don't mind doin' a little work.*

Maybe we could even help Uncle John around the farm. Immediately, Kate felt she should let Aunt Bobbie know what assets two girls could be around the house and the farm, even if they were a little on the young side. "Aunt Bobbie, we'll help out around here a lot. I know we're young, but we're hard workers--"

Aunt Bobbie interrupted Kate's pitch. "Oh, you stop that right now, you hear me, Katie Rhea? You're our nieces, and we are tickled to death to have you girls stay with us, whether it's for a week or for a year or for forever! You hear me?" As Aunt Bobbie said this, she held Kate by the shoulders and looked her directly in the eye. "We are happy you girls are gonna be here with us. You know how long it's been since I had some company around here, little girl? Your Uncle John's workin' all the time. It gets sa lonesome around here sometimes I think I'll lose my mind if I don't get somebody to talk to!"

Aunt Bobbie seemed sincere. This only confused Kate more.

"I'm gonna wake Birdie up and tell her what's goin' on," was the only response Kate could muster.

Aunt Bobbie sat silent for a moment studying Kate. "Alright." She smiled. While you're tellin' your sister the good news I'm gonna go make y'all somethin' for breakfast. Any requests?"

Kate thought for a moment. "Whatever's easiest - Aunt Bobbie? Have you seen a little gold necklace with a K on it anywhere? I think I mighta lost it."

Chapter Twelve

It took a while for the two girls to get used to John and Bobbie's sincerity. Kate and Birdie, by this time, had become accustomed to either feeling like they were a burden or worrying they would be left alone to fend for themselves. But the girls were surprised to find Uncle John and Aunt Bobbie seemed happy to have them in their home.

Kate had been mortified a day or two after they'd come to John and Bobbie's to discover that - along with their heaping paper bags full of dirty laundry - their drunk mother, and insatiable appetites, both girls had shown up on their doorstep infested with head lice. But, true to her word, Aunt Bobbie bore both girls' troubles with infinite patience. She even went to the store and bought the fancy head lice remedy instead of doing what Mom had always done, which was to spray the girls' heads with roach spray several times a day until the infestation seemed to dissipate.

Once the unwelcome critters had been dealt with, Aunt Bobbie announced one day that she was going to charge the girls with a task. *Oh, finally, here it comes*, thought Kate, relieved that, at last, she would know these people's true motive. *I can handle it,* she figured. *No matter what it is, I can handle it. They're feeding us. They're letting us stay here. Whatever they want us to do, I can handle it. And I can help Birdie Kay get through it.*

Kate braced herself for whatever new hell awaited her and her sister.

Kate and Birdie were both seated on John and Bobbie's brown and tan velveteen couch expecting the worst. Though there was plenty of room on the couch, they sat close, clutching each other's hands.

Uncle John sat across from them grinning, reclining against the large, plush back of his easy chair. He took a large gulp from a tall glass of iced sweet tea. As he set it down, the ice clinking to the bottom of the nearly-empty glass, Bobbie walked over to the girls holding a thick, heavy-looking catalogue. She seemed excited. This worried both girls.

"Alright, girls. Me and your Uncle John been talkin' and we think it's about time for y'all to help us out with some things around this place." Both girls eyed Aunt Bobbie and Uncle John suspiciously. "You see this book?" She gestured toward the catalogue she was holding, and Kate noticed Aunt Bobbie's finger was stuck inside the catalogue marking a certain page. She strode over and squeezed herself between the two apprehensive girls. "We can't have y'all laid up in the living room on the couch every night. It just ain't right," Bobbie sighed. Uncle John, eyes closed now, nodded heartily in agreement with his wife.

Oh no! thought Kate. *Are they gonna make us stay out back in a shed? Or in the barn with the cows where it's all dark and scary? Birdie Kay might not be able to handle that*, she panicked. *She's still just a little girl. Maybe I can talk them into letting her stay in here. I'd be okay with that. But what if there are rats out there? Or snakes?* Kate immediately started forming a plan for Birdie and her to run away. *Where will we go?* She asked herself. But, before Kate could get too far into her escape plan, Aunt Bobbie interrupted her thoughts.

"Okay, girls. It's time to decide. They've got these nice oak beds that're just beautiful, and I will be okay with whatever you decide. They're your beds. But I just have to say that I love these white ones! They are so feminine!" She flipped through catalogue and revealed a dog-eared page displaying a little girls' matching bedroom suit with two white, twin-size beds, intricate flowering designs etched across the headboards. Each bed boasted a soaring white canopy and was bedecked with a plush, baby blue and white quilt on top of soft baby-blue sheets. Matching white nightstands, topped with reading lamps squatted beside the beds, and in the corner, loomed an ornate chest of drawers. Both girls, on either side of Aunt Bobbie, sat staring wide-eyed at the bedroom they were sure every little girl dreamed of having. Neither spoke.

Hurriedly, Aunt Bobbie explained, "Y'all don't have to get what I like. It's *your* bedroom. You get to pick. I just really like this one. But it's up to you. Whichever one you want is fine with us."

"Oh, Aunt Bobbie, we don't need nothin' like that," Kate stammered. "That must cost a fortune." She didn't know what to think or how to respond. Were these people they barely knew considering buying this elaborate bedroom for them? "We're not even gonna be here for that long. I'd hate for you to waste your money on something so expensive. We're as happy as can be right here on the couch. Really. We couldn't ask for more. Huh, Birdie Kay?" Kate looked at her little sister expectantly. But Birdie was completely entranced by the picture of the dream bedroom. "Huh, Birdie Kay!" Kate repeated more forcefully.

"Oh!" Birdie said, roused from her dreams. "Oh, yeah. Kate's right, Aunt Bobbie. We don't need alla that. Anyways, Mom'll be back to get us in a day or two," she offered sweetly, if half-heartedly.

"Girls," Uncle John chimed in, somewhat uncomfortably, "your mamma's not gonna be back to get y'all for quite a while. She's off tryin' to get herself better. She's had a pretty hard time since your daddy went away," he said in a gentle voice. "I know y'all miss her. And you ought to. She's a real good lady. But how 'bout let's just go on like it might be a long time 'til she comes back? Then, if she comes to get y'all earlier it'll be a real nice surprise? But 'til she does how 'bout we just pretend y'all are gonna live with us for a while? How would that be? Ya think ye could do that?"

Uncle John had such an earnest look in his eyes, and, truthfully, both girls were quite content to stay with their aunt and uncle for as long as it took that neither of them had the heart to object, even though they both desperately missed Mom and (surprisingly) Beverly.

The least we could do is be happy while she's gone, thought Kate, even though, in the back of her mind, she felt unexplainably guilty that she was happier with Aunt Bobbie and Uncle John than she had been with Mom in years.

"Is she okay, Uncle John?" Kate asked.

"Baby, your mamma is fine. And she don't want y'all mopin' around here the whole time she's gone. She knows Uncle John's gonna take good care a you girls. It's alright for y'all to have a little fun, y'know."

"Yeah!" Aunt Bobbie chimed in. "You girls are our family. We love you. We want you to feel like you're at home when you're with us."

"I sure do like those beds," Birdie whispered, eyes wide. "They're so pretty!"

John, Bobbie, and even Kate laughed. It was true. The beds were beautiful. And if it made these sweet, sweet people happy to give her and Birdie this bedroom set, who was Kate to deny them that? It made her happy to make them happy. "I like them too," she stated.

"Then it's settled!" cried Aunt Bobbie. "I knew y'all'd like the white!"

Chapter Thirteen

For the first time in what felt like a very long time, the girls could act their age. They fought over silly things. They went to picture shows downtown to see scary movies. After they saw Dracula, they lay in their matching twin beds and talked about how scared they were, which in a strange way seemed like a luxury. It was nice to fear something imaginary instead of being scared of the really terrifying things in life, like knowing they'd have nothing to eat the next day and no Mom to make sure they were safe.

The best thing about living with Aunt Bobbie and Uncle John, by far though, was that they could play. They were once again free to pretend. Aunt Bobbie and Uncle John gave them a dime every week as allowance for doing chores. At first, this seemed ridiculous to both girls. Allowance? For making sure they did silly little things like helping with the dishes after dinner? Both girls had a hard time getting used to this. At first, they hoarded their dimes, both saving up for when they were back with Mom and they needed to eat. They competed fiercely with each other to see who could save the most money, both picturing the day when Mom came back into their lives. Who would she be the proudest of for managing to provide the most food? But, after a few weeks, the girls got a little more comfortable and started to let go of a little money at a time. Eventually, they gave into temptation. Of course, Birdie was the first to cave. She'd had her eye on a Barbie doll for weeks. Every time Aunt Bobbie took them to the general store downtown Birdie took her dimes with her, intent on buying herself her first Barbie. Kate would encourage her to buy it, always mindful of their competition, knowing Birdie's purchase would give her the edge she desired. Aunt Bobbie, ever patient, would wait on the girls, listening, amused, to their conversations about the purchase. Time after time, Birdie talked herself out of it. Until the day a new Barbie arrived, wearing a matching pink jacket and skirt, complete with a pillbox hat. It was more temptation than any seven-year-old girl could resist.

Kate lorded her loot over Birdie for less than a week. The more she watched Birdie play with her new Barbie, the weaker she got. It took exactly one week for her to follow in her little sister's footsteps. The first opportunity she had, she bought the same Barbie, only hers wore a blue outfit. The dolls were so beautiful. They cost two dollars and seventeen cents apiece, and neither girl ever even considered buyer's remorse.

Aunt Bobbie seemed to enjoy the girls' new purchases even more than the girls. She spent one whole Saturday afternoon helping them construct a Barbie house from old cardboard boxes. Even Uncle John got in on the fun that night.

It was early August and the heat in Oklahoma had become stifling. "Girls, ya did a good job on this house for yer dolls, but yer missin' somethin'." Uncle John disappeared and all three girls forgot that he had even commented on their construction until he came back into the living room with one of Aunt Bobbie's hairspray cans. They all watched curiously as he opened the front door, stepped out, and began spraying her hairspray into the air for no apparent reason.

"John! What in the world are you doing with my hairspray, honey? You're wastin' it!" cried Aunt Bobbie, running to the door.

"You'll see! Hang on a second, woman!" Uncle John chided teasingly. They all looked on curiously until

Uncle John brought the can back into the house, empty. He then kicked off his cowboy boots and spread himself out like a little boy on his stomach on the living room floor in front of the Barbie house. "Where's the bedroom?" he asked. Kate pointed to a corner of the cardboard box meant to be Barbie's upstairs bedroom. Uncle John placed the can on the outside of the "house" and pointed the nozzle into the bedroom window, pressing down on it.

Amazed, Birdie exclaimed, "It's an air conditioner, Kate! Our Barbies have an air conditioner in their house!" Uncle John grinned, knowing he was the hero in the room. Aunt Bobbie looked at him like he had just rescued her from sure death. They all sat on the living room floor playing Barbies for the rest of the evening.

Eventually, the Barbie house was relegated to the girls' bedroom, but they didn't mind. Kate and Birdie spent hours every day playing. Their bedroom, with its new furniture, felt like it belonged to someone else. It was always so clean. It never smelled bad, and there was always enough light during the day coming through the large plate glass window when they pulled back the curtains that they didn't even have to turn on the lights. The soft, green shag carpeting was clean and comfortable. There were many times when Aunt Bobbie had to drag them from their bedroom to eat or bathe, both activities that, before coming to Bobbie and John's, they would have jumped at. Sometimes it would dawn on Kate that she was playing pretend and enjoying herself. It seemed to her she was living in an alternate reality. She rarely even felt the need to cuss anymore. At first, she told herself she was just doing it to entertain her little sister, but, after a while, she couldn't deny she was having just as much fun as Birdie. The best times were the times when she would look up and catch Aunt Bobbie standing in the doorway secretly watching them.

The first time it happened, Kate looked up and saw Aunt Bobbie standing there watching them like they were the only two little girls who existed, like they were something rare and special. She couldn't remember ever seeing an adult look at her that way, not like she was a bother, an annoyance, an unwanted responsibility, but like she was something special, something wanted. Someone who mattered. She didn't know what to think of the feelings this evoked deep in her gut. She had never felt anything like it before. At least she couldn't remember ever feeling anything like this. But surely she had. Surely, Mom had looked at her like this before. Hadn't she? Or Dad? Of course, they had. She'd just been too young to remember it. At these times, she forced herself not to think of Mom or of Dad. She simply let herself enjoy these rare moments because she figured they wouldn't last.

***

"You girls wanna go see your sister?" asked Aunt Bobbie one day, out of the blue.

"Yes!" Exclaimed Birdie. "Beverly!"

Birdie obviously missed Beverly. Kate didn't answer. She hadn't thought about Beverly in weeks, and the mention of her name brought feelings of guilt. *What if Beverly isn't having fun?* she asked herself. She had been so wrapped up in letting John and Bobbie spoil her that she hadn't even given Beverly's situation a second thought. And she was appalled at herself when she caught herself dreading seeing Beverly. The past several weeks had been so relaxing. She hadn't had to worry about anyone but herself, and she was ashamed to admit to herself that she was reluctant to have to go check on her own sister. But then Kate remembered she had a question for her sister.

"Well, y'all go get ready! We're going to Mother and Papaw's this afternoon to visit! Y'all can take your

Barbies if you want," Aunt Bobbie yelled from the bathroom. She was, as she called it, "gittin' dolled up."

The drive was surprisingly short. Who knew they had only been living a few minutes away from their sister this whole time? Mother and Papaw were not strangers to the girls. They knew who they were; they just hadn't seen their grandparents since they were barely old enough to remember them.

"Aunt Bobbie, how come we call our grandma 'Mother'?" asked Birdie. She wrinkled her freckled nose at Kate, giggling about the strange title. Kate giggled back.

From the front seat, Bobbie craned her neck to look Birdie in the eye. "Well, little girl, I'm not sure why. Why don't cha ask yer uncle?" She smiled in John's direction, a questioning expression on her face.

Uncle John, not taking his eyes off the dirt road ahead, said, "You know what, Birdie Kay? I never thought of it before. All us kids called 'er that our whole lives, so I guess y'all always heard yer mamma call her that."

"Oh," answered Birdie. "That makes sense." She shrugged.

Mother and Papaw lived on the other end of the farm, it turned out. They resided in an old, two-story farmhouse that was small and faded, but quaint. As they pulled into the dusty, red dirt driveway, Beverly ran out the front door. She was the same old Beverly, only fatter. She grinned from ear to ear, and when she slung open the car door to see her sisters, they both immediately noticed Beverly's new accessory: shiny, black tap shoes. *Real* tap shoes.

Mother and Papaw kissed Kate and Birdie and hugged them tightly. They kept commenting on how beautiful they both were and how much they had grown since the last time they had seen them. Mother even cried.

"Have you talked to my mom?" Kate asked Mother.

"No, baby girl. We haven't heard from your mamma. But she's doin' okay, I can tell ya that," said Mother kindly. Her soft blue eyes seemed like they were on the verge of tears at the mention of her only daughter.

Beverly was pulling on Kate's arm. She wanted to show her and Birdie her new room, and she wanted to play a new game with them.

"Oh, girls!" cried Papaw. "She has been so excited to see her sisters. That's all she's talked about for three days," he teased, smiling, seemingly proud of Beverly.

While the adults sat outside on brightly colored lawn chairs visiting, Beverly dragged her sisters by the forearms into the little farmhouse, grinning from ear to ear. As they entered the house, Beverly's tap shoes hit the linoleum floor of the small entryway and made delicate little tapping sounds with every step that she took. Both girls were a little envious.

"Whadda y'all think?" she asked, beaming, once they had entered her bedroom. There was an iron framed bed in the middle of the room, the mattress covered with an elaborately sewn quilt. It was beautiful. Her room looked so homey and soft. Both girls, though they thought their room was much more stylish and modern, said they were happy for their sister and that they loved her bedroom. In addition to the bed, the room contained a beautiful, old, solid, cedar armoire and a small desk situated in the corner of the room complete with a matching chair.

"This is my school desk," boasted Beverly. "It's where I do my work. Y'all wanna play school?"

"Sure," both girls answered at once, excited to play a new game.

"Come on," she said, leading them through the sparsely furnished little farmhouse and out the back door into the backyard where they stopped at a small patch of cement about as big as a living room rug.

"I'm the teacher," said Beverly. "You have to do what I say."

Both girls, out of their element and happy to see their sister, willingly complied.

"Every morning when you get to school, I start out the day by doing a little dance for my students," explained Beverly. "Go sit down," she commanded.

Both girls obediently sat on the irregularly shaped concrete pad. Once they had been instructed to scoot this way and that, when they were seated according to their sister's intricate instructions, Beverly began. She stomped and waved her arms soulfully. For five minutes, then ten minutes, then fifteen minutes. Both girls watched, at first amused, then bored, then (after being scolded by their older sister for not paying enough attention) miserable. They had to admit that she had stamina. Her little chubby legs wobbled and turned red. Her shorts rode up higher and higher on her inner thighs as she danced until there was nowhere left for them to go. Beverly didn't seem to notice; she kept right on going, dancing to a tune that, apparently, only she could hear.

Once the performance came to an end, Beverly bowed elegantly and awaited her applause. Kate and Birdie clapped obediently, not knowing quite what to say after such a passionate performance. Normally, they would have laughed at such a ridiculous spectacle, but they both somehow knew that Beverly needed to be indulged just as Bobbie and John had been indulging them over the past several weeks. So, they held in their laughter until the end of the evening.

Once John and Bobbie announced they were going home and the goodbyes and promises to return had been made and they were safely in the car and out of Beverly's sight, they could finally let out their real feelings. They were barely out of the driveway when they finally made eye contact. Once the girls started laughing, it was hard to stop. Birdie had tears rolling down her cheeks. After the giggles had subsided, they couldn't look at each other or it would start all over again.

Back home and in their bedroom, there was a brief relapse. Finally, the girls were able to compose themselves and discuss their evening.

"Did you ask her about your necklace?"

"Yeah," Kate replied. "Mom took it."

"What? Why?"

"Bev said Mom went around the house right before they left taking things here and there. When she took my necklace off me, Bev was too scared to ask her why. Maybe she wanted something to remember me by." Kate shrugged her shoulders.

"Yeah, I bet that's it. She'll give it back when she comes to get us."

"Yeah, I know. I just hate not havin' it. It always reminded me of Dad."

"I know. Hey, did you see how fat Bev's gettin'?" asked Birdie, eager to turn the subject away from such a sad subject.

"Yeah, she's humongous!" exclaimed Kate. "Are *we* gettin' fat?"

Birdie looked down at her own stomach. "I don't think so. Do I look fatter to you?"

Kate appraised her little sister's midsection. "It looks the same as it always has," she shrugged.

"You look the same too. I wonder why Beverly's gettin so big."

"I don't know," Kate frowned in deep thought. "Did you notice her teeth?"

"Yeah, I saw 'em. I think they're rotten."

"Yes! The edges of the front ones are all black and crackly-looking." Kate sighed. "I'm so glad Mom left us with John and Bobbie instead of Mother and Papaw, aren't you?"

"Yeah!" Birdie started to giggle again. "Just think, we'd be big and fat like Beverly, and our teeth'd be black! Ew!" she laughed.

"Mother and Papaw seem nice though, don't they? You don't think they're mean to her or anything, do you?" Kate asked.

"No way! I think they're really nice. Maybe too nice, y'know? I mean, Aunt Bobbie makes us brush our teeth every morning and every night whether we want to or not. Sometimes I wish she wouldn't be so strict about it, but now after seeing poor Bev's teeth, I guess I'm glad she makes us do it."

"Yeah, I guess so. Maybe that's why she's getting so fat too. Mother and Papaw just let her eat sweets and bad food all the time. Aunt Bobbie always makes us eat all our vegetables before she lets us eat her cakes and pies. And they're so good that I always want to eat more than one piece, but I guess her not letting us is a good thing, or we'd look just like Bev."

Birdie seemed to be deep in thought. "Kate, do you miss Mom?" Birdie asked, tears suddenly appearing in her eyes.

"What made you think of Mom?" Kate asked.

"I don't know. Talking about Bev bein' fat and havin' rotten teeth just made me wonder what we'd be like if we were still with Mom. I never brushed my teeth when we were with her. And then once I thought that, it made me think of Mom. I wondered what she's doing right now. And then I wondered if she even misses us. And it made me remember that *I* miss *her*." Both girls sat in silence for a moment, just looking at each other. "Do you?" Birdie asked.

"Yeah. I miss her." Kate admitted. "But that doesn't mean I want to leave here. Uncle John and Aunt Bobbie are so good to us. Sometimes I lay in bed at night and think I'd be okay if we never saw 'er again." Birdie looked surprised at Kate's naked honesty, but she remained silent as Kate continued. "Sometimes I miss her so bad that it makes my stomach clench up. But I don't think I want to go back with 'er.'"

In all the time since they had left Bloom street, the girls had never discussed Mom's behavior and the lifestyle they had been forced to live over the past few years. They had all three instinctively known that their job was not to judge their mother, but to protect her at all costs, even at the expense of their own welfare. And talking about it, feeling sorry for themselves, would only make things seem worse. So, they didn't. Ever. Now that their basic human needs were being met and they had adults in their lives they could depend on, they were starting to feel safe enough to look back at the past few years, even talk about it.

"I don't want to go back with her either, Kate," Birdie whispered conspiratorially, her hazel eyes wide, like she was afraid she was going to get in trouble for even uttering the words. "I love it here."

At the mention of possibly betraying Mom, Kate felt a rush of guilt. She felt like she had to say something in Mom's defense. "Yeah, but do you think she would be okay without us? I mean, we take care of her. What would she do without us?"

"Is it bad that I don't really care anymore? I mean, she's our *mom*. Isn't *she* supposed to be the one who takes care of *us*?"

"Yeah, but I mean, she's having a hard time. She was a good mom when Dad was around. She's just sad. And what kinda kids would we be if we just thought about ourselves all the time?"

Birdie thought about this for a moment. "Yeah, I guess you're right. I just like it here so much, Kate. I don't ever want to leave. And do you think we'd get to take our stuff with us if she came back to get us? And where would we live?" Birdie chewed her bottom lip, worried about her bed and her Barbie doll.

Kate rolled her eyes at her sister's naivete. "Birdie Kay, you're so dumb! What's Mom gonna do? Tie our big fancy beds to the top of her old car?" She laughed at the absurdity of it.

Birdie looked offended. "I don't know! Maybe." She seemed hurt that her sister was laughing at her when they were supposed to be having a heart-to-heart discussion.

Kate felt bad for hurting her little sister's feelings. "Well, I want to stay here as bad as you do," she offered as kindly as she possibly could.

"Maybe she won't come back."

"Yeah, maybe. Come on. Let's go brush our teeth."

Chapter Fourteen

The next morning, the girls walked in on an intense conversation between Uncle John and Aunt Bobbie.

"John, I know we can't afford it, but I also know we could find the money *somewhere*. You know your mother and dad live on a lot smaller income than we do. We've got to figure this out, honey. We can't let that little girl walk around with ever' tooth in her head rottin' out."

Oooohhh... they were talking about Beverly's teeth.

"Bobbie, I know we have to figure something out. I'm just tellin' you that I don't know where we're gonna come up with the money. Do you know how expensive that's gonna be?"

"Well, we don't even know how much it'll cost yet. Maybe I should take her to the dentist first, and then at least we'll have some idea of what it's gonna cost."

"Yeah, I guess you're right. Maybe it won't be that expensive. They look pretty bad though, Bobbie. I had to get some work done almost ten years ago, and you remember how expensive that was. And I don't think that was anywhere near as extensive as what Beverly's gonna need."

"I know, John, but it's got to be done. There's no tellin' how bad it is. I saw they were bad when they first got here, but they've gotten a lot worse in just the little bit of time that they've been here."

Were they that bad when we got here? Kate asked herself. *Are ours bad?* She ran to the bathroom and climbed up onto the sink counter. She put her face as close to the mirror as she could and pulled her lips far away from her teeth with her fingers until it became painful and examined her teeth, one at a time. She had lost most of her baby teeth and her adult teeth still had jagged edges, but they didn't look bad. She felt another presence in the room and saw Birdie beside her in the reflection of the mirror. She climbed up beside her sister and began examining her reflection as well. Kate relaxed her lips and helped her sister. She looked closely at Birdie's teeth and nodded her head, indicating that she found her sister's oral health satisfactory. They climbed down from the sink together and walked back into the kitchen to catch the end of John and Bobbie's conversation.

"I guess you're right," Uncle John sighed. "I guess they all three need to go in and have 'em looked at. I know my sister probably hasn't taken 'em in years."

Aunt Bobbie flicked her cigarette ashes into a heavy-looking green glass ashtray and took a sip of her coffee. She glanced over at the girls, smiled and winked.

The very next week, Aunt Bobbie announced that they had an appointment that afternoon. After lunch, she laid clean, ironed outfits out on the girls' beds. She brushed and braided each girl's hair with extra care and insisted on standing over each of them as they thoroughly brushed their teeth. "Git 'em good now. Make sure ye get them back ones. And don't forget to brush your tongue," Aunt Bobbie commanded. All this scrubbing and shining seemed a bit like overkill to Kate and Birdie, but they indulged their aunt, smiling secretly at each other, stifling giggles. They were excited. None of the girls had ever been to the dentist. Mom had always been good about making sure they brushed their teeth when they were back in Arizona, and there had never been any need for them to visit a dentist.

Once Aunt Bobbie was satisfied with the girls' appearance (after she'd made Birdie change her shoes and Kate change her shirt...twice), they finally left the house.

"We just have to stop by your Mother and Papaw's house real quick to pick up your sister, and then we'll be on our way!" Aunt Bobbie announced.

Beverly was waiting on the front porch when they pulled into the driveway. She hopped up and ran toward the car as soon as she saw Aunt Bobbie's Oldsmobile.

"Oh, my lord! What is that child wearin'?" Aunt Bobbie exclaimed.

Kate and Birdie Kay looked at each other and laughed. Beverly's hair was obviously uncombed, and there was a rat's nest so big in the back of her head that it was visible from the front. She was wearing a white shirt with bright yellow and red diagonal stripes running from her right shoulder down to the left side of her abdomen; it was very dirty. It looked like she had rubbed chocolate ice cream all over the front of it. Her purple shorts, also filthy, were too short and too tight. And, as both girls had suspected (and secretly hoped - to satisfy their own amusement), Beverly was proudly prancing to the car wearing her shiny black tap shoes.

Bobbie turned around to look at the girls. For the first time since they had been with her, she seemed upset with them. "You girls stop that laughin' right now, you hear me? She can't help it. She dudn't know no better! I'm gonna run in the house and help your sister comb her hair and find somethin' decent to wear right quick. You two sit *right* where you are," she said, pointing one long, frosted pink fingernail in their direction, "and I want you ta think about how mean you're bein' to yer sister right now! When she gets in this car, I don't want to hear even one giggle come outta either one a yer mouths, young ladies! You oughta be ashamed a yerselves!" she scolded as she turned and opened her car door to get out. Before she shut the door, she turned and bent down so that she could see their faces. "I *mean* it!" she slammed the car door and walked briskly inside.

Kate and Birdie sat stunned and silent for a moment. Aunt Bobbie had never said a cross word to them before. "Do you notice that when Aunt Bobbie gets mad, she talks even more country?" Kate whispered, holding back a smile. Birdie sat staring at her lap and nodded her head. "Did you see her?" Kate whispered. And both girls lost control. They were laughing so hard they were snorting. "We gotta stop, Birdie," she managed through snorts and giggles.

"I know, but I can't," Birdie laughed.

"We got about two minutes to pull ourselves together," Kate said, trying to compose herself. "Aunt Bobbie'll be so mad if she comes out here and we're still laughin'!"

"I know! I'm *tryin'*!" Birdie struggled to pull herself together.

They both calmed down, but only after applying great effort.

"Are we mean?" Kate asked Birdie.

"I don't know. Maybe."

"That was funny, right?"

"Sure was," Birdie replied flatly.

Ten minutes later, Beverly, looking much more presentable, and Aunt Bobbie got into the car.

"Hey, Bev," Birdie greeted her sister.

"Hey," Beverly pouted. She was obviously upset Aunt Bobbie had insisted she change her clothes, as well as wash her face and comb her hair.

"Y'all ready?" Aunt Bobbie cast fierce eyes at both girls in the rearview mirror, daring them to let even one smirk escape.

"Yep. All ready to go," Kate replied, attempting to convey an apology with her eyes.

Kate and Birdie each had one cavity, which Aunt Bobbie said wasn't bad, considering they had been on their own for the past few years as far as dental care went. Both girls did have a little decay starting at the edges of their front teeth, but the dentist thought he could fix this with minimally invasive procedures. Both girls were back in the waiting room in no time.

Beverly's appointment was a different story altogether. It took over an hour before Aunt Bobbie popped her head out the door. "Just checkin' on y'all. It's gonna be a few minutes. Y'all okay?" Aunt Bobbie asked.

"We're fine. How's Bev?" Kate asked.

Aunt Bobbie glanced back toward the room where Beverly was and said, "She's fine, sweetheart. It's just gonna be a little while, that's all. Y'all gonna be okay for a little bit longer?"

"We're okay, Aunt Bobbie," answered Birdie.

Aunt Bobbie nodded and closed the door.

"I feel bad about laughin' at her now," said Birdie.

"I don't," Kate lied. "She shoulda took better care a her teeth, like we did. Shoot, we're younger'n her an' we had the good sense ta brush our teeth, even when we all had to share the same toothbrush and use bakin' soda or peroxide or just water. We still *did* it. You remember all those times I'd tell her she needed to brush her teeth? She never would! She'd always tell me to leave her alone, that I wasn't her boss. Remember that?"

"Yeah, Kate, but you had to tell me to brush my teeth too or I wouldn't 've ever done it either."

"Yeah well, that's different, Birdie Kay. You were little. She's older than both of us. You didn't do it on your own because you were too little to know any better. She didn't do it cuz she was lazy. That's why she doesn't comb her hair and clean herself up at Mother and Papaw's. They're old. And they're too nice. And Bev just goes around doin' whatever she wants all day long. They can't make her do anything, and she knows it. I don't think she's doin' 'em right, Birdie Kay. They're lettin' her live there and feedin' 'er and buyin' 'er clothes and tap shoes and God knows what all else!"

Birdie was trying not to laugh.

"What are you laughin' at, Birdie Kay? It's true and you know it!" Kate announced, indignant.

"Yeah, it's true," Birdie managed. "Do you notice that you talk just as hick as Aunt Bobbie when you get mad?" Birdie teased.

***

"Well, Dr. Jones said he can't save her teeth. Said the only thing to do is pull 'em all. They can either give her implants, which is what he recommended, but it's a lot more expensive, or we can get her dentures. That's the cheapest way to go. But he said either way they've all got to come out. He said there's all kindsa infections brewin' in there," Aunt Bobbie said to Uncle John that evening.

Uncle John was quiet for a moment, then he sighed and asked, "They've *all* got to come out?"

"Yep. Ever' one of 'em. He said the front ones that look so bad are the healthiest teeth in her head. Said he wasn't sure how Beverly was even eatin'. He said it must be painful ever' time she chews somethin'."

"Poor kid. Sure is a shame," Uncle John said as he shook his head slowly from side to side, staring down at the countertop he was leaning on. "Is there any *good* news?" he asked, a sarcastic half-smile on his face.

"Well, Kate and Birdie just need one trip, and the girl makin' appointments said we could get 'em both in before school starts," offered Aunt Bobbie.

"Well, that *is* some good news," Uncle John said as he turned his attention to Kate and Birdie. "How was your first trip to the dentist, girls?"

"It was fine," Birdie replied.

Kate said nothing. Something Aunt Bobbie said had diverted her attention from teeth talk. *School?* Kate silently asked herself. In the time that they had been staying with Aunt Bobbie and Uncle John, Kate hadn't considered school, not even once. *Will we go to school here? In Oklahoma? What if the kids don't like us here? What if we don't have any friends? Do they do school different in Oklahoma? What if we don't know any of the stuff they teach here?*

Worried, Kate walked to her bedroom without even a second thought about their upcoming dentist appointment, which had, before the mention of school, been causing her some mild anxiety.

She situated herself on the bed, flat on her back, her best thinking position. Out of habit, her hand automatically went to the spot where the golden K used to dangle, even though she knew it was no longer there. Absently, she hoped it was bringing Mom some comfort, but she didn't dwell on her. Kate had bigger things to worry about at the moment. Since they'd left Arizona, back in May, they hadn't had to worry about school. It would be so different in Oklahoma.

Interrupting her musings, Birdie burst into the room. "Hey, they're gonna have to put Bev to sleep when they pull alla her teeth out," she announced breathlessly. "They're doin' it soon too. The dentist said they need to do it as soon as possible. He said Bev could get real sick from havin' rotten teeth!" She stopped suddenly and realized Kate wasn't even listening to her. She jumped up onto the foot of her sister's bed and reached out and shook Kate's leg. "Hey!" she yelled. "What's wrong with you?"

"Nothin'!" Kate said, more forcefully than she had meant to. "I'm just thinkin'. Leave me alone."

"Aw, come on, ol' girl!" Birdie said, smirking, mocking the way Uncle John talked to the cows when he was trying to get them to do something they didn't want to do.

Kate got Birdie's joke and half smiled. "I just didn't think we'd be here long enough to have to worry about goin' to school here. Aren't you kinda worried about it?"

Birdie thought about it for a moment, wrinkling her brow, pursing her lips, and rolling her eyes toward the ceiling as she did so. "Not even a little bit," she replied.

"Birdie Kay, be serious. What if they don't like us here? What if they think we're dumb because we didn't learn the same stuff in Arizona they learn in Oklahoma? How can you not be worried?"

Birdie put her hand on Kate's leg and cocked her head to the side. "Sister, think about it for a minute. We'll have freshly cleaned teeth, we won't have to get ourselves up and off to school all on our own, and we won't have to worry about Mom all day long every day. Even if we're learnin' stuff we've never seen before it'll be easier than it's ever been. Plus, you know Aunt Bobbie. She's gonna make sure we have nice clothes on every single day!"

All these things were very true. Kate hadn't considered the positive aspects of school since they were going to be living with Bobbie and John. Feeling surprisingly better, Kate smiled. "Y'know, for a little sister, you sure are smart sometimes."

"I know," Birdie smiled back proudly.

"Oh Lord, don't get the big head now!" Kate teased as she sat up on her bed. "Wanna play Barbie?"

Chapter Fifteen

"You girls are gonna be on your own for a little bit today," Uncle John announced one morning a few days later. "Yer Aunt Bobbie took Beverly to the dentist this mornin'. She's gonna git some a her teeth took out."

"Why just some?" asked Kate. "I thought they had to take them all out."

"Well, little girl, it's such a big job they're gonna have to do it in stages. Dr. Jones said he's gonna take the worst ones out first, the ones in backa her mouth that're givin' 'er the worst trouble. Said it oughta relieve some a the pain she's been havin'. Then they'll go in two more times ta get 'em all outta there. Then she'll go in one more time and come out with a set a brand new, pearly white choppers!" Uncle John grinned and leaned toward the girls, chomping his big, white teeth at them. Birdie laughed.

Pain? I didn't know she was ever in any pain, thought Kate. *She never complained.* But then, when she really thought about it, who would she have complained to? Mom was so often either gone working or off on one of her drunken escapades Beverly could have been in pain for weeks and nobody would have noticed. And when Mom *was* home, they all three tried their hardest not to be a bother to her because they were afraid she'd leave again. Even Birdie, the youngest, hadn't complained when her eardrum had been injured. If her sisters hadn't spoken up, she might never have told Mom about it.

Uncle John slid the girls' breakfast plates, which had been warming in the oven for them, across the counter. *Pancakes, yum,* thought Kate. *I love it here.*

"Now I'll just be out in the barn if y'all need me." Uncle John placed his old gray cowboy hat solidly on his large, blond head. "Or, if y'all want, you can come help me around the dairy when you get done here."

Both girls said that they would meet Uncle John out in the barn after they'd eaten and dressed. It still gave the girls a giggle every now and then when Aunt Bobbie or Uncle John had to leave the house for a little bit and asked if they would be alright. Did they not know that the girls had been on their own for weeks at a time before? It seemed so ridiculous that they had to laugh.

They spent the day helping Uncle John around the dairy. When they'd first arrived on the farm, Kate had thought the cows would be scary because they were such huge creatures. In reality, they were extremely gentle. They seemed oblivious to other beings' presence. All they really seemed to want to do was eat. The girls found the milking process, especially, extremely interesting once they got past the moist, pink udders, which seemed disgusting at first.

They swept the barn and the floors of the milking area for Uncle John, and he said they did such a good job that he thought they were ready to help with a very important job. He led them outdoors to a small pen. As they walked, he grabbed two large bottles filled with milk and two rubber contraptions neither girl recognized. Inside a pen were two small calves, which the girls found adorable.

"Kate!" Birdie squealed, "Baby cows!"

"*Calves*," Uncle John corrected, smiling down at his youngest niece.

While the girls had been busy oohing and aahing over the calves, Uncle John had taken the rubber contraptions he'd grabbed earlier and attached them to the tops of the milk bottles.

"Their mammas ain't feedin' 'em, so we got to do it by hand. Come on," Uncle John said, as he unlatched the gate to the pen. He held the gate open for the girls and handed them each a bottle of milk. He patiently taught them the proper way to feed a calf and then left them to their work, closing the gate behind him.

As she was feeding her calf, Kate realized her cheek muscles were sore from all the smiling she had done that day. She looked around her at the big, empty blue sky, the other cows, grazing in the fields. As far as she could see, there was only land and sky and cows. The air around her was hot and heavy, and it smelled of alfalfa hay, a scent she had not experienced before coming to the farm. The sun was so bright, she had to squint when she looked out at the fields beyond, and it warmed her skin. She took a deep breath and smiled, even though it hurt her cheeks. She was happy, truly content and happy. She glanced over at Birdie, and judging by the look on her face, she felt the same way.

***

Aunt Bobbie didn't make it home until after dark that night. She looked exhausted and seemed upset. Her shirt was untucked and wrinkled, which the girls had never seen on Aunt Bobbie before.

"It went that good, huh?" asked Uncle John.

"Oh, Lord, John. I don't think it coulda gone any worse." Bobbie dropped her purse in front of her and walked over to Uncle John who wrapped his arms around her, engulfing her slim frame in his strong embrace. "It was awful," Bobbie muttered into her husband's chest.

"Here, sit down." Uncle John pulled a wooden stool out from under the bar, where the girls ate breakfast every morning. "Tell me all about it. She okay?"

"Yeah, she's fine, I guess. The doctor said the actual procedure went fine. He warned us that when she woke up from the anesthesia, she might be cranky. He said that was just a side effect of the medicine that put her to sleep. But, John, you shoulda seen her. She threw a fit when she woke up. She was cussin' everybody and throwin' things. Your mamma tried ta calm her down, but Beverly didn't want anything ta do with any of us. She kept hollerin' for us all ta git outta there 'n leave 'er alone. She kicked at a nurse. Lord, I didn't think we'd *ever* git 'er calmed down. Once we finally did, the doctor tried to talk to her, and she went after *him*!

"And the poor little thang was in sa much pain, I couldn't hardly look at 'er. After she settled down a little, it was even worse because then she realized how much she was hurtin'. Little ol' thang just laid there and bawled. There didn't seem to be anything we could do to get it to stop hurtin'.

"John, she swears up and down that she ain't going back for the rest of it. She said she don't care if ever' tooth in her head falls out. She ain't going back. I don't think she's kiddin', John. I ain't ever in all my life seen a kid that dead set against somethin'. Said she'd run off and wouldn't any of us ever see 'er again if we tried ta make 'er go back. Mae and Pete didn't know what ta do. Hell, I didn't know what ta do either."

"Well, she's gotta go back, Bobbie," Uncle John said, matter-of-factly.

"*I* know that, and *you* know that, but try tellin' *her* that." Bobbie propped her elbows on the countertop and let her head fall into her hands.

Chapter Sixteen

Beverly's next appointment came and went, and, true to her word, she did not go back. She kicked, she screamed, she even spit and slapped. Finally, Mother and Papaw said they would let it go for the time being and revisit the issue in a few months.

Kate's tenth birthday came right before school started. It was the complete opposite of her ninth birthday. She hadn't expected anything, hadn't even mentioned it to Aunt Bobbie or Uncle John. They had already done so much for her and Birdie, and Aunt Bobbie was already starting to buy them both school clothes. She really couldn't have asked for anything more. But, on the morning of her tenth birthday, she woke to find Bobbie, John and Birdie standing over her, grinning.

"Wake up, sleepy head," said Aunt Bobbie. "Just because you're ten years old now it don't mean you can lay around the house sleepin' all day, young lady."

Kate sat up, sleep still in her eyes, and smiled. They had remembered.

"Ha-aa-py birthday to you..." they all sang in unison.

After the song was through, Aunt Bobbie asked, "What would the birthday girl like for breakfast?"

"Say pancakes," Birdie whispered around a wide, snaggle-toothed grin. She had begun losing her baby teeth and, thanks to the tooth fairy, was again ahead in the girls' contest to see who could save up the most money.

"Pancakes," Kate replied.

"Pancakes, huh?" asked Uncle John. "I thought when ya turned ten you'd get a taste for coffee and cigarettes." He raised one eyebrow mockingly, eyeing Kate.

"No," she said, trying to keep a serious look on her face to match Uncle John's. "Pancakes." Then she laughed.

After breakfast, Uncle John headed out to his dairy duties. Aunt Bobbie instructed the girls to go get dressed while she cleaned the kitchen. Back in their bedroom, the girls giggled and scuffled as they hopped around their beds; excitement was in the air. It had been a long time since one of them had had a properly celebrated birthday. Aunt Bobbie's usual routine, whenever cleaned anything, was to put on one of her many beloved country music albums. The girls could hear Lynn Anderson's song, "I Never Promised You a Rose Garden" begin to blare from the record player in the living room. Both girls knew the song by heart. They joined in, singing loudly and dancing all over the room, even on the beds. At one point, Birdie slipped and fell off the mattress. Both girls squealed in delight; out of breath, they dissolved into the kind of rare laughter that makes people's stomach muscles cramp up.

Kate looked up to find Aunt Bobbie in the doorway, arms crossed, leaning on the door frame. She cleared her throat to make sure she had both girls' attention. "What is all this racket?" she asked in that country accent that the girls had grown to love. She turned her head and looked sideways at them, suspicious. But she couldn't hold the serious expression for very long. She burst into giggles of her own and ran for the nearest child, which happened to be Birdie, attacking the little girl with tickles.

They spent most of the day in Bobbie's enormous, pink bathroom. She painted each girl's fingernails and toenails with the greatest care. She even placed cotton balls between each girl's ten toes. She helped them to wash, dry and curl their hair. They listened to Aunt Bobbie's records all day. Conway Twitty was her favorite, and they listened to "Hello, Darlin'" six times in a row, each time all of them singing along at the top of their lungs.

"Aunt Bobbie," this is my favorite day, Birdie said as she watched her aunt teach her sister how to apply lipstick. "I don't want it ever to end," the little girl whispered as she played with the back of Aunt Bobbie's short, blonde hair.

Aunt Bobbie put down the lipstick and turned her attention to Birdie. "Oh, sweetheart. This is my favorite day too. And I hope it never ends." She hugged Birdie. Kate watched them and realized that she felt the same exact way as her sister.

"Ye know, I gotta git in that kitchen and git to work on your sister's birthday dinner and a cake!" Bobbie exclaimed as she looked at her watch. Both girls seemed disappointed that their girl time with Aunt Bobbie was coming to an end. Bobbie saw this and commented, "It sure is gonna be a lotta work. I don't know if I can get a roast on and bake a cake all by myself. You girls think you'd mind helpin' me a little?"

Both girls' eyes lit up. They smiled and hobbled behind Aunt Bobbie to the kitchen, keeping their gleaming pink toenails raised so that they didn't mess them up.

"Aunt Bobbie," Kate said as she was carefully peeling potatoes the way her aunt had taught her, "I want to be just like you when I grow up."

Surprised, Bobbie asked, "What for, honey?"

"Well, you're just so nice. And your house is so pretty. And you're so pretty."

"Well, thank you, sweetheart," Bobbie said as she expertly prepared a roast to bake. "But, y'know, I had things I wanted to do when I was a younger woman. Don't get me wrong: I'm real happy with my life and your Uncle John. I've had it good, but sometimes I wish that before I'd got married and had kids I'da done somethin' that was just mine, y'know? Somethin' I did to make my mark on the world. Y'know what I mean?"

Blankly, Kate looked at Aunt Bobbie. "No. Not really. What did you want to do?"

"Oh," Bobbie smiled. "I don't know, maybe go to college? Teach school? Be a nurse?" she asked no one in particular, a far-off look in her eyes. "It's silly, I guess. I just wanted to know that I could take care a myself, make my own way. I look at *you* girls, and I think you could do anything you want with your lives. Y'all got any ideas about what you want to be when you grow up?"

"I sure don't want to be a school-teacher," Birdie piped up." Bev makes us play school when we go visit her, and it's not fun, Aunt Bobbie," Birdie pronounced, a serious look on her face as she shelled peas into a large, ceramic mixing bowl. "You have to be real mean, too. Well, I *guess* spankin' the kids might be a *little* bit fun," she said thoughtfully. Bobbie and Kate smiled at each other knowingly.

"Kate, what do you want to do?"

"I don't know. I never really thought about it," she answered honestly. The thought had literally never occurred to her. After she considered her options for a moment, Kate said, "I think it might be fun to work in a grocery store. You get to push all those buttons on those neat cash register machines. I think I'd like that a lot."

Aunt Bobbie smiled. "Well, girls, your ol' Aunt Bobbie's gonna give you some advice. You won't have much use for it right now, so just listen real hard and stick it in your back pockets for another day."

This time, the girls smiled knowingly at each other. Aunt Bobbie had all kinds of funny sayings like that. But she had never offered them advice before, so they both did as she said and listened carefully.

"School is real important, girls. I wish somebody'da told me that when I was your age." She was silent for a moment while she placed the roast in the oven and adjusted the temperature. "You know what school is, girls? School is the only way a girl's got of makin' her own way in this life. You go to high school and make the best grades you can. Then you go to college. You make the best grades you can there too."

Here Kate interrupted. "College? Aunt Bobbie, me and Birdie Kay can't go to college. Mom says that's just for spoiled rich kids. The boys go so they can keep bein' rich, and the girls go so they can find a rich husband who'll take care of 'em."

"Well, little girl, I'll tell ya this: a lotta people think that. But it ain't true. You girls can be anything you want. And I'll tell ya what college is: it's your way of livin' your own life." Aunt Bobbie took another large mixing bowl out of the cabinet in front of her and began collecting various ingredients from other cabinets to start on the birthday cake. From the looks of the ingredients, Kate guessed it was going to be a chocolate cake. "A girl oughta have a way to support herself. Gettin' a college degree means you'll always have a job, which means you'll always have a way ta make it on your own. It means you get the choice to live your life the way you see fit. A girl ought never have to depend on a man to support 'er. Now, me, I got lucky with your Uncle John. He's good to me. He thinks of me as his partner." Bobbie had been measuring and adding cake ingredients into the mixing bowl as she spoke. She was quiet for a moment while she searched yet another cabinet for a box of baking soda. Both girls waited expectantly. Neither of them had ever heard a woman talk like this. Kate thought it seemed so modern. "Anyway," Bobbie picked up when she was back in front of her mixing bowl, "say one a you girls grows up and gets married, has a couple kids, then your husband starts beatin' on ya, pushin' ya around 'n' whatnot. What're you gonna do? If you don't have a way to make money and provide for you an' your babies, what're you gonna do? You're stuck.

"Now, say the same thing happens, but you went to school an' got yourself a degree. Well, then you got options. You don't have to hang around there lettin' some mean ol' thang smack ye around. Ye get out. Y'all see what I'm sayin'? Don't ever depend on a man to take care of you. I've known too many people who ended up stuck somewhere with somebody that treats 'em like dirt, an' they just gotta smile an' take it because it's the only option they got. Y'all don't have to ever be put in that position if you go to college. This mean ol' world can strip us of all we got. Everything. But, no matter what, can't nobody ever take that away from you. That degree's yours, no matter what life throws atcha. If you girls don't ever remember a word your Aunt Bobbie says, you remember that, y'hear me?"

Chapter Seventeen

Kate's birthday ended up being the perfect day. She and Birdie stayed in the kitchen, talking with Aunt Bobbie and helping her to prepare the meal all afternoon. When Uncle John came in from the dairy, they ate. Everything was delicious, especially the cake. Uncle John lit ten birthday candles, and, as Kate blew them out, she wished they could stay with their aunt and uncle forever.

When she opened her gifts, Kate was elated. Aunt Bobbie had picked out three stylish, very grown-up looking school dresses for her, which she loved. She also got three new pairs of knee socks and a pair of shiny, black patent leather Mary Jane shoes to wear with her new dresses. She didn't know what to say. Birdie squealed and clapped her hands, happy for her sister's good fortune.

Later, after the girls had gotten ready for bed, Aunt Bobbie came into their room. She had a small, wrapped package in her hand.

"Hey, girls. Y'all ready for bed?"

"Yeah. What's that?" asked Birdie.

"Something' I wanted to give your sister in private," replied Aunt Bobbie, as she took a seat on the edge of Kate's bed.

Worried, Kate asked, "What is it?"

"Open it and see."

Kate unwrapped the brown paper package and found two small, dainty, white bras, one on top of the other. "What are these for?" she asked as she held one up to the light to get a better look at it.

"Well," Aunt Bobbie said, smiling, "they're for you to wear. You're ten years old now, won't be too long before you start becomin' a young lady. You're gonna be needin' those here before long."

"Oh," said Kate, unsure of what her response should be.

Aunt Bobbie laughed. "Oh, honey, don't look sa upset! You don't have ta start wearin' 'em tomorra. I just thought ya oughta have 'em for when the time's right." She smiled kindly at her niece.

This made Kate feel a little bit better. She smiled back at Bobbie. "Thank you, Aunt Bobbie. But - well, how will I know when the time is right?" she asked, slightly embarrassed.

"I'll tell ya when it's time, Kate," beamed Birdie. "When you get big giant boobs!" The little girl held her arms straight out in front of her, leaning back as if she were balancing a heavy weight on her chest, then she fell over on her bed giggling.

"*Oh*," laughed Aunt Bobbie. "It dudn't happen like that, you silly girl! What am I gonna do with you, child?"

She looked at Kate. "I'll letcha know when it's time to wear 'em, and I'll show ya how they work," Bobbie reassured Kate as she patted the girl's arm. "For now, you two need ta get your little tail ends in the bed!" she clucked, as she rose to go.

"Thank you, Aunt Bobbie," Kate said as she watched her aunt shut the door behind her, looking back one last time to say goodnight.

As the girls lay in bed that night, they were too excited to sleep. They talked of boobs and school and clothes and, eventually, Mom.

"Did you miss her today?" asked Birdie.

"Yeah. Did you?"

"Yeah. But I still don't want her to come back. Do you?"

Kate sighed. "I don't know. I still miss her. But I don't want us to have to leave Aunt Bobbie and Uncle John."

"Maybe we could all live here together," Birdie said innocently, even though she knew as well as Kate that would never happen. "Hey," Birdie said, changing the subject, "you know how Aunt Bobbie was talkin' today about us gettin' jobs and takin' care of ourselves when we grow up?"

"Yeah?" Kate asked, yawning.

"What if we opened our own diner like Mom and Dad's?"

"Would you really want to do that?" asked Kate. "They always worked so hard."

"Yeah, but they were happy."

"Yeah, that's true. We might could do something like that," she smiled to herself. "We could call it Kate & Birdie's Diner."

"No way. We'd call it Birdie & Kate's Diner! Or - or - what about Barbie's Diner? Huh? What about that? Everybody likes Barbie!" Birdie informed her sister, excited now.

Kate laughed silently in the dark. "We'll see."

The girls talked late into the night, dreaming about their futures. As Kate drifted off, she realized that this was the first time she had ever thought seriously about being a grown-up. She had never had any dreams before. She'd been so fixated on just surviving from day to day for so long that she'd never really had the time to consider the future.

Chapter Eighteen

On the first day of school, Aunt Bobbie woke the girls extra early. She gorged them on bacon, eggs and pancakes. She rushed around the house, laying out clothes, re-ironing shirts, wiping down shoes that had never even been worn. She seemed more nervous than the girls. "Y'all better eat. Yer gonna get hungry right smack in the middle of the mornin' if ya don't," she clucked. She had packed each girl a lunch and went over the contents of their bags with them, instructing them to eat everything she had packed so that they wouldn't be starving by the time they got home from school.

Finally, Uncle John, who, until the moment he spoke, had been all but ignored the entire morning, teasingly scolded Aunt Bobbie. "For God's sakes, Bobbie! You're gonna have them girls sa full, by the enda the day they'll look like stuffed 'n' scrubbed chickens! Let 'em alone," he laughed, shaking his head at his wife's fussing.

When it was time to walk them to the bus stop, Bobbie talked the entire time. Kate was grateful for the chit-chat. It kept her mind off what school was going to be like. "Y'all's cousins Rick and Randy used to walk to this bus stop ever' day. I'm just goin' with ye cuz it's your first day. After today y'all'll walk by yourselves, alright?"

"Okay," said Birdie, obviously apprehensive about her first day of school in a new town. "Will you be here when we get back?"

"Wouldn't miss it for the world, little girl," Bobbie replied. This seemed to comfort Birdie. "It's gonna be fun. I promise," said Bobbie. "If it's not, I won't make ya go back. How's that sound?"

"Good," Birdie smiled.

Kate, content to listen to Bobbie and Birdie's back-and-forth, walked alongside them silently.

"What're you so quiet for, young lady?" asked Bobbie.

"I don't know," Kate answered. "Just nervous, I guess."

"Me too." Aunt Bobbie smiled down at her niece.

They walked the rest of the way down the red dirt road toward the bus stop in silence. Their summer together had been full of laughter, new experiences and camaraderie. They had been so excited about the clothes the girls were going to wear and the friends they were sure to make that they had been able to avoid considering the fact that their endless summer had, inevitably, come to its conclusion. Even though the day was ripe with possibility, it was also full of melancholy, and all three were faced with this fact as they made their way toward the bus stop.

Silence settled in once they had reached their destination. Though they had gotten up hours early, they'd spent so much time preparing for the day that the bus was already pulling in and all three silently wished for more time. The other children, who had been waiting there already, began to board the bus as soon as it came to a stop. But Kate, Birdie and Bobbie stood side by side, unmoving, watching the other children.

"Well, I guess it's that time," Aunt Bobbie finally said. "Y'all better get goin'."

Birdie couldn't fight off the excitement any longer and ran to catch up with the other children. "Bye, Aunt Bobbie!" she hollered over her shoulder. "Come on, Kate! Let's get a seat together!"

Reluctantly, Kate followed her little sister.

"Bye!" yelled Bobbie. "Y'all have a good day! Love you!"

This stopped Kate in her tracks. Filled with emotion, she turned and ran back to her aunt. She stopped short just in front of Bobbie. Not knowing what to say, abruptly, she hugged the woman, hard. Not wanting to let go, holding back hot tears with all her might, she whispered, "I love you too, Aunt Bobbie."

Just as abruptly, the little girl turned without looking her aunt in the eye and ran to catch up with her sister.

Kate held Birdie's hand the whole bus ride, pretending to comfort her small sister, but taking as much solace as she was giving; both girls were nervous. *She loves us*, Kate thought. She quickly realized she wasn't going to be able to let herself dwell on this thought because, for some reason, even though it made her happy, she had the urge to cry when she thought about it.

She turned to her other worries. *What if they don't like us? What if the girls are mean to Birdie Kay here like they were at our last school? I'll have to fight somebody. Aunt Bobbie'll be so mad. Or, even worse, so disappointed. But I can't let anybody be mean to my little sister. I won't ever let that happen again. She wouldn't be able to take that again.* Kate looked down at her little sister. *How could anyone not like her?* She asked herself. She was "dressed to the nines," as Aunt Bobbie would say, in a dark green and navy, plaid pinafore with a crisp, white collared dress shirt underneath. Aunt Bobbie had really outdone herself. Complete with new, white knee socks and black leather Buster Browns, Birdie looked adorable. She not only looked as good as all the other little girls, but better. Aunt Bobbie had carefully washed and braided both girls' hair. Birdie's thick, shiny, golden brown locks were the perfect mix of coiffed and mussed. As the bus bumped along the dirt roads, stopping now and then to collect more children, Kate continued assessing her little sister's appearance. She had lost some of her front teeth over the summer, and the permanent ones were surfacing. That, along with a tan and the little freckles sprinkled over her nose and cheeks from their time outdoors on the farm with Uncle John, gave her a healthy, all-American-girl look that was sure to attract attention and earn her the friends she was so looking forward to making. No one would ever have guessed that just a few short months ago this little girl had looked more like a mangy, feral cat than the fresh-faced farm girl sitting beside her now.

All this focus on Birdie's appearance caused Kate to feel the need to address the way she looked today. When, at Aunt Bobbie's prompting, the girls had gone into her and Uncle John's bedroom to look at themselves in Bobbie's full length mirror, Kate could hardly believe the girl staring back at her was the same one who had arrived on John and Bobbie's doorstep a few months ago. She looked like one of the well-dressed young ladies in the catalogues Aunt Bobbie always had around the house. She wore one of the dresses she'd gotten for her birthday, also a pinafore, but it was red. In addition to her own crisp, red, white and blue checkered shirt, new white knee socks, and her new Mary Janes, Kate also wore one of her new bras. She hadn't really needed it yet, but it made her feel grown-up, and she was glad she had worn it.

As she looked down at herself, she realized she had changed a lot too over the past few months. Her blonde hair, sun-bleached now, felt shiny and healthy instead of always being filthy and snarled. Bobbie had parted Birdie's hair down the middle and braided it on each side, adding white satin ribbons to the end of each braid and combing her bangs down straight across her forehead. Kate had wanted hers the same way, but Bobbie had insisted that she was too old for that and, instead, French braided it loosely down her back. Kate approved of the results wholeheartedly. She felt it made her look sophisticated.

Sometimes the girls used to go days at a time with barely anything in their growling little stomachs, which had caused Kate to grow somewhat wiry. But now, well fed and able to enjoy the fresh air and sunshine, she looked healthy and felt strong.

Still, though both girls' appearances had improved, Kate felt the same as she always had on the inside: insecure. Worried thoughts skittered through her mind. *What if we can't do the work here? What if the teachers don't like us? What if the kids don't like us? What if they make fun of us?* All kinds of terrible scenarios tortured Kate throughout the bus ride. She considered escape routes. She had to make sure that if something went wrong the girls would be able to find each other and get away from whatever it might be that threatened them.

Though it was still early morning, the bus felt hot and stuffy. The tiny, white hairs at the nape of her neck were beginning to stick uncomfortably to her skin. Between the points where the girls' skirts ended and before their socks began, the outer parts of their bare legs touched. Sweat mingled between their skin and made it feel warm and slimy. The bus windows were down. This should have provided some degree of relief, but only hot air, rife with dry, red dust swirled in, whipping thick, long braids and carefully ironed first-day-of-school, stiff collars around like slips of loose-leaf notebook paper in a tornado.

Finally, after picking up its last passenger, the bus pulled into the parking lot of the elementary school. Kate didn't know whether to be relieved the ride was over, or terrified that the day was about to begin. The girls had not left each other's sides all summer. Now they were about to be separated for an entire day.

"Here, don't forget your lunch," Kate said, as they stood and prepared to exit the bus, facing each other. Kate noticed that Birdie's eyes were wide with apprehension. "Look at you," she said, deciding to take the approach that usually worked best with Birdie. "You look so nice. I bet you make all kindsa new friends today," Kate smiled, handing her sister her brown paper lunch bag. "Don't worry. You're gonna have so much fun, the day's gonna fly by!" Kate attempted to sound cheery. She reached out, obeying a maternal instinct, and smoothed down Birdie's windblown bangs.

"I know." Birdie met Kate's eyes. "It's easy to make friends. All you gotta do is pick a girl who looks nice, walk up to her, and say, 'Hi. My name's Kate. Wanna play?' Is that what you're scared of?"

Oddly, Birdie's astute observation of her sister's inner turmoil, as well as her startlingly simplified solution to a problem that had seemed so complicated, calmed Kate. She didn't know how to answer her sister's simple question, though. "Yeah. No. Oh, I don't know!" Kate responded in exasperation. "Mostly, I guess, I'm worried about you."

"Really?" Birdie asked, surprise evident in her voice. "I was worried about you! I was afraid you might get into a fight or somethin'. I was gonna ask you to be nice and make some friends today so we could stay here for a while. I'm just scared it's all gonna be over before we really even get to have any fun."

"All right, girls," a voice from the front of the bus startled both Kate and Birdie. "Summer's over. Let's go." They looked over to find the bus driver standing, waiting impatiently, hand on hip, for them to exit the bus, and they realized, embarrassed, that they were the only kids left onboard. They looked at each other one last time, both took deep breaths, smiled, and headed down the aisle toward the waiting bus driver.

"Here we go."

"Here we go."

They held hands all the way to the door and let go just in time to make sure none of their new classmates saw.

***

Several weeks had gone by in the blink of an eye. Both girls' teachers loved them. Birdie had started out a little behind in reading, but, with help from Aunt Bobbie, she caught up with her classmates in no time. Kate's teacher, Mrs. Benson, was impressed with what a hard worker she was, and she told her so. Kate had never been complimented by a teacher, and it made her feel good about herself. She worked even harder to make a good impression and, if she was being honest with herself, to get more compliments too.

Kate and Birdie had thought they would see Beverly at school, but she never showed. When they asked Bobbie about it, she said that Mother and Papaw had decided to let Beverly take her lessons from home because her teeth were still bothering her. Bobbie assured the girls, who were visibly upset by the news, they all were working hard to convince Beverly to go through with the rest of the dental work she desperately needed, and that they would be seeing her at school in no time. The girls readily accepted Aunt Bobbie's explanation, thankful they didn't have to worry about their sister.

They saw Beverly on the weekends when they went to visit Mother and Papaw. Each time, they noticed her behavior was more and more odd. She had become wild and even more flighty than usual. Her hair was always unkempt, and her clothes were perpetually filthy. Beverly had begun obsessively washing her hands after Dad had left, but now she was so obsessed with this ritual that she could barely concentrate on a single conversation. She was constantly disappearing. Every time the girls went to look for her, they found her in the bathroom, in the dark, scrubbing her hands with soap and hot water. Mother and Papaw said they had tried and tried to convince Beverly to stop doing this, but the more they begged, the more she scrubbed. Her hands were always pink and raw. It looked painful. Kate and Birdie also tried to talk to Beverly about her obsession, but their sister refused to even acknowledge the subject. Eventually, the girls learned to ignore it, even though it became increasingly disturbing to see their sister like that.

Bobbie talked to their doctor about Beverly, and, after a few visits with the girl, he claimed that, combined with Mom leaving, the dental procedure had simply been too much for Beverly to handle psychologically, so the coping mechanisms, which she'd developed when her father had been removed from her life, had returned with a vengeance. He said he thought these behaviors would likely get worse before they got better. He assured Bobbie that it was just comforting for Beverly, and, if the adults in her life remained patient and didn't call attention to it, she would stop when she was ready, when she felt safe and secure. This explanation made everyone feel a little more at ease with Beverly's strange behavior, and, as a family, they decided to let Beverly heal in her own way, on her own schedule.

***

In stark contrast to their sister, Kate and Birdie fit in with their new classmates as well as they did with their teachers. Birdie made lots of friends quickly. Kate, though it took her a little longer, made friends too. She wasn't a social butterfly like Birdie, but she was content with that, especially since she had made one very good friend. Her name was Tammy, and she lived just down the road from John and Bobbie's house, so the girls would meet halfway and then spend time at each other's houses. Tammy liked to spend time at Kate's because Uncle John let them feed the baby cows. Kate enjoyed spending time at Tammy's house because she had a treehouse. They did this several times a week. Tammy's family had even invited Kate to spend the night with them the following week to celebrate Tammy's upcoming birthday.

The girls were ecstatic about the sleepover. Tammy's parents had promised they could sleep in the treehouse. In the week leading up to the big day, the girls spent every recess meticulously planning every minute, careful not to waste any of their precious time. Kate, it was decided, was going to ask Aunt Bobbie if she could take along some of her nail polish. It took one whole recess for the girls to agree on the color they were going to paint their fingernails and toenails. Tammy's mission was to talk her mom into letting the girls bake chocolate chip cookies. Between the two of them, they were sure they were old enough to do this independently.

The night before the sleepover, Kate was so excited she could barely stay in her bed. Bobbie had agreed to let her take the nail polish if she promised to be very careful not to spill it. Tammy's mother had agreed to let them bake the cookies with minimal supervision, a compromise the girls decided they could live with. Kate had gone back and forth when trying to decide what pajamas she would wear. Aunt Bobbie had been the tie breaker. She picked the white gown with big, pink roses on the bodice. It wasn't the prettier of the two (the other was powder blue with a satin bow on the neckline), but it was warmer, which was smart since the girls would be in the treehouse.

As Kate was contemplating whether she should bring her Barbie, she heard an unfamiliar noise that seemed to come from the living room. She hadn't been scared since they'd first come to live with John and Bobbie, but this noise made her heart beat hard inside her chest. *It's probably just one of the cows too close to the house,* she told herself. But, as she lay in her bed listening, the sound became more familiar to her ears. *It's the doorknob jiggling*, she thought, terrified. She lay still for several minutes, and, though she listened intently, she heard nothing more. Finally, Kate began to feel drowsy. *Maybe it was just the wind*, she told herself. After a few more minutes of no more noises, she rolled to her side and began to drift, still halfheartedly listening for anything out of the ordinary. *You big ol' silly*, she laughed to herself. *Fraidy cat! How're you gonna make it a whole night in a tree house if you can't even fall asleep in your own bed?*

She had to have just fallen asleep because she was jarred awake suddenly by the definite sound of the front door's knob jiggling, this time more insistent. She was contemplating running to Bobbie and John's room when she heard footsteps in the hallway between the bedrooms. She froze with fear. Her bedroom door swung open.

Uncle John's voice boomed in the dark. "Kate? Birdie Kay?"

"Uncle John?" Kate whimpered. "Somebody's at the door. They're trying to get in the house."

"You sure it ain't Birdie trying' to get out?"

"No, she's asleep, Uncle John," Kate half whispered-half yelled. "It's somebody outside. They're tryin' to come in."

Aunt Bobbie joined Uncle John in the doorway of the girls' room. They listened for a moment. They heard nothing but Birdie's deep breathing as she slept peacefully.

Then it happened again. The doorknob was jiggling. Kate gulped and covered her head with her blanket. Aunt Bobbie rushed to the bed and sat down beside her. "Call the police, John!"

When Uncle John switched on her bedroom light, Kate saw that he held a large, menacing gun in his right hand, the muzzle of the barrel pointed toward the floor. She couldn't decide whether this was a comfort or whether it made her feel even more terrified. *He seems comfortable holding it. He must know how to use it,* she thought. The light must have woken Birdie. "What's wrong?" she asked sleepily.

"Nothing," they all three answered simultaneously, all eager to reassure the youngest person in the room, as well as themselves.

"Y'all stay here. I'm gonna go look out the window."

"No, John." Aunt Bobbie insisted. "Call the police!"

"Oh, hush. It's probably nothin'. If somebody's out there I'll call 'em then."

"John--" started Bobbie. But Uncle John had already headed toward the living room and shut the bedroom door behind him.

Birdie jumped into the bed with Bobbie and Kate. She scooted in beside her sister and helped herself to the cover, squishing in as close as she possibly could to her big sister, the person who had always protected her. Then she wrapped her arms tightly around Kate and said, "I'm scared." They all were. They waited in silence, the bedroom light glaring, it seemed, on such a still, dark night.

"Goddammit!" It was Uncle John shouting from the living room. They all three jumped and stared at each other, not sure what they should do. Then, "Woman, you scared the dog shit outta me!" Uncle John sounded angry, but unafraid.

"I'll go see what's goin' on." Bobbie rose from the bed and opened the door cautiously. She hadn't made it halfway down the hall when the girls heard Aunt Bobbie say, "Oh, my lord, Joyce! You scared us half to death!"

Kate and Birdie looked at each other. It was Mom. She was back.

Chapter Nineteen

1975

It was starting to get chilly, chilly enough that, to smoke a cigarette comfortably on the front porch, Kate had to wrap an old, tattered scrap-quilt around herself, even cover her head. She laughed when she thought about what she must look like to the passersby, a fourteen-year-old girl wrapped in a quilt, nun-style, seven months pregnant and smoking a cigarette. *I might cause a wreck.* She laughed to herself again. Since Beverly's baby had been born earlier that month, Kate and Birdie had been smoking their cigarettes on the front porch at their sister's insistence. Mom had smiled, puffing away, when Beverly had asked her to smoke outside.

"When you start payin' the bills around here, little mamma, you can tell me where I can and can't smoke my cigarettes," Joyce informed her eldest, appraising her through half-squinted eyes, making sure she didn't dare balk at Mom's snide reply. Of course, Beverly knew better than to cross Mom if she hoped to keep the peace in the house.

It had been years since Mom had shown up at John and Bobbie's house in the middle of the night and demanded her children be returned to her, behaving as if she had been wronged in some way. Kate let her mind wander back to that night, as it often did. She liked to daydream sometimes about how different things would be if Mom had never come back into their lives.

"Joyce, honey, you're outta line. You've had too much to drink tonight," Uncle John reasoned. "Why don't Bobbie make up the couch for you, and you can sleep it off, and we'll talk about all this in the mornin'?" he asked as he placed his hand comfortingly, but firmly on Joyce's shoulder.

Mom jerked her body backward and, with an offended look on her face, said, "How dare you, you sonofabitch? Ya steal my babies out from under me and then have the gall to tell me I'm outta line for wantin' 'em back?"

The girls had climbed out of bed cautiously and now stood in the doorway of the living room, half in shock that Mom was actually back. Aunt Bobbie had walked over and was standing protectively in front of them.

"Now, Joyce, just calm down. We didn't take these girls from you; you asked us to look after 'em for a while, remember?" asked Uncle John. "So, you could get yourself together. Don'tcha ya remember that?"

"I don't remember any sucha thing!" Mom yelled.

"Listen, now," Uncle John tried again. "Them's your girls. Me 'n' Bobbie's always knowed that. We wouldn't never try to take your girls away, sister. We love you, Joyce. They're your girls, and you can have 'em back any time you want. I was jist thinkin', since ye been drinkin' 'n' it's sa late that it'd be better if ye waited 'til in the mornin', that's all."

"Goddammit, John! If I'd wanted ta git 'em in the mornin' I'da come 'n' got 'em in the mornin'!"

To everyone's surprise, after a few moments of silence, John started to laugh. He shook his head and said, "Lord, girl. Ya look like hell! Yer hair's all messed up; yer dressed like a damn hippie! What in th' world 've you been doin'?" John put one hand on his hip and rubbed the top of his head with the other.

Joyce seemed taken aback by her brother's disarming demeanor. Even more surprising to their shocked audience, Joyce started laughing too.

"You want a drink?"

Joyce sighed. "Don't I always?" She smiled, calmed.

John made his way to the kitchen to make his sister and himself a drink, shaking his head and chuckling to himself. He looked over at Bobbie and the girls, who still hadn't said a word and said, "You girls go say hi to yer mamma and then gitcher little hind ends ta bed. It's late and ye got school in the mornin'."

The girls looked from John to Joyce, but they didn't move. Bobbie stood stock still, staring in disbelief at her husband, mouth half open. "Are you kiddin' me, John Smith?" She turned to the girls. "You two stay right where you are," she said in a low voice. Then she turned and followed John into the kitchen, which left Kate and Birdie exposed.

Joyce, in the meantime, had seated herself on the couch, waiting patiently for the drink her brother had promised. She sat there wordlessly, staring at Kate and Birdie. "Well, look at you two," she said. "Went 'n' got big on Mamma, didn't cha?"

The girls continued to lurk in the doorway of the living room, unsure of themselves. Kate wished her aunt hadn't left them there alone with Mom. Bobbie had sounded mad when she'd spoken to Uncle John, which was very out of character. Kate could hear both their voices coming from the kitchen in a heated discussion, but they were talking so low that she couldn't make out what they were saying.

"Y'all jist gone stand there starin', or ye gonna git over here 'n' give yer mamma a kiss? I ain't seen y'all in a month!"

Actually, you haven't seen us in over five months, Kate thought as she grabbed Birdie's hand. Until that moment, she hadn't realized she'd been keeping track of how long Mom had been gone. Together, Kate and Birdie walked awkwardly toward their mother. When they reached her, they stood in front of her, silent, not knowing what to expect.

Joyce reached out and grabbed both girls, hugging them. She smelled like liquor and sweat. She held them for a long moment and then, keeping her hands on their arms, leaned back to look at them. Uncle John had been right. She really did look like hell. She seemed to have aged several years in the time she had been away from them. "Whatsa matter with you girls?" she asked. "Ain'chall happy ta see yer mamma?" She looked surprised and disappointed, almost hurt.

Kate could hardly stand to be this close to her mother. The desire to run tempted both girls. They didn't want her here. *Why are you here?* Kate kept asking over and over in her head. *You're gonna ruin everything.* When she looked over at her little sister, big fat tears were rolling down both cheeks.

Finally, John and Bobbie came back into the living room. John was carrying two glasses and Bobbie looked upset. "Here ya go, sister," said John as he handed Joyce one of the drinks and sat down in his chair.

Joyce took a long drink and said to the girls, "Y'all ready to go home?"

"No," Birdie said through her tears. "I'm not ready, Mom."

Kate was shocked that Birdie had the guts to say it out loud.

Mom looked like someone had slapped her in the face. Birdie's blunt answer seemed to instantly sober Joyce. No one spoke. The tension was palpable.

Finally, Bobbie spoke. "Girls, it's gettin' late. Y'all go on to bed 'n' letcher mamma 'n' us catch up. Y'all c'n visit with 'er all ye want tomorrow."

The girls looked from their aunt to their mother, not sure what to do. Joyce, expecting them to defer to her, was pleased. Seeing that they still knew who the boss was seemed to buoy her spirits. She smiled, took another long drink and said, "Y'all heard yer aunt. Go on now; do what she said. I'll see y'all in the mornin'."

Relieved, the girls wasted no time in exiting the room, but, as she turned toward Bobbie, Kate gave her a look that said thank you. Bobbie nodded slightly in Kate's direction as if to say, *You're very welcome. And I'm sorry.*

Kate held her little sister as she cried herself to sleep that night. They didn't talk. They both knew their break from Mom was over. The only difference between the two was that Birdie had still been young and naive enough to believe they could really have stayed with John and Bobbie forever. Kate had known all along that their days here had always been numbered. She didn't cry that night. She didn't think about anything, really. She just stared into the darkness, trying to soak up as much of her last moments in this bed, this room, this house as she could.

Let Down

Chapter Twenty

To her credit, Bobbie fought valiantly for the girls to stay with her and John, but, in the end, Joyce won. She and the girls stayed with Mother and Papaw for a few weeks, which wasn't terrible. It was nice for them all to be together again, and the girls enjoyed getting to know Mother and Papaw better.

Mom was strange. She never said where she had been or what she'd been doing for all the time she was gone, but it was obvious she hadn't given up drinking. If anything, she was worse off. She was always pensive and brooding. Mother and Papaw catered to her every whim, but the more accommodating they were, the more demanding and ungrateful their daughter became. She'd send Papaw to the liquor store with a list and when he returned, she'd scold him for buying the wrong brand of vodka or the wrong size bottle. Mae and Pete were getting on in years, and Kate found it sad that Mom was so disrespectful toward them - couldn't seem to even speak civilly to her own parents.

Joyce took to screaming at the girls and even started getting physical with them. One day Beverly was walking through the house in her tap shoes minding her own business when her mother grabbed her roughly by the forearm as she passed by. "What the hell's wrong with you, huh?" she asked, slurring her words.

"Nothin', Mom," Beverly replied, confused.

"What the hell's wrong with your goddamn teeth? Ain'tchu been brushin' 'em? You know how goddamn embarrassin' that is for me?" Mom asked angrily, still squeezing Beverly's arm tightly. "Looks like you ain't been taught no better! Does that make you happy? *Huh?*" she asked loudly as she yanked Beverly closer to her. "Ta make ever'body think you got a terrible mother who dudn't care enough ta teach 'er own daughter ta brush 'er goddamn teeth?"

"No, Mom," Beverly replied, squeezing her eyes shut, cowering in front of her mother. "I'm sorry," she cried. "You're a good mom."

Joyce let go of Beverly's arm, shoving the girl away from her. "You're goddamn right I'm a good mamma." She leaned back on the couch, crossed her arms, and turned her head away from Beverly, closing her eyes and lifting her chin slightly, as if she was disgusted by even the sight of her daughter.

Hurt inside and out, Beverly crept out the back door so softly, her tap shoes didn't even sound on the floor. Kate and Birdie had heard the exchange from the bedroom the girls had been sharing and looked at each other.

"You think she's okay?" asked Kate, scared to leave the room, but knowing she needed to go check on Beverly.

"No," said Birdie. "But, if we're gonna go talk to her we have to walk past Mom, and I'm scared, Kate."

"Me too," she sighed. "We can't just leave her out there though. You know her feelins are hurt."

Birdie looked down at her hands, resting between her legs. She was sitting cross-legged on the bed. Resignedly, she said, "Let's go."

Mom didn't say a word as the girls passed in front of her. Kate was relieved by the fact that she seemed oblivious to their presence.

Beverly sat in the tire swing Uncle Buddy had hung for her shortly after she'd moved in with Mother and

Papaw. To Kate and Birdie's surprise, Beverly was smoking a cigarette.

"Where the hell'd you get that?" Kate asked, her voice a mixture of surprised and impressed.

"Stole it from *her*." Beverly pointed her chin in Mom's direction. "I hate that bitch," she said, as she watched her feet scrape the dirt back and forth as she swung aimlessly on the tire swing.

Both girls nodded their heads sympathetically, acknowledging their sister's wrongful scolding in the way siblings do. Especially when they're children, siblings seem to know each other so well that, many times, words are simply unnecessary. Kate thought about this as she and Birdie stood in solidarity with their sister, who swung and smoked and sobbed. She guessed this bond between brothers and sisters was why Uncle John had behaved so strangely the night Mom came back. He simply knew his sister, knew the best way to handle her drunken tantrum. He probably knew her better than the girls knew her. He had grown up with her, lived with her his whole childhood. Mother had told the girls an interesting story about Mom that they'd never heard before.

The girls had been sitting in the front yard with Mother one evening when Mom was being particularly cantankerous. Papaw had suggested they all go outside and enjoy the nice evening and let Mom have the house to herself for a little while.

Once outside, they were all glad for Papaw's suggestion. It was a beautiful night, probably one of the last warm ones, Mother had told them.

"I want'chall ta know yer mamma wudn't always like this," Mother began. She smiled then, a memory bringing momentary happiness to her normally sad, blue eyes. "Yer mamma was sa perty. I wish y'all coulda seen 'er," she said, looking off into the distance as if she were watching her daughter in an old movie that only she could see. "John and Buddy had all kindsa friends comin' outta the woodwork once yer mamma got ta high school, didn't they, Pete?"

Papaw laughed, exposing perfectly white false teeth. "Bo-uh, they shore did," he said, shaking his head and leaning forward in his lawn chair, both hands resting on the walking cane he had recently and reluctantly been using. He'd had it for a few years, but had insisted he didn't need it until his arthritis got so bad he could no longer go without it. "We had more teenage boys here than they did on the football field on Fridee nights!"

"Y'alls granddaddy's sa scandalous, he'd put 'em ta work!" Mae laughed.

"Well, hell, Mae! We was feedin' two or three of 'em ever' night there for a while. I had ta reduce our losses any way I could," he said, pretending to be offended. They both chuckled, remembering a better time when they had been in their prime and all their children still lived at home.

"Anyway," Mother continued, "she was sa perty there was always some ol' silly love-struck thang a comin' around, bu'cher mamma wouldn't have nothin' ta do with a one of 'em. An' I'll be damned if that didn' jist make 'em pine after 'er even more.

"She couldn' even go downtown without ever' pair a pants in the place turnin' toward that girl. She even had a lady run out of a beauty parlor after 'er one day. Told 'er she'd do 'er hair fer free, 'n' all she had ta do was tell people where she's havin' it done."

"That girl never paid fer nothin', did she, Mae?" Papaw interjected.

"She shur didn'." Mother sighed. "When she's born, I thought she'd break us 'cause she's sa perty I couldn' resist buyin' her nearly ever dress I saw. But the older she got, the pertier she got 'n' bo-uh people shore do like a perty little girl. Seemed like ever' time we went to church some lady or another'd brought us a new dress. Kid had sa many clothes by the time she's six years old I had ta ask the preacher ta make an announcement one Sundee from the pulpit 'n' ask that the ladies take a break from buyin' 'n' makin' little Joyce Smith any more clothes for a while because me 'n' Pete didn' have nowhere else ta put 'em."

"Really?" asked Kate, amazed. How had she never heard any of these things about her own mother?

"Yep." Papaw assured her. "When she's out for them three days I betchu nerly ever'body in this town was here at this house at one time or another ta check on her."

"Every'body loved that little girl," Mother said dreamily, a sad, closed-mouth smile stretching across her face.

"*Out* for three days? Whaddya mean?" asked Kate.

"Where'd she go?" asked Birdie. Both girls were hanging on their grandparents' every word. They could listen to stories about their mother's glory days all night long. In a strange way, it made Kate miss her mother, even though she sat right inside the house.

Mother laughed in response to Birdie's question. "Not out like she was gone, Sweet Pea. Out like she wouldn' wake up."

"*What?*" the girls asked in shock.

"Yeah," said Papaw. "Three whole days. We was scared ta death. Doctor come out 'n' looked at 'er. Said she's breathin' alright 'n' ever'thing looked alright with her; she's jist asleep. Wouldn' wake up."

"Nope. She shore wouldn'. Jist laid in the bed like that three whole days. I's terrified," Mother said. "I's afraid she might never wake up. Lord, I swear all I did fer three days was pray 'n' cry, pray 'n' cry."

"Well, what happened to her?" asked Kate, impatient with her grandparents now.

"Well," said Papaw, "her 'n' 'er girlfriends was a runnin' around on the dairy causin' a ruckus, gittin' inta trouble, pesterin' 'er brothers. I think one them girls musta had eyes for John or Buddy, 'cause them girls that day would not leave them boys alone fer nothin'.

"Finally, when John was headin' out to the west pasture, I couldn' take 'em a runnin' around there no more, a gigglin' 'n' carryin' on the way they were. Told John ta take 'em with 'im. So, he got in the truck 'n' the girls all jumped in back. I didn' think nothin' of it. Kids always rode in the backa the truck. They's always fine.

"Well, I guess John was a feelin' ornery cause he started weavin' around, drivin' crazy, a slingin' them girls around in the backa the truck. Well, he didn't see a big ol' dip in the pasture 'n' the truck hit it just right 'n' it throwed y'all's mamma clean outta the truck. Knocked 'er clean out."

"It shore did," Mother chimed in. With that far off, haunted look in her eye, she said, "Doctor said she's fine when she woke up, but if you ask me she ain't never been the same since that happened."

***

Standing at the tire swing with her sisters, Kate thought about this story and understood why Uncle John had been so patient with Mom. He felt the same about his little sister as she felt about Birdie. Maybe he even felt guilty about her falling out of the truck, like he hadn't protected her.

"Wonder why she's so mad at everybody." Birdie said to no one in particular.

"I was wonderin' the same thing," said Beverly, grinding the cigarette she'd finished smoking into the ground with the toe of her tap shoe.

"I don't know," said Kate. "It's weird. It's like she's mad at us because we were happy while she was gone."

"Well, what'd she expect us to do? Lay down and die?"

"Probly," Kate replied. "You got any more a those cigarettes, Bev?"

Chapter Twenty-One

Mom soon grew sick of Mother and Papaw's hovering and found a little rent house in town. She demanded Pete and Mae give her the money for her first month's rent, and they gave it to her, probably, the girls suspected, to get rid of her. Kate couldn't blame them. That was all she'd wanted to do ever since the first night she saw Mom again at John and Bobbie's house.

Mom supervised while the girls loaded what was left of all their belongings into the car. They couldn't do anything right, according to Mom.

"Bo-uh, I swear, y'all sure got lazy," Joyce yelled as the girls tried to pack too many boxes into the trunk and get it to shut. "Stay with yer aunt 'n' uncle for a few days 'n' all of a sudden y'all don't know how to do a damned thang, do ye? Makes me sick seein' my girls sa spoiled!" Joyce said. She was sitting in an old, ratty lawn chair alternating between barking orders and taking big gulps from a large glass bottle with clear liquid inside. The girls bore their mother's insults, trying not to ruffle her feathers.

The rent house wasn't very far away from the dairy, but this fact did little to comfort Kate and her sisters. As they pulled into the drive, it felt like staying with John and Bobbie and Mother and Papaw had been a dream. Their new home looked like all the other dumps they'd stayed in with Mom over the past years. To Kate, their new house represented their old life. It wouldn't be long before the girls were on their own again. As everyone was getting out of the car, a sickening feeling crept its way into Kate's stomach, and she wondered if she would be able to do it again.

"It won't be so bad this time, Kate. We got people here who'll watch out for us," Birdie reassured her big sister. "You'll see." Birdie always seemed to know when Kate needed to be reminded that all hope was not yet lost. She wished she could believe her little sister, but that too-familiar sinking feeling refused to budge.

Kate's hand instinctively went to her neck, the place where the K necklace Dad had given her used to rest. When she was feeling scared or anxious, she used to fiddle with the K. It was a comfort to her. Right after Mom had come back, Kate worked up the courage to ask her about the necklace. She'd assumed Mom had taken it to feel close to the girls, as a reminder of her connection to them, but she was wrong.

"You mean that cheap little piece of tin yer daddy gave ye? Hell, they wouldn't even give me a nickel for that piece a shit at the pawn shop."

Kate couldn't even register her mother's words. She wondered how anyone could be so cruel and selfish. Surely, she had heard her wrong. "Well, if they wouldn't take it, you've still got it. Can I have it back? Where is it?"

Mom, bothered, rolled her eyes when she answered. "God, I don't know, Kate! I guess I musta lost it. I can't be expected to keep up with alla your shit for you. Now go on 'n' play. Mamma's busy."

A few weeks later, after they'd gotten settled in the new rent house with Mom, Kate met up with Birdie on the walk home from school, as usual. All three girls had been feeling low over the past few weeks, but this day was different. Birdie was bursting with excitement, and, from a block away, Kate could see that her little sister was beaming.

"Hey!" yelled Birdie.

From this distance, Kate could see that Birdie still looked like a kid with a normal life. Kate had learned from Aunt Bobbie how to braid and had taken to fixing Birdie's hair for her every morning before school. They still had all the nice clothes Bobbie had gotten them for school, and Kate made sure she laid out her little sister's clothes for her every night. Before they'd left, Aunt Bobbie made sure they had their toothbrushes and a new tube of toothpaste. Kate stood over her little sister every morning and every night to make sure Birdie brushed her teeth thoroughly and that she didn't waste any of the toothpaste. As she neared her sister, she wondered how long they could keep up their charade.

"Guess what! Guess what!" Birdie yelled excitedly, hopping up and down, grinning from ear to ear. She waved a piece of blue cloth as she jumped up and down in place.

"What?" asked Kate, pleased to see her little sister in such a good mood. "What is it?"

"I won! I won!"

"Won what?" Kate asked, finally close enough to her sister to identify what she'd been waving in the air. It was a blue ribbon, a first-place ribbon. She took it from her sister's willing hand and examined it closely. "You won this?" she asked.

"Yep!" Birdie blurted. "It's a spelling bee ribbon! Look at it! It's real! We had a spelling contest today, and I won first place!"

"That is so neat!" exclaimed Kate. "You did good, Birdie Kay."

"I know! I did, huh? Mom's gonna be so happy!"

Kate doubted this. Mom used to at least wait until it was dark out to start drinking, but lately she'd taken to cracking one open as soon as she rolled out of bed, guzzling steadily throughout the day and night until she passed out on the couch. She didn't even try to work anymore. She didn't cook; she didn't clean. She just sat on the couch all day drinking and chain-smoking. She barely acknowledged any of the girls unless she felt the need to berate one of them.

Luckily John and Bobbie stopped by once or twice a week to bring groceries. Kate was sure they would have all starved by now if it weren't for her aunt and uncle. She felt sorry for them every time they came for a visit, especially Aunt Bobbie. Mom seemed to hate her brother's wife. Every time they came over, Joyce found a new way to insult Bobbie. It was obvious that it hurt her feelings, and Kate wasn't sure how much longer her poor aunt would be able to take the abuse. Joyce called her every foul name she had ever learned. She seemed instinctively to know the girls had grown to love Bobbie, and she hated her for it. Sometimes she wouldn't even let Bobbie or John in the house. She'd stand at the door, take whatever gifts they bore, and unceremoniously tell them to get off her front porch.

Kate was surprised to see her aunt and uncle every time they came to visit, and she was sure it was the last time she'd see them every time they left. But, week after week, they showed up. On the rare occasion Bobbie got Kate alone, she'd ask how she was doing. She'd make sure the girls were brushing their teeth and ask Kate if there was anything specific she needed.

On one visit, Mom happened to be gone on one of her drinking sprees. Bobbie wanted to take the girls home with her and John, but John said that would only make things worse for the girls when Joyce returned. Reluctantly, everyone had to agree. Instead, they took the girls out to dinner. They got full on burgers, fries and milkshakes. Their time together was precious and far too short. Bobbie and John wanted to know every detail about school and their friends. Kate cherished these times with her aunt and uncle. It was almost painful to be with them because it only reminded her of the life she and her sisters might have had.

Once, on one of John and Bobbie's rare visits without Mom there to run them off, Bobbie asked Kate to sit out on the front porch with her so they could have a talk.

She told Kate that her body would start to change soon and gave her some feminine hygiene products.

"These are for just in case," Bobbie said, looking Kate in the eye. "Now don't be scared. It happens to every girl when she's around your age. There ain't nothin' ta be scared of. As long as yer prepared, it ain't even a big deal. Ye hear me?"

Kate trusted her aunt. The things she was telling her seemed a little scary, but Kate remembered the talk she'd had with Aunt Bobbie about the training bra. It had seemed scary at first, but when the time came for her to start wearing a bra, she had been expecting it, and that made it less scary.

"Well, now that that unpleasantness is over, I want ta give ye somethin' else. Ye might not want ta show this ta yer mamma. She might not like it." Aunt Bobbie pulled a small package wrapped in tissue paper out of the bag that had also contained the feminine hygiene products. Gingerly, she handed it to Kate.

Kate held the package in her hands, relishing the fact that someone thought enough of her to bring her gifts that were wrapped. She fought the urge to smell the paper. She wanted to remember every second of this exchange. These small, stolen moments with Aunt Bobbie were what got her through the hard times with Mom.

Slowly, she removed the delicate, white tissue paper from the small, rectangular package. Inside, was a gold picture frame that was just a little bit bigger than her hand. It contained a black and white picture of Birdie and Kate on their first day of school when they had lived with Bobbie and John. Kate remembered that Aunt Bobbie had insisted on taking the girls' picture that morning, even though Uncle John was giving her a hard time for making such a big deal of their first day.

Kate stared at the picture in silence for several minutes. *Was this really just a few months ago?* She asked herself. *We look so different, so happy, so normal.*

Finally, Aunt Bobbie spoke. "Do you not like it?" she asked, confusion evident in her expression. "I thought you'd love it. Y'all both look sa cute. I'm sorry, honey."

"No, Aunt Bobbie. I do! I love it! Thank you so much!" Kate said as she wrapped her arms around her aunt, gripping her with all her strength. "It's beautiful. I can't believe that's us."

"Well, sweetheart, that's y'all alright. You're beautiful girls." She took the picture from her niece and examined it. "Y'all sure do take a pretty picture." Then she looked Kate in the eye, turning her body toward her niece. "Baby, I've tried and tried ta talk yer mamma into lettin' ye come back and live with me and Uncle John, but she ain't gonna let y'all. I even went and talked to the sheriff to see if there was anything I could do, but, long story short, there jist ain't nothin' can be done. She's y'all's mamma, and if she wants y'all ta live with her, then y'all have to. Lord, if yer Uncle John knew I did that he'd probably kick me out on the street! That man is blind as a bat when it comes to his baby sister. She can't do no wrong in his eyes."

"I know, Aunt Bobbie. It's not your fault," Kate said. She could see how upset her aunt was, and, in a strange way, this comforted Kate. She knew her aunt would do anything within her power to make sure that Kate and her sisters were safe and properly cared for. That meant a lot to Kate.

"Well, I wantcha to remember that it's not yer fault either. And I want you to remember that you're strong, Kate. You're one of the strongest people I've ever met. The way ye take care a yer sisters, the way ye make sure ever'body around ye's taken care of, those are signs that you're a strong person, Kate. Don't you ever forget that, little girl. It ain't fair that a little ol' thang your age has all that on 'er shoulders, but if there's anybody can handle it, it's you."

"Thank you, Aunt Bobbie." Kate said this because she wasn't sure what else to say. She didn't know how to process what her aunt was telling her. In her young mind, it sounded like a goodbye.

"I mean it now. You might not understand what I'm tellin' ye right now, but someday it'll all make sense. The first time I met you, I didn't know what ta make of ye. You looked like a nine-year-old little girl, but when ye talked ye seemed like some kinda old soul, like ye were a lot older on the inside. I didn't understand it at first, but I do now. I think God knew what you'd have to go through in this life, so he gave ye some extra wisdom. It's what's gonna help ye to make it through the hard times. But I want ye ta promise me something, Katie Rhea. I want ye to promise me ye won't let alla this stuff change ye. Don't let it make ye mad at the world. Ye hear me? Cuz then ye become somethin' else, something' hard and mean. And yer too sweet for that. You got a good heart. Can ye promise me you'll keep it like that?"

Kate thought about what Bobbie had just said. She honestly didn't know if she could keep a promise that she didn't really understand. But she didn't want to disappoint the person she looked up to more than anyone else in the world, so she said, "I promise I'll try, Aunt Bobbie."

Bobbie ruffled Kate's hair. "That's all I can ask of ye, little girl."

***

"Kate!" yelled Birdie, pulling her sister out of her own thoughts. "Don't you think Mom'll be proud that I won the spelling bee?"

Kate couldn't help but laugh, looking down at her little sister. "I don't know about Mom, Birdie Kay, but I'm real proud of you!"

This was enough for Birdie. She smiled and turned in the same direction that her sister was headed. Home.

Chapter Twenty-Two

"We-ll, ain'tchu special!" was Joyce's response to her youngest daughter's triumph. "I betcha think yer better'n the rest of us now, don'tcha?" Mom asked as she blew smoke into the already musty living room air. "I've about had it with you girls a'struttin' around this house with yer damn noses up in the air! Ever' one a you thinks yer hot shit nowadays, don'tcha? Makes me sick."

Kate had been afraid this was going to happen. She braced herself for the tirade. She said a silent prayer for her little sister, but she knew there was nothing she could do for Birdie, except comfort her when it was all said and done.

Birdie stood frozen. The blue ribbon that had just minutes before been so important to her now dangled from her hand by her thigh, as if it were no more important than a piece of trash she was on her way to throw in the garbage. She bowed her head, waiting for Mom to finish.

"I wish I'da never sent y'all ta stay with yer aunt 'n' uncle. Yer all sa disgustingly prouda yerselves for wipin' your own asses, I can't hardly listen to ya talk anymore. Won a goddamn *spellin'* bee! Hell, ye *oughta* be able ta spell! Y'all go ta school with a buncha goddamn hillbillies! Ye oughta be bringin' one a those goddamn ribbons home ever' *week*!" Joyce noticed that Birdie was staring at the floor. "Oh, has Mamma hurt your little doll-baby feelins, *puddin'*?" she asked, mocking her daughter.

Birdie, continuing to focus on the toes of her shoes, did not look up.

"Goddammit, I'm talkin' ta you! When yer *mamma's* talkin' to ye, ye look 'er in the *eyes*, ye hear me, little girl? That's the *least* ye can do!"

Still, Birdie trained her eyes on her feet.

Joyce stood then, incensed at the gall of her youngest child. She walked toward Birdie and roughly grabbed the small girl's chin, yanking it up until Birdie had no choice but to look her mother in the eye. Two large tears made their way down her cheeks.

"Oh, *hell*! Are you really cryin' *again*? My God, girl. Ain'tchu eight years old? You've gotten sa goddamn tender, I can't even talk to you anymore." Joyce shoved Birdie's chin away from her so hard the little girl stumbled backward several steps. The only thing that kept her from completely falling down was fear.

Kate watched the interaction in horror. Mom had never been this cruel to Birdie before. She wanted to help her little sister, but she was just as scared as Birdie. She couldn't have stepped in if her life had depended on it.

"You know what?" Mom asked no one in particular. "You girls have had it far too easy around here for far too long." Her voice was too loud for the small living room. It echoed off the dingy rent-house walls. "I tell you what. It's about time y'all learned how good you have it. Time ta start earnin' yer keep around this place. I'm sicka doin' everything around here. From now on, if you wanna eat, you'll find it yerselves. Goddamn, if you don't know how to fight in this world you ain't ever gonna have nothin'!"

Dread crept its way up Kate's neck. *This is gonna be bad,* she thought to herself.

"You two are gonna walk your little pampered asses downtown today and git yer mamma a new bra."

Surprised, Kate thought, *That doesn't sound too bad. We walk everywhere we go now. That's no big deal. She must be drunker than I thought.* Kate let a sigh of relief escape. She risked a glimpse at Birdie and could see that she, too, was relieved.

Both girls stood waiting.

"What the hell are y'all standin' around for? Birdie Kay, turn yer good ear toward me, for God's sake!"

"I heard you just fine, Mom," Birdie replied. The defiance in her tone was subtle, but Kate recognized it easily. "You didn't give us any money."

Mom cut her eyes at Birdie and stepped so close to her that Kate was sure her sister could feel their mother's hot breath on her forehead. In a low, menacing voice, Joyce said, "I *know* I didn't give you any money. Yer so smart -" Here Joyce jerked the blue ribbon from Birdie's grasp and slammed it into the girl's chest. "Figure it out."

Both girls immediately knew what their mother was implying. *She wants us to steal it.* The relief they had both been feeling only seconds earlier vanished as the reality of the situation dawned on them.

"And don't you dare bring your sorry asses home without one."

With that, the girls knew they were dismissed. They scurried out of the house.

"Kate, what are we gonna do?" Birdie fretted. "I don't wanna steal."

Kate felt as confused and frightened as her sister, but she also knew that it would do them no good to fight the inevitable. Mom had demanded something, and the reality of the situation was that Mom always got what Mom wanted.

Kate decided the best way to approach the situation was to toughen up and get it over with. "Stop whining, Birdie Kay. We both know we gotta do it. It won't do us any good to whine about it."

Birdie looked at her sister with hurt in her eyes. "But, Kate, I don't want to be a thief."

It bothered Kate to do her sister that way, but she knew she couldn't baby Birdie in this situation. "Remember when we lived in Arizona? You were so good at stealing cigarettes from behind the counter. This'll be just like that. Piece a cake."

Birdie did not reply.

As they walked down the road toward the downtown area, Kate couldn't help but feel that she had betrayed her little sister. She had crossed some invisible line, and she worried that she might not be able to cross it again to get back to where she wanted and needed to be. *But I don't have a choice*, she told herself. "Quit bein' a big baby. Let's go get this done so she'll quit bitchin'."

Birdie looked at her sister, surprised, but said nothing. It was obvious they didn't have a choice. "You know why I don't wanna do it, Kate?" she asked her sister.

"Why?" asked Kate, thinking she knew the answer.

"Because I don't want to like it too much."

This surprised Kate. "What do you mean?" she asked, confused.

"I *was* really good at stealing. And I *liked* it. It made me feel good. Strong, I guess, y'know? I don't want to be one of those people who steals all the time." She paused for a moment. "I don't wanna be like Mom."

Kate understood what her sister meant. She thought it had only been her who felt the pull of a darker existence. Now she knew they all struggled with the knowledge that a life like Mom's would be easier. It was easier to lie, to cheat, to skirt the system. "I know what you mean," she confessed.

As they approached Cohen's department store, the two girls developed a plan. Kate would distract the clerk while Birdie slipped the bra down the front of her dress. Then they would look around for a while so they didn't arouse any suspicion, and then they'd stroll out of the store just as innocent as could be.

The plan did not go as well as the girls had hoped. First, Birdie was so nervous that her hands were shaking. Instead of looking like a kid who had wandered in off the street to peruse the merchandise, she looked like a sweaty, nervous wreck. And Kate wasn't any better. She was so nervous that she stood and stared at the store clerk for an uncomfortable amount of time. And Birdie did nothing to improve the situation as she tried unsuccessfully to appear nonchalant.

Kate had to do something, or her sister was going to get caught. She swallowed the knot in her throat and spoke up. "Do y'all have any of the new go-go boots here?"

"Excuse me?" asked the young girl who was working after school as a clerk in the department store. She looked bored, slightly annoyed that, for money, she had to be nice to some kid just in case she actually had the money to buy something, which the store clerk highly doubted.

"Do y'all have go-go boots?" Kate asked again, self-conscious.

"I'm not sure," the clerk responded, obviously anxious to get rid of the kid. "If we do, they'll be over in the shoe department." The girl pointed in a random direction toward the back of the store.

Kate wasn't sure what she should do. The plan was for her to keep the store clerk occupied while Birdie did her dirty deed. But Kate didn't have to tarry long in her decision- making because just then Birdie darted out the door past them.

The clerk looked on disinterested and, a bit confused, watched through the store window as Birdie ran for dear life. "Wonder what's wrong with her," she said to no one in particular.

Kate stood, frozen staring at the girl in front of her.

"You gonna buy something?"

Kate heard the clerk's question, but she couldn't answer. She just stared back like a mute idiot. The only thing she could make herself do was walk slowly backward, unable to break the awkward eye contact she and the clerk had established. Eventually, she bumped into the cold, glass door with her butt. Feeling something solid snapped Kate out of her stupor. She turned and ran for all she was worth.

Birdie was waiting a few blocks down, bent over with her hands on her knees, catching her breath. "Where the hell were you?"

Kate had no excuse. *I'm such a chicken shit*, she thought. *I can't believe I froze like that! Maybe Mom's right. Maybe we did get spoiled being at John and Bobbie's.* Shame held her tongue. She could only look at Birdie.

"Where the hell *were* you?" Birdie asked again. "I thought something had happened to you!"

"Did you get it?" This was the only thing Kate could think of to say that would steer the conversation away from the fact that she couldn't even do something as simple as be a decoy for her sister, the one doing all the heavy lifting.

"I got the damn thing," Birdie replied, disgust and disappointment lacing her voice and radiating from her eyes as she looked at Kate.

"Well, ya did good," Kate coaxed, hoping the compliment would soothe her sister, whose feathers were justifiably ruffled.

"I know I did good, goddammit!" Birdie yelled, surprising Kate. "What the hell were you doin'? You're the one who told me to stop bein' a damn baby! And then you couldn't even keep that stupid teenager talkin' for five minutes so I could get that stupid bra? What the hell has happened to you, Kate? You used to be so good at stuff like that."

They had begun walking in the direction of their house; neither girl had much to say. Kate risked a sideways glance over at her sister's face after a few minutes to see if she could tell from the expression on Birdie's face whether she was still mad. Birdie's silhouette shocked Kate. Her baby sister seemed to have grown a large bulge in her crotch. She looked like a normal little girl from the waist up, just minding her own business, walking down a neighborhood street. But then she had a large vulgar lump right at her crotch. Kate realized quickly that the bra Birdie had stuffed down the front of her dress had slipped during her getaway, but it didn't make it any less funny. Despite herself, Kate began to giggle.

Birdie looked over at her sister, surprised that she was laughing. "What the hell are you laughin' at?" She cut her eyes toward her partner in crime. She was still mad enough that she wouldn't even give Kate the courtesy of turning her head toward her. Chin raised, eyes half shut, she was using the facial expression they had always seen Mom use when she was upset with someone and wanted to make sure they knew it.

"Look down at your crotch," Kate answered, genuinely trying not to completely lose her composure out of respect for the master thief walking beside her.

Curiosity got the best of her, and she looked down and saw where the bra had ended up. Birdie tried valiantly not to let herself smile, but, even though she'd grown up a lot that day, in the end, she was still just a little girl. They hadn't walked ten steps before they were both so tickled that they had to stop in order to regain their composure.

***

Mom wasn't impressed when they made it home and proudly presented their spoils. "'Bout damn time y'all gotcher asses back here. I got places to be," she snapped as she snatched the stolen bra out of her youngest daughter's hand and examined it. "Got the wrong damn size too, didn'tcha?" They both suppressed a snicker.

Chapter Twenty-Three

Aunt Bobbie died unexpectedly when Kate was twelve. Uncle John said it was something called an aneurism. Kate didn't have any idea what that was, but she did know that she felt a hole in her heart. Mom, true to her style, got drunk for the occasion of Bobbie's funeral. It was the only time the girls ever saw their uncle lose patience with his sister. They had the funeral at Bethel, the church the Smith family had founded near the turn of the century. Every family member since then had married there, and they all attended Bethel religiously; Mother and Papaw were no exception. The Smiths also had all their funerals there.

John was distraught over the loss of his wife. He could barely speak before the funeral. Kate wondered how he had even managed to get himself dressed and to the church that day. Though she could sympathize with her uncle, she herself felt nothing but an unsettling numbness. She had loved her aunt more than almost any other person in her world. She looked around at all the people crying and she wanted to be one of them, but the tears just wouldn't come.

Even though she was obviously drunk, Joyce insisted on singing a song for Bobbie. She seated herself at the piano in front of the expectant grievers. Kate, nervous, looked around at the people sitting near. She saw Rick and Randy, John and Bobbie's sons, sitting with their wives and children. Both were visibly shaken. Kate couldn't blame them. How could anyone not have loved Bobbie, especially the two boys who were lucky enough to call themselves her sons? For an instant, Kate felt jealous of Rick and Randy, but just as quickly she chastised herself for being so selfish.

Kate distracted herself by looking down at the dress she was wearing. That morning, when she'd picked it out, she had thought Aunt Bobbie would have liked it. Though it was far too tight and too short for her now, she had struggled into it because it was one of the last dresses Aunt Bobbie had picked out for her. It was the dress she'd worn to her first day of school in Oklahoma.

When it was time for Joyce to sing her song, all three girls sat on pins and needles, silently praying that Mom wouldn't embarrass them. *At least she looks nice*, thought Kate. She was wearing a fitted, black, tea-length, sleeveless dress with matching black heels. Joyce was always able to pull herself together when the odd occasion was deemed worthy. She somehow managed to look like a respectable lady when she wanted to.

Joyce, obviously pleased by all the appreciative glances she was receiving, sat down at the piano and began to play "Amazing Grace." The girls had sat and listened to her play this song on the guitar many times. Kate breathed a sigh of relief. She knew Mom could play this song, no matter how drunk she was.

The piano and Mom's voice were perfect. Kate even started to feel herself getting choked up thinking of all the times Aunt Bobbie had made her feel like she was special. Halfway through the song, however, Mom missed a note on the piano, and Kate was jolted back to the present. Joyce didn't seem bothered. She just kept going. Most people probably didn't even notice since it was such a minor mistake. But then she made another mistake. And another. And another.

Maybe her behavior after that was because she was embarrassed, or maybe Joyce was throwing a fit because her performance hadn't gone the way she'd wanted it to. Either way, after about two minutes of Mom banging on the piano keys with all the force she had in her now frail body and screaming the words to "Amazing Grace," Uncle

John had heard enough. He strode swiftly between the pews and up to the front of the church, snatched his sister up by the arm, and half-dragged her out the door, ignoring Joyce's protests. The look on his face was grim. And frightening. Humiliated and unsure of what they should do, the girls left their places in the designated family pew and followed Mom and John outside.

They were shocked at what they stumbled onto. Uncle John still had ahold of Mom's arm, and he was shaking her roughly. "What in the hell is wrong with you, Joyce?" he asked, hurt causing his voice to crack as he tried to hold back his tears. "My *wife* just died. Our *sons* are in there. Your *daughters* are in there." John's piercing blue eyes were concentrated on his sister. They seemed to be begging for an answer, any answer that would explain Joyce's behavior. But she had no answer. She wore a look of shock and amusement.

Finally, when he saw that he couldn't talk any sense into her, John let go of Joyce. He turned away from his sister, sadly shaking his head and went back to his wife's funeral.

"What the hell are y'all standin' there for? For God's sake, get in the goddamn car!" Mom yelled, seemingly unphased by her brother's emotional reaction. The girls hesitated, Kate for the longest. She stood staring at the church door, torn. She felt that she should go back in and apologize to her uncle. Her heart ached for him. She had never seen this strong, capable man look so broken. But what could she say? There were no words to ease his pain. Maybe she should just go with Mom and let the man grieve in peace. He had probably had enough of all of them anyway.

Reluctantly, Kate made her way to the car and climbed in beside her sisters. Mom gunned the engine, squalling the tires, throwing up red dirt behind them, and drove away from the church.

Chapter Twenty-Four

Kate didn't think she'd ever get over Aunt Bobbie's sudden death. They didn't see Uncle John again for months. She worried about him, and she thought about Bobbie constantly. Mostly, she thought about the last real conversation they had ever had. Over and over, she silently promised Aunt Bobbie that she would remember her advice and make a good life for herself.

But Kate's promises got harder to keep as time went by. Mom was home more, but she was always drunk. She didn't stay away for days at a time anymore, but she would leave early in the afternoon all dressed up and come home in the wee hours of the morning. She started bringing strange men home with her. Kate, always the night owl, could never sleep until she knew Mom was home safe.

The first night she heard a man's voice in the other room, she naively thought maybe Dad was home. She hadn't heard his voice in so long that she had forgotten what it sounded like. *It could be him,* she told herself, even though something felt off. She got up from her spot between Birdie and Beverly and crept to the bedroom door. The voices turned to strange sounds through the cheap paneling of the hollow door, someone breathing heavily, a soft moaning. For some reason she couldn't quite pinpoint, once she got closer, she realized the man on the other side of the wall was not her father. Stealthily, she padded back to the bed she shared with her sisters and climbed in. She tried to sleep, but sweet oblivion would not show its elusive face. She lay there for what felt like hours listening to the strange sounds in the other room. And then, as suddenly as they'd started, the noises stopped.

The next morning, Kate pretended to be asleep so that Birdie or Beverly might do some unwitting reconnaissance. But neither of the girls, after returning from the kitchen, said anything about a strange man being in their living room.

After several days of no one mentioning this bizarre occurrence, Kate began to doubt herself. *Maybe I just dreamed the whole thing.* But something deep inside told her she hadn't dreamed it and that she should be wary.

Several nights later, Kate was awakened by a strange sound again, but this time it was a different sound, and it seemed much closer. It sounded like metal clanking against metal. She opened her eyes to find a man crawling up on the bed with her and her sisters. She squeezed her eyes shut tight, sure she was dreaming, but if it *was* a dream, it was a very realistic dream. She could feel their cheap mattress bouncing with the extra weight of a large, moving human being. Cautiously, she opened her eyes into tiny slits. A shirtless man whose jeans were unbuttoned and unzipped, a leather belt with a large belt buckle dangling loosely to the side, was hovering over Birdie, staring down at her. The sound she had heard was his belt buckle, loosened, clanging against itself.

It was warm most nights with three bodies sharing one bed, so the girls slept without covers, even on nights when it was cool out, and they usually only slept in panties and light shirts. This night was not out of the ordinary in this respect.

"Well, lookie what we got here," the man whispered, grinning to himself in the dark. "Three perty little flowers ripe for the pickin'." He reached down and caressed Birdie's torso. Kate wanted to tell the man to stop, but, like so many times before, she froze with fear.

She watched, horrified, as the man, poised on his knees above Birdie, moved her sister's panties to the side.

Her mind wouldn't work. She just kept telling herself over and over, *Do something, you idiot. Do something.*

Kate was so overwhelmed by what was happening that it took her a few moments to notice that she felt something warm underneath her body, something warm and uncomfortable.

For once, she was relieved her older sister was a bedwetter. Beverly had chosen that very moment to pee the bed. It was just what she needed to shake her from her stupor. Kate's eyes opened wide. She knew what she needed to do.

Just then, the man noticed he wasn't the only one awake in the room. In no hurry to stop what he was doing to Birdie, he looked Kate in the eye and said, "Well, lookie here. We got ourselves a little pervert. You like to watch, sweetheart?" he crooned.

Kate had no idea what the man was talking about, but she knew what she had to do to get him away from Birdie. She took a deep breath, opened her mouth, and screamed. She screamed like her life depended on it. This woke Birdie and Beverly instantly, and as soon as they saw the man, half naked, hovering over them with his hands in Birdie's underwear, they both followed their sister's lead and began to scream as well.

Within thirty seconds, the man was outside starting his car and skidding out of the driveway. Birdie was inconsolable for at least half an hour. Beverly said she didn't see what the big deal was. He hadn't hurt anyone, after all. She dragged a pillow over to a corner of the room and went back to sleep. For once, Kate was glad to have sheets to wash. It gave her time to think about what had happened and to form a plan to make sure it didn't happen again. And, in some odd way, Beverly peeing the bed comforted her. At least she knew how to deal with that.

Kate's eyes were still wide open when the sun came up. She couldn't let herself fall asleep, even though the events of the night had left her drained and exhausted. If she wanted to keep herself and sisters safe, especially Birdie, she had to toughen up.

Through it all, Mom never even lifted her head off the arm of the couch. The next morning, she yawned, stretched, and said she had slept like the dead.

Well good for you, Kate thought to herself sarcastically as she and her sisters headed off to school.

Chapter Twenty-Five

Winters in Oklahoma were hard for the girls to get used to. When it was hot, it wasn't much different from Arizona, except everything seemed to sweat more. But the winters were a different story. It wasn't out of the ordinary to wake up and look out the window to find the entire world painted white, the temperature thirty or forty degrees cooler than the day before. At first, the white stuff seemed exotic and beautiful to three girls who had never seen snow. But, upon further inspection, they realized it was not soft, powdery snow, but tiny, rock hard crystals of ice. Everywhere. Icicles hung from every elevated surface, as well. Schools and businesses would close their doors. Pipes would freeze, and there would be no water. The roads would be deserted. The whole world grew silent, desolate on these days.

It was mid-January. Aunt Bobbie had died the summer before, and Kate was still raw with the knowledge that she wasn't coming back. She, Mom and the girls had all been stuck in the house for days, waiting for the latest round of ice to melt. They had no electricity. It wasn't hard to see why. Icicles a foot long were hanging from every power line in their neighborhood. Kate felt lucky that a neighbor passing by a few nights earlier had warned her about the next storm headed their way and told her that if she kept the water dripping from her faucet the pipes wouldn't freeze up. She was sure this was the only reason they still had running water. Kate made a mental note to thank the neighbor the next time she saw him. She also made a mental note to make sure the faucets were still dripping before she went to bed that night.

Mom was in a particularly foul mood because she had gone through all the liquor in the house and was down to her last beer. But she wasn't the only one in a mood. The girls had begun snipping at each other the day before and were still going strong. The resentment Birdie had begun to feel toward Kate that first day Mom had made her steal the bra had only festered. Although Kate had gotten better at being a distraction so that Birdie could fulfill her now common duties for Mom, there were other ways Kate was letting her little sister down. One thing in particular had angered Birdie. Kate's old friend, the one she'd made when they lived with John and Bobbie, Tammy, had invited Kate to her house to play. Mom had said she could go, but she had to take Birdie with her. Begrudgingly, Kate consented, knowing she didn't really have a choice in the matter.

Kate and Birdie found themselves on the roof of Tammy's house not long after they'd gotten there. It had been the place Kate and Tammy told each other their deepest secrets, their hopes and dreams. It had been the place where they had cooked up the sleepover that was never to be.

The conversation had lagged, and Kate, desperate to win back her only real friend, decided she had to make Birdie and Tammy like each other. *Maybe if they like each other she'll start inviting both of us over,* thought Kate. Then they could go to Tammy's house more often and avoid Mom a little more. Kate needed to think of a way for Birdie to impress Tammy. This was difficult because Birdie was only ten. A ten-year-old impressing a twelve-year-old was near impossible.

Kate, scouring her brain for just the right story to tell, remembered that when they had been best friends a few years back, one of their teachers had a candy drawer. Tammy was always trying to come up with a plan to break into that drawer. Even though a few opportunities did present themselves, Tammy always chickened out at the last minute. She never could work up the nerve to follow through. *That's it!* thought Kate. *I'll tell Tammy about what a good thief Birdie is.* "She can steal anything." she began, casually gesturing in Birdie's direction, careful not to appear too eager.

"*Birdie* can?" asked Tammy, intrigued.

"Yep."

"*Really?*" She regarded Birdie with palpable doubt.

Birdie sat silently, observing the exchange, obviously confused about why her sister was divulging one of their most diligently guarded secrets.

"She'll pretty much do anything you dare her to." *Yeah, that sounds good. Say she won't back down from a dare.* Kate was on a roll. "Anything. She doesn't care. If you dare her to do it, she'll do it. I dare her to steal stuff all the time, and she never gets caught!" Kate bragged.

"Like *what?*" Tammy asked, skeptical.

"Anything. I've dared her to do anything I can think of, and she always does it."

Tammy turned to Birdie. "You'll do *anything* I dare you to do?" she asked.

"I guess. Maybe. I don't know," Birdie said.

"Okay then, I *dare* you to jump off this roof," Tammy challenged, triumph dancing in her eyes, sure she would prove Kate wrong.

Shit, thought Kate. She looked at her little sister. She was trying to figure out a way to get her out of this mess, but her mind was blank. She had not seen this coming.

"No way," Birdie replied. "*You* jump off the roof!"

"I'm not the one who said she'd take any dare, *chicken,*" Tammy retorted.

Birdie, her cheeks tinged with shame, tilted her small chin toward the sky. "I'm not a chicken." She stood and walked toward the edge of the roof, looking down at the ground. "It's too far. I'll get hurt," she said more to herself than to Kate or Tammy. She backed away from the edge of the roof and sat back down between the two girls.

"That's what I thought, chicken shit," Tammy said, leering at Birdie. She turned to Kate. "She's not gonna do it, ya big liar."

"Yeah she will!" Kate retorted, her pride wounded now too. Despite the unrealistic demand, Kate was ashamed of her little sister. "Why won't you just do it? It's not that far down." She looked Birdie in the eye, hoping her sister could see her silent plea. *Please do this for me, sister,* she begged with her eyes, not realizing until just then how desperate she was. *Please help me save this one last normal thing in my life. A friend. That's all I want: just one normal thing, just one measly little friend. Is that really too much to ask for after all I've done for you?*

But Birdie turned away from Kate. Her answer was clearly a resounding *no way, Jose.*

Birdie's outright refusal angered Kate. *After all I've sacrificed for this little shit, she has the gall to refuse this one, small request?* Before she even knew what she was doing, Kate stood. "You're just a goddamn coward," she screamed, her face hot with a pent-up rage she hadn't even realized was there before that moment.

Tammy seemed to enjoy the exchange between the sisters. She picked up where Kate left off, chanting, "Coward, cow-ard, cow-ard," over and over, getting closer and closer to Birdie's face every time she sang the word. Birdie was able to ignore it when it was just Tammy, but then her sister, red in the face, inexplicably angry with her, joined in. They were both yelling in her ears, one on either side of her, "Cow-ard, cow-ard!" sang the girls. They were doing the same thing the mean girls had done to Birdie at school back when they were in Arizona, when they had burst her eardrum. Finally, unable to endure the teasing anymore, especially from Kate, her ally, her partner in crime, Birdie leapt up from her spot on the roof, ran to the edge, and jumped.

Somehow, Birdie landed on her feet, but the impact was so forceful that her teeth slammed together hard enough that if her tongue had listed to the side a little, she would surely have bitten it off. She howled as pain shot up from the bottoms of her feet, through her body, and out the top of her head. She clapped her hands over her ears and squeezed her eyes tightly shut as she staggered around aimlessly. She appeared disoriented, like she had forgotten where she was.

Staring down at Birdie, Kate felt disgusted with herself. The sound of two cupped palms rhythmically pounding out genuine appreciation interrupted her inner self-loathing. Kate turned and saw Tammy peeking over the edge of the roof, grinning and clapping for Birdie. Kate realized two things: one, her plan had worked, and two, her sister would never forgive her for this.

***

Now that they were all stuck in the house together because of the ice storm, Birdie's animosity toward her older sister was getting harder for Kate to overlook. It started out as little arguments here and there, Birdie digging in and refusing to follow along with Kate's ideas any longer, arguing with Kate about little things. The girl's bitterness over her sister's betrayal swelled with the passing days.

No one was surprised when Mom announced she was going to the store. In truth, they were all relieved to see her go. None of them expected her to come back if she was able to find an open bar.

Kate peeked out the window after a few minutes of not hearing the car roar to life. "I guess she walked," she said. "The car's still out there, and I don't see her."

"Who gives a shit?" Beverly responded. Kate and Birdie looked at their sister, surprised at her indifference. Beverly had been acting even more strangely than usual.

She'd taken up with a red-headed boy. Mom referred to him as "that worthless hippie." Beverly, who had always been one to retreat into herself when things got tense, had become even more stoic lately. And both girls had noticed she was getting fat again. Not long after they were all back together, she slimmed down almost immediately, but now she was packing the pounds on again. All she did was sleep during the day, and they both knew why. She was slipping out at night to see that boy. She'd stay gone all night sometimes.

No one knew if Mom noticed Beverly's unexplained absences, or if she even cared. But Kate and Birdie noticed. Her comment about Mom walking to the store had been the first thing she'd said to either of them in days.

"We-ll," teased Kate. "Look who's finally talking to her sisters."

"Shut up, Kate," blurted Birdie, not really interested in taking up for Beverly, but looking for any reason to let Kate know they were not on the same side anymore.

"*You* shut up, you little shit. Nobody was even talking to you," she replied, spite dripping from her words. *God, when is she gonna get over it? It's been months since that crap on the roof, and she didn't even really get hurt. I'm done apologizing.*

"Why don't you both shut up?" Beverly asked, surprising them both. "I'm so sick a y'all fightin' all the damn time."

"Well, guess what, little miss high and mighty," responded Kate, knowing she sounded like Mom but not caring. "We're sick a your stuck up ass prancin' around here like you're better'n everybody all the time anyway! "Oh, look at *me*," Kate sang in a high, annoying voice, mimicking her older sister. "I'm sooo fancy. I got myself a red-headed boyfriend! I'm jist so much fancier than everybody, I don't even know what to do with myself! My little sisters are so stupid now. I can't even bring myself to even talk to 'em!" Kate pranced back and forth in front of Beverly, twisting around on her tiptoes. She held her pinky in the air and kept the other hand on her hip. Her eyes were closed, and she held her nose up in the air, mustering a mock disdain for the people around her that even made Birdie laugh. "Look at me. I'm soooo fancy! I'm so much better than the people I live with!"

Kate was drawing energy from Birdie's laughter and from Beverly's seething anger. The madder Beverly got, the bolder it made Kate.

Beverly yelled for Kate to stop it, to shut up. But Kate couldn't seem to make herself stop. She didn't *want* to stop.

Finally, unable to take the teasing anymore, Beverly leapt forward from her seat on the couch and lunged for Kate's throat. She pinned her younger sister in a matter of seconds, her hands around Kate's neck.

Shocked by her sister's rage, Kate struggled to breathe. She looked to Birdie for help, but her little sister was lost in a fit of laughter; she was enjoying the show, the *whole* show, not just the part Kate starred in. She looked up into Beverly's eyes and saw cold, unyielding anger. Beginning to see stars now, Kate's eyes rolled back toward Birdie, who had stopped laughing, but still did not move to help her.

Just then, Birdie yelled, "Beverly! Stop! Listen." Birdie squinted her eyes in concentration.

Good, Kate thought. *Distract her so I can get up and kick her ass!*

Beverly, however, seemed not to even hear Birdie. She just kept choking Kate.

Birdie got down on the floor beside Beverly and grabbed her arm. "Really, Beverly. Stop for a minute. Listen."

Kate had to hand it to her little sister. She was a good actor, totally devoted to her part. Personally, Kate would've preferred it if Birdie would have just jumped on Beverly and ripped her off her, but she was in no position to be picky.

Beverly finally heard Birdie and paused in choking her younger sister to death, listening intently.

It was such an odd scene. Kate imagined someone walking in right now and seeing them. All three girls sat silent as stones, Beverly straddling her sister's torso, hands still poised in their strangling position, and Birdie on her knees beside them both with her "shhh" finger to her lips.

Kate still thought Birdie was acting when a mewling sound so faint that she thought she might be imagining it captured her attention, and she realized Birdie was telling the truth. *Does that mean if she hadn't heard a strange sound my sister would still be sitting as a spectator watching our oldest sister strangle me to death?* Kate wondered, shock registering on her face as she realized Birdie had a cruel streak lurking just beneath the surface.

"Ohhhhhhh…."

Everyone heard it this time. It was faint, but it was definitely there.

All three girls strained their ears to hear it again.

Silence.

Then, "Ohhhhhh…"

"What the hell is that?" asked Beverly, still straddling Kate.

"I don't know. It sounds like an old female cat squallin'," replied Birdie.

They all listened intently, wondering if they'd hear it again.

"Ohhhhh…"

"There it is again!" Kate shouted. "Get your fat ass off me!" She said to Beverly as she now easily rolled her sister to the floor beside her.

Beverly willingly let her sister buck her off, curiosity and a small amount of fear replacing the anger she'd given in to just moments before.

"Do you think it's a person?" asked Birdie. "Someone hurt, maybe?"

"Sounds like an ol' cat in heat to me," replied Beverly. "We heard 'em all the time when I stayed with Mother and Papaw. They scared me at first because it always sounded like a lady screamin'. But it never was. It was just them ol' barn cats. But Papaw always said it was worse in the spring. Said that's when animals went into heat. I can't imagine 'em wantin' to do anything but keep warm on a night like tonight."

Kate was unsure of what it meant to be a cat "in heat," but this sounded like a person in trouble to her.

"Go look out the window, Birdie," Kate said, now perched on her side, still lying on the floor.

"*You* go look." Birdie said, still in the habit of defying her traitorous sister.

"Just go," demanded Beverly.

Probably still a little frightened by Beverly's display of strength, Birdie obeyed without question. She crept to the window and, moving the ratty, mustard colored curtains aside, peered out at the white, frozen landscape. "I don't see anything," she reported.

But then they heard the sound again.

"Ohhhhh…."

"Somebody's out there," Kate said.

"Well, go out there then!" cried Beverly. "If it's somebody who's hurt, we can't just leave 'em out there."

"Why not?" asked Kate. "It's not our job to save some big ol' idiot who went out in the snow 'n ice!"

"What if they're really hurt?" asked Birdie.

"So what? Why's it our problem?"

"Well, we can't just sit here listenin' to 'em bellerin' all night!" yelled Beverly. "It's not like we'll be able to sleep with them out there hollerin', throwin' a fit all damn night!"

God, she's cranky lately, thought Kate. "I guess we could go out and look around," she offered, hoping to placate her hostile sister for a little while.

"It's probably just an ol' cat anyway," chimed in Birdie. "I'd sure sleep a lot better if it was. We could at least go run it off."

"Oh, hell!" cried Kate. "Fine. Come on then. Let's get it over with. It'll take two weeks for me to get warm again, but if it'll make you two puddins sleep better, for God's sakes, let's go run that goddamn cat off!"

Neither of her sisters said a word, but they both put on their coats, following their sister as she stomped ahead of them.

Kate, cautious, slowly opened the front door. They were immediately met with the sound again.

"Ohhhh…"

"That's no cat." Birdie's hazel eyes were wide, frightened.

"Come on," Kate said, sounding braver than she felt.

The girls followed the sound. Kate led the pack, wanting to get this over with as soon as possible. She crept forward praying she'd find some old cat but knowing there was no way that was what they were hearing. She was several paces in front of her sisters, and, to their surprise, she slipped on the ice and fell.

"Goddammit! It's about damn time y'all brought your worthless asses out here ta help a feller! Ohhhhh…!" said a voice from across the yard.

Surprised, Kate, flat on her back now, looked over to see Mom sprawled on the ice. From her struggle to get back on her feet, her dress had hiked itself up around her waist, and her long, skinny, white legs were splayed, spread eagle, on the ice and snow. Her old powder blue house shoes were haphazardly strewn some feet away. *Who goes out in an ice storm in a flimsy nightgown? And house shoes?* Kate asked herself as she stared over at her irate mother.

Beverly and Birdie cautiously leaned over and helped Kate pull herself to her feet. It was Birdie who first let out a chuckle. This got Kate and Beverly tickled, and once they'd started, they couldn't stop. All those months of pent up frustrations and anger seemed to have chosen that moment to release their hold on the sisters. *It feels so good to laugh*, thought Kate.

"I guess we solved the mystery," Beverly managed through snorts and squeals.

"Goddammit!" yelled Mom. "A feller lays out here on the cold ground almost freezin' ta death and all you ol' worthless thangs can do is laugh? Ungrateful sonsabitches!" Mom spat, lying helpless on the ground.

Mom's tirade, combined with the very unladylike position in which she lay, her white panties shining for the world to see, threw the girls into a fit of hysterics, despite the freezing cold temperatures. The fit was only intensified when Birdie, during a particularly intense bout of giggling, bent down, lost her balance, and succumbed to the icy sidewalk below. She crashed to the ground loud and dramatic and carefree, her newly long, skinny arms and legs flailing wildly. This only made the girls laugh harder.

Beverly, the only one who remained on her feet, cautious as always, bent, hands on her knees, trying to collect herself, but she was gloriously unsuccessful.

Mom was so mad, she was fuming, probably melting the ice beneath her. "Goddammit! Are y'all gonna laugh all night or ya gonna help yer mamma?"

Though it was freezing out, Kate looked around at the still, dark night, felt the pure, cold air stinging her nose, and realized she wanted to savor this moment. She watched her beautiful sisters smiling so hard that it probably hurt their faces and found herself wishing time would stop right where it was. Just for a moment. She felt like she could see every single star. Despite the chaos, she felt at peace for one small moment. For some reason she could not pinpoint, Kate thought of Aunt Bobbie. She pictured her aunt looking down on her, laughing too, happy to see her nieces happy.

Eventually, the girls dragged Joyce to her feet and got her back into the house, fighting residual giggles all the way. Mom never stopped cussing them, but, as they started up the porch steps, Kate glimpsed Mom's profile, and, though it was hard to see past the tangled mass of snow-streaked hair, she could have sworn Joyce was stifling the tiniest hint of a smirk.

Chapter Twenty-Six

Even though they'd shared a laugh over Mom in the ice storm, the animosity between the girls was still very much alive. Mom, of course, picked up on this, and, instead of calling them down, she encouraged the fighting. She even went so far as to egg them on. She seemed to enjoy watching her daughters antagonize each other.

One day the following spring, when Birdie and Kate had been bickering non-stop, Mom ordered them into the front yard with her. She had been telling them all day long they should settle their latest argument with a fist fight, but none of the girls' disagreements had ever come to blows. Not yet anyway.

Kate and Birdie stood in the front yard, still mad at each other, awaiting Mom's instruction. They wouldn't even look at each other.

Mom stood on the front porch, reigning over her little ramshackle kingdom, every bit the queen of her domain.

Both girls looked on expectantly. *God, what the hell does she want now?* wondered Kate.

"Well, what are y'all waitin' for? You been wantin' to fight for days now. Here's your chance. Let's see watcha got."

Both girls stood staring at their mother. *She wants us to fight? Out here? Now?* Kate asked herself, looking around their small, overgrown front yard.

"Git to it!" shouted Mom, one hand on her hip, the other gesturing in the girls' direction. Her brows were raised, and she held her eyes open wide. She cocked her head to the side to show them she meant business, that she was serious.

Kate didn't believe Mom actually wanted them to fight, so she decided to call her bluff. Lazily, she closed the gap between her and Birdie and gave her little sister a solid shove. Birdie side-stepped, stumbling a few times, but was otherwise unaffected.

"That all you *got,* girl?" Mom yelled from the porch, quickly becoming agitated.

The girls stood next to each other, both staring at their mother in disbelief. *Shit,* thought Kate. *This is not going to end well.*

Mom descended her throne and walked toward Kate, never breaking eye contact, her black hair shimmering in the bright spring sunlight. She always walked with her chin tilted slightly upward, shoulders back, as if she knew exactly where she was going and didn't have to look anywhere but straight ahead. It seemed to Kate that not even the ground dared swell in her mother's path.

When she was standing face to face with her daughter, who was now only a few inches shorter, Joyce raised her hand, swiveled her torso back, and slingshotted around like a taut rubber band suddenly released, slapping Kate across the face so hard her head swung violently to the right, her wheat colored hair whipping across her face and over her eyes. The pain radiated through her cheekbone and down to the corner of her mouth. The sensation, combined with hot embarrassment, caused Kate's eyes to tear up, but she didn't dare let emotion get the best of her now. That would only goad Mom into doing something worse. Kate managed to push her emotions down by swallowing hard and forcing herself to stare straight at the ground

Once she'd mastered the mask, she turned her face back toward her mother, keeping her eyes averted. Even though she was careful not to look at her mother's face, she could sense the radiating waves of satisfaction rolling off

Joyce. Her mind's eye could picture those cat eyes sparkling with delight.

"Look at me, goddammit!" Shouted Joyce.

Reluctantly, Kate raised her eyes to meet her mother's. What she saw made her stomach hurt. *She's holding back a smile?*

"You wanna be tough?" Joyce asked her daughter. "Here's your chance." She nodded her head in Birdie's direction. "Kick her little ass. Show 'er who's boss."

Kate was disgusted. *I'm not gonna beat up my little sister, the only person around here I even halfway like.*

Joyce must have seen through Kate's expressionless veneer and sensed what she was really thinking because, again, lightning quick, before she could even brace herself, Kate felt the forceful sting of her mother's open palm across her face. A drop of blood trickled from the corner of her mouth, and as she reached up to wipe it away, Joyce's hand came up again. Kate flinched, but her mother only grabbed her wrist this time.

"Leave it," said Joyce. "Don't you ever let anybody see that it bothers you to bleed a little." Kate could smell the liquor on her mother's breath, hot and sweet in her face.

"Okay." she said, understanding that acquiescence was expected, no, required.

Kate realized then that she did not have a choice. She would have to fight her sister to get Mom to stop. She turned toward Birdie. "I'm sorry," she mouthed.

I know, said the worried look on Birdie's face.

Now that she had her back to Mom, Kate used her tongue to covertly assess the damage to the corner of her mouth. The small cut tasted metallic, and the pressure of her tongue caused it to sting even more. *She's gone too far this time,* thought Kate. *She's been a shitty mom for a long time, but now we gotta put up with her hittin' us too?* She found herself welling up with a blinding rage she had never experienced before. *I can't take this anymore*, thought Kate as she doubled up her fist, pulled her bony elbow back, squeezed her eyes tight, and drove her knuckles forward until they made contact with the soft flesh of Birdie's left cheek. Her eyes flew open just in time to see her little sister grimace in pain.

Stunned, Birdie stumbled backward a few steps but recovered her balance before she went down. She wasn't able to keep tears from springing to her eyes and spilling down over the already reddening flesh of her cheek, but she was able to reign in what must have been an almost overwhelming desire to cry out.

Birdie looked to Mom. Kate could see that the question in her sister's eyes echoed her own. *Is that enough? Are you satisfied?*

Joyce stared back, unmoved. The look on her face asked the question, *Well? Why'd y'all stop?* And they both knew Joyce's thirst for blood had not yet been quenched.

Kate knew Birdie was well aware she couldn't get away with not fighting back. Kate also knew that, somewhere deep down, Birdie *wanted* to fight back. She watched her little sister muster all her strength and ready herself to return the blow. She did her best to stand still. *Take it like a man*, Kate told herself. But at the last second, she flinched and stepped to the side so that Birdie's fist was unable to make full contact.

Kate knew Birdie had been holding in a lot of anger over Kate deserting her in that store when Mom had first started making the girls steal for her. Her mind went back to that day when Birdie had confided in her that she wanted to be good, like Aunt Bobbie had taught them to be. Then her memory wandered back even farther to the day on the roof. Birdie had wanted to say no when Tammy dared her to jump. *God, I'm such an asshole*, thought Kate. *I was her only protector, and both times I failed her. I deserve to be paid back for betraying her like that.*

When Birdie tried again, rearing back for a second shot at Kate, Mom yelling in the background, urging Birdie to take advantage of Kate's hesitation, she made full contact. Kate's chin whipped violently to the right, crashing into the soft meat of her small shoulder. And, for the second time in just a few minutes, she felt blood trickle from the corner of her mouth.

Before Kate's body even had time to register the pain that was sure to come, she knew it must be bad from the look of regret on Birdie's face.

But this time, when the pain did come, it came with an unexpected, overwhelming anger, a white hot, unreasonable rush of emotion that demanded an outlet, a blinding fury that would settle for nothing less than immediate and all-encompassing vengeance. And this time, no matter how hard she tried, Kate could not push it down.

Before she knew what was happening, she felt herself land another blow squarely on her sister's nose. It was as if Kate was a spectator, floating outside herself, watching herself do to Birdie what she wanted to do to her mother.

Birdie fell to her knees, both hands cupping her nose. She hunched her shaking shoulders forward and tried valiantly not to cry.

"*Yeah*! Kick her *ass*, Kate!"

"Get up," Kate said, breathlessly. The rage hadn't left her as she'd hoped it would. If anything, the pain in her knuckles from smashing them into the cartilage of Birdie's nose fueled inside her a lust for more. It was as if a dam had finally broken and out rushed all the frustration and helplessness and hopelessness she had ever felt. After so many years of nothing making sense, of everything feeling wrong and out of whack, Kate suddenly felt like it was all so simple. She had been so full of these feelings for so long, that now that they were being released, the only thing she could do was hide and watch, hover outside herself as a spectator. She did not feel guilt. She did not feel shame. She did not feel anything, except raw physical release.

"Get up, goddammit!" Kate said, more forcefully this time, poised and ready. "You hate me, remember? You've wanted to get ahold of me for a long time now! Here's your chance. Get up!"

Still, Birdie knelt, holding her nose.

Desperate for more, Kate finally resorted to what she knew would get Birdie mad, fighting mad, the one thing that always made her insanely angry. "I said, get up, *chicken shit.*"

Birdie's head shot up. Plain hatred radiated from her eyes. Slowly, she rose, and they both got what they wanted.

***

Kate ended up besting her sister, but barely. They were both exhausted by the time Mom called the fight. Kate knew the only reason she got the best of Birdie was because she was younger and still tender, but she didn't care. Panting as she made her way onto the front porch steps, she felt satiated, like she'd finally scratched an itch that had been plaguing her for weeks.

Mom favored Kate for several days after she won the fight. The girls quickly realized that the new way to Mom's heart was to be the winner in her little battles.

There were many more days like that first day in the front yard. They fought valiantly every time she told them to. Sometimes Birdie won, but most of the time Kate emerged victorious. She had become vicious. She did anything she had to do to win. She even tried to gouge out Birdie's eye with her thumb once. When she was fighting, she felt free. She felt alive. At first, she tried to tell herself she fought with Birdie because Mom made her do it, but after some time, she had to admit that, while that might have been true in the beginning, now she truly enjoyed having an outlet. She also enjoyed feeling like Mom's special daughter again. She couldn't deny that fact, even though she knew what Mom was doing to them was sick.

Leave a Feller Standin' in the Rain

Chapter Twenty-Seven

1974

Even though she had started physically maturing last winter when she was still twelve, Kate felt no closer to becoming a woman. That seemed strange when she thought about it because, even though she didn't feel like she was anywhere close to adulthood, she did feel very old, much older than the kids at school. She had nothing in common with any of them, really. They all seemed naive to her, ignorant to the way the world worked.

Joyce wasn't the least bit surprised when boys started coming around to see Kate. After all, she was her mother's daughter. Of course, she was beautiful. Kate, in sharp contrast to her mother, was very surprised. They hadn't even been in school for a month when, every week or so, a boy from her class, or a boy from the class next to hers, or sometimes even an older boy in a higher grade would show up at their house, knock on their door and ask to see Kate.

She never knew what to say. She never let them come in the house. She was embarrassed enough for them to see the *outside* of it. She'd never live it down if one of them went to school and told all the kids about the inside of her home. Or, God forbid, about Mom. She didn't know what Mom would do, but she was sure the woman could think of a thousand and one ways to humiliate her daughter in front of a boy. Kate was also sure that nothing would please her mother more.

So, she would sit out on the front steps with the boy for what was only a few minutes, but always felt like an agonizingly long time. Sometimes a boy would work up the nerve to ask her on a date. She always said no. She wasn't quite sure why she always declined. It might be fun to go to a movie theater or to a restaurant, or whatever it was kids did when they went on dates. But she was positive she wouldn't have any idea how to act or how to dress or even what to say. She guessed that had something to do with it, but she didn't really spend much time thinking about boys or dates, or even friends.

Since Aunt Bobbie's death, Kate had been thinking about her a lot, about the things Aunt Bobbie had said to her and Birdie. About them being able to make their own lives better. In her free time, when she wasn't helping Birdie steal for Mom, or fighting for Mom, or worrying about her sisters because of Mom, she was trying to figure out what she was going to do with her life, her grown-up life, the one that would someday belong to her and her alone.

Kate knew she wouldn't always be tied to Mom, and, in a way, that was a scary thought. What would she do with herself? Who would take care of Mom? Of Beverly and Birdie?

There were too many questions to which she didn't know the answers, and this made Kate nervous. She needed to plan and figure things out. When the time came for her to go, she needed to have a direction.

Another thing keeping Kate busy these days was driving Mother to the doctor. Her grandmother was in bad health, and her doctor, a kindly older gentleman named Dr. Smith, wanted her to see him once a week. Mother always said she trusted him because his name was Smith, and, though he was no relation, Smiths were good people.

Since Papaw, Uncle John, and Uncle Buddy were busy with the dairy, and Mom could never be bothered to do anything for her mother, the responsibility of driving Mother to the doctor every week fell to Kate, who had learned to drive years ago. Even though she was a few years away from being able to drive legally, everyone in the family agreed she would be fine driving in Wewoka. It was a small, laid back farming community, and it was not uncommon to see younger teenagers driving in town. The consensus seemed to be that as long as the underage driver was behind the wheel for work or for family, and not for fun, it was okay.

Kate, seated on the front porch after a boy from her class had paid her an awkward visit, chuckled to herself thinking back to the time she had let Birdie go to a doctor visit with her and Mother that past spring. Birdie had begged to go. Kate hadn't minded the company at all. It got extremely dull sitting in the car alone, sometimes for over an hour, waiting on Mother to finish her doctor visit. At first, she had gone in with Mother on every appointment, but the waiting room was unbearable. At least Kate could listen to the radio if she stayed in the car.

Birdie had been excited to miss school and ride in the car with her sister. She seemed to find this weekly appointment she was typically excluded from exotic and mysterious. She seemed to suspect Kate was doing something secretly fun without her, and this made going along even more enticing for the youngest sister. Kate remembered hoping Birdie wasn't too disappointed when she saw how boring Mother's trips to the doctor really were.

When the day arrived, Birdie had been excited because it was raining. She was obsessed with driving at that time and had said she was anxious to get some tips from Kate for traveling on wet roads. Kate remembered being suspicious of her sister, thinking Birdie was surely going to want to do more than watch once they hit the dirt roads on the way to pick up Mother. It was no secret she had been itching to get behind the wheel.

Sure enough, as soon as they had turned off the paved road, Birdie started to beg. "Please, Kate! Pleeease! I promise I'll be careful."

"Alright, but don't go too fast." Kate had already decided she was going to let Birdie drive. Why shouldn't she? Kate had been much younger than Birdie when she'd had to teach herself to drive so that she could find their drunk mom and drag her home.

Birdie did well for her first time. Kate didn't have to tell her very much at all. The girl had obviously been paying close attention for a while now.

They pulled into Mother and Papaw's driveway and hurriedly switched seats, one sliding over and one sliding under across the old, dirty upholstery of Mom's worn, green Cadillac. When Mother hobbled out the door and into the rain, appearing old and frail despite her large frame, she was none the wiser.

Once they were at Dr. Smith's office downtown, Mother gave the same speech she did every week. "Now, I don't mind y'all sittin' in the car listenin' to the radio, but dontchu go nowhere, ye hear?"

"Yes, ma'am." Both girls rolled their eyes in unison, smiling as they chanted the expected response.

Birdie was begging again before the hem of Mother's dress was through the doorway of the doctor's office. "Kate, please! You get to drive every week."

"No way, Birdie!" Kate replied sternly. "This is different. We're right in the middle of town. Somebody'll see us and tell Papaw!"

"Oh, hell! Nobody'll see us, and you know it! You just don't want me to have any fun!" Birdie pouted. "I know you probably go all over the place when you're by yourself." She crossed her arms and turned her head to stare out her window on the passenger side.

Kate knew not to try to talk Birdie out of her mood. She had become so stubborn over the past few years that Kate knew when she shouldn't waste the energy to try to talk to her sister.

She didn't want Birdie to be sad though. She had so looked forward to this day. And, truth be told, they probably wouldn't get caught. Both girls looked much older than they actually were, plenty old enough to drive. And it was raining steadily, so other people probably wouldn't be able to see them anyway. *We've got at least thirty minutes,* she said to herself.

"Oh shit, ya big baby! Here." Kate took the keys out of the ignition and leaned across the seat so she could dangle them in Birdie's face.

"Eeeeek!" Birdie screamed! "Thank you, thank you, thank you! You're the best sister in the whole world!"

The girls drove all over town, Birdie at the wheel, of course. They cruised up and down Main street, followed winding roads to the outskirts of town, drove through residential areas, all the while blasting the radio. They heard Lynyrd Skynyrd, Creedence Clearwater Revival, Otis Redding. Given they didn't get to listen to the music of their generation very much at home, Birdie was impressed with Kate's knowledge in this area. She seemed to know all these songs by heart.

"How do you think I pass the time while Mother's in the doctor every Tuesday?"

Both girls looked at each other wide-eyed at the mention of Mother.

"Shit!" They both screamed it at the same time.

"How long do you think we've been gone?" asked Birdie, pulling to the side of a residential street to let her sister take over.

"Hell, if *I* know," yelled Kate, clambering over her sister to trade her places.

Kate sped to Doctor Smith's office, praying Mother was still inside. But, as she neared the parking lot, there stood Mother in the pouring rain, arms crossed at her middle, her jaw clenched.

"Shit," Kate muttered under her breath, turning the wheel, pulling into a parking space. She looked over to see Birdie with her head down, brown hair hiding her face, her hand covering her mouth. Then a teardrop hit her arm. *Is she really crying?* Kate made a mental note to have a talk with Birdie later. *She's getting too old to be crying at the drop of a hat, especially over something silly like this. Sure, Mother'll be mad, but I doubt she'll tell Mom.*

Mother knew her daughter could be cruel to the girls, and, though she was too old and insignificant in Joyce's eyes to be able to do anything to stop her, she was far too kind-hearted to do anything to make her granddaughters' lives any harder than they already were.

The worst she'll do is make us feel guilty for forgetting about her, thought Kate. Maybe Kate had gotten to know Mother a lot better than Birdie had with all the time they'd spent alone together over the past several months driving back and forth to the doctor.

Kate had to look away from Birdie to finish parking the car, but she said, "Birdie, don't cry. It's not that bad."

Birdie said nothing but kept her head down.

Mother, her nose in the air, face dramatically turned away from Kate, seated herself in the backseat. She was soaking wet. *Now I know where Mom gets that look from,* Kate thought, remembering all the times Mom had used that same expression to let one of the girls know she was mad at them. When Kate tried to explain, Mother simply ignored her, wouldn't even look in Kate or Birdie's direction.

Kate couldn't look directly at Mother because she was afraid she might start laughing, and she didn't want to hurt the poor old woman's feelings any more than she already had. But she couldn't escape the thought of how funny Mother looked. She brushed the image of her soaking wet, sulled up grandmother out of her head as best she could and tried again, careful to avert her eyes. "Mother, please don't be mad! I'm sorry. We just wanted to drive around the block real quick."

Mother still wouldn't look at Kate. Her white, thinning hair was soaking wet and plastered to her face. Kate knew the woman must barely even be able to see because her bangs suctioned over her eyes. Water dripped steadily from her chin.

"Mother, stop bein' ridiculous! Look at poor little Birdie Kay! She feels so bad she's cryin'!"

Kate gestured toward Birdie, whose shoulders were shaking. She kept her head bowed.

Finally, Mother turned her head toward Kate, but didn't lower her chin or uncross her arms. "Leave a feller a standin' in the rain," she said slowly, in a low voice. Then she turned her head away from her granddaughter again and stared out the window.

Kate was glad for this, because when she turned back toward the front of the car, Birdie snuck a peek at her. That's when Kate realized Birdie wasn't crying at all. She had been trying desperately to hide the fact that she was laughing uncontrollably, so hard that actual tears were running down her cheeks!

Somehow, they both managed to keep their laughter at bay until they dropped Mother back at her house. Kate even struggled through one last apology, which Mother completely ignored.

The girls made it about a quarter of a mile down the road before Kate had to pull over. They sat on the side of the dirt road laughing so hard that they were both choking and crying. Finally, an old farm truck snapped them back to reality when the driver had to honk at them to get them to move.

For days after that, Kate and Birdie would make eye contact at random times during the day and one of them would say, "Leave a feller a standin' in the rain." Then they'd get tickled and laugh all over again.

That was the one and only time Birdie was allowed to go with Kate and Mother to the doctor.

Chapter Twenty-Eight

1974

They started getting food stamps, which was nice because now they had food in the house sometimes, at least when Mom couldn't find someone to sell them to.

Of course, Joyce was too proud to use the food stamps herself, so she made the girls do it. They didn't mind though. It was a little embarrassing, but they were all so happy to have food in the house, they quickly got over their embarrassment.

They always went to the grocery store across town, hoping this would reduce their chances of running into someone they knew from school. One day, while they were checking out at this grocery store, a boy walked over and started bagging their groceries. Kate found herself wishing he hadn't come over to their line. He was handsome in an innocent sort of way, and she didn't want him to see her paying with food stamps. Her cheeks burned as they got closer to the last bag.

The boy kept glancing at her. She was terrified he was going to say he knew her from school.

Beverly had run to the back of the store to get butter, which, even though it had been on their list, they somehow had forgotten. As she returned, out of breath, she placed the butter triumphantly in the basket, grinning because she'd gotten back before the clerk was done checking them out. Everyone was in a good mood on the days when they bought food, even Beverly.

"Hey," Beverly said, eyeing the boy who bagged their groceries. "I thought we had to bag our own groceries at this store."

The checker looked nervously from the boy to Beverly and Kate. "You do. Is he not with you?"

The boy started to laugh. Kate noticed he had the prettiest blue eyes. It was almost like she could see right through them, they were so clear. He was blushing.

"You don't work here?" she asked.

"No," the boy said shyly. "You're just so pretty, I didn't think you oughta have to bag your own groceries." Now her cheeks were red too.

Kate didn't know what to say. It didn't help that Beverly was standing next to her staring at the boy like an idiot, a big silly grin splitting her face. She elbowed Kate.

Of course, since Kate's mortification wasn't complete just yet, Birdie chose that moment to run up to the counter, throwing a loaf of bread down. "What's everybody grinnin' for?" she asked, looking cluelessly from face to face. Kate wanted to beat the hell out of both her sisters.

Birdie looked at the cashier. "When did y'all get bag boys?"

"They didn't," Beverly said conspiratorially to Birdie, but loud enough that everyone could hear her. "This boy just thinks Kate's too pretty to have to bag her own groceries." Beverly waggled her eyebrows up and down.

Both girls began to giggle at their sister's obvious discomfort.

"We-ell," Birdie drawled in that teasing way they had all developed since moving to Oklahoma.

The boy, watching the sisters' exchange, amused, finally spoke up. "Can I take these to your car for you?"

Kate figured out a way to staunch the flow of humiliation spilling from every pore in her body, and she seized the opportunity. She turned to Beverly. "Will y'all stay here and pay?" she asked, shoving the change purse with the food stamps in it toward her sister.

Beverly, still grinning from ear to ear, took the change purse. "Yeah, sure, Katie Rheaaaaa," she drawled.

God, I like her better when she's pissed off all the time and not speaking to anybody, Kate thought as she followed the boy who was pushing their groceries out of the store for her. *Now what am I gonna do about him?* She asked herself.

Out in the parking lot, the boy slowed and looked back, waiting for Kate to catch up. When she did, he let go of the basket with one hand and held it out to her. "Hey, Katie Rhea. I'm Dean. Nice to meet you."

His shoulder-length, reddish-blonde hair whipped around his face in the hot Oklahoma wind, which seemed to be refusing to acknowledge it was way past time for summer to make its exit. He smiled, and, at that moment, Kate decided she liked him. A lot. "My name's not really Katie Rhea. That's just a dumb nickname my mom gave me when I was little," she stammered. "My sister was just trying to embarrass me." She found herself laughing. She was surprised at how comfortable she felt around this boy. He seemed different, more like her than any other boy she'd ever met.

"So, what's your real name?" Dean asked, still smiling, looking her dead in the eye.

"Oh," Kate realized, embarrassed that she'd been lost in her own thoughts and forgotten to tell him her name. "It's Kate."

He laughed. "So, Kate, do you think you'd be interested in maybe hangin' out sometime?"

Of course, Beverly and Birdie chose this moment to interrupt them.

"He-ey, pretty girl!" teased Birdie.

Kate flashed an apologetic look at Dean. He smiled back patiently.

She turned her face toward her sister. "Hey, *asshole*," Kate whispered to Birdie in an even, warning tone. Louder, she said, "Y'all wanna start loadin' the car? I'll be there in just a second." *I can't wait 'til the next time*

Mom's got us out in the yard, she tried to convey with her eyes. *You're dead.*

Birdie smiled sweetly, but her eyes were sending out a completely different attitude altogether. They seemed to say, *Yeah, but it won't be today!* "Sure, lover girl," she replied, enjoying being able to tease her sister with the virtual guarantee that there would be no immediate reprisals.

Ahh, sisterly love, Kate thought. She sighed and watched her sisters take the cart full of groceries from Dean and wheel it away, fighting over who would get to push it through the parking lot.

When Birdie and Beverly were busily loading the car, Dean asked, "So how 'bout it? Wanna go do somethin', pretty girl?" he teased.

"Yeah," Kate answered, surprising herself. "Whaddya wanna do?"

"You're the boss. Anything you say."

Kate wanted to say something witty, but, like every other time she needed her brain to work fast, it failed her, and she was left staring back at Dean, no words.

"I know!" Dean sounded excited. "You think about it and surprise me when I pick you up Friday night."

Relieved, Kate agreed. She gave him her address, and they parted ways.

She had five days to think of something cool for them to do. At least she had school to keep her busy, and she would get some time alone to think when she took Mother to the doctor that week.

School was agonizing. Every day seemed to crawl by slower than the one before, but there was one bright spot in the week. During lunch on Wednesday Kate was walking out of the cafeteria alone, as usual, when a boy named Tommy Jones stopped her in the hall.

"Hey, you're that Bloom girl, right? John Smith's niece?"

She was caught off guard that this handsome, older boy was speaking to *her*, a kid who was usually completely invisible at school, especially since her friend, Tammy, had gotten a boyfriend and stopped having time for her friends. Kate just stared at the boy, unsure of how to make her mouth work.

The boy revealed sparklingly white teeth when he did this half-smile thing that made Kate's insides twist.

She thought he would shake his head at her mute response and walk away thinking about what a complete idiot she was, but he only leaned against the wall, put his hand in his pocket, and coolly waited for her to gather herself.

The boy was so devastatingly handsome that Kate wanted to shake her head to clear it, but she didn't dare. She forced herself to speak. "Yep, that's me," she finally replied. *Real smooth*, Kate. *The first time anyone at school's talked to you in a month, and this cute guy tries to start a conversation with you, and you come back with the goofiest response you can possibly think of. Great job, dumbass.* She rolled her eyes at her stupidity and then, too late, realized he probably thought she was being a smart aleck in answer to his question since she added that nice eye roll to an already clipped-sounding response.

Tommy's smile faded only slightly at her awkward answer, but he didn't move to walk away. He kept leaning against the wall, staring at her. He seemed so calm, so confident.

Finally, the silence between them became so awkward that Kate had to either say something or walk away. "John's my uncle. How do you know him?" She still sounded like a smart ass, but at least she wasn't standing there staring at him anymore like there might be something wrong about her in the head.

"He just gave me a part-time job on the dairy," Tommy responded, still standing against the wall, relaxed, sure of himself, seeming more like a grown, successful man than some redneck teenager. Kate reminded herself of this fact, and it made her feel a little less self-conscious.

"Oh." It wasn't much, but it was all Kate could think to say. At least she wasn't standing there completely silent, practically drooling. *Victory! You have conquered your fear of speaking to teenage boys, Kate! Congratulations!* She wanted the floor to open up and swallow her whole at that precise moment.

Thankfully, Tommy didn't seem to notice. He continued. "Yeah, when he hired me, he said he had a couple of nieces who go to school here. Said your last name was Bloom, and I thought I remembered a couple of new girls named Bloom were runnin' around here somewhere. Your sister's younger, right? Cute little freckle face with shiny brown braids, right?"

She hasn't been that for a few years now, Kate thought to herself, but, still, she felt a bit comforted. *I can do this. I can have a two-minute conversation about my uncle,* Kate told herself. *He's just trying to be polite because my uncle is his boss.* For a minute there, she had thought this boy, who was way out of her league, was going to flirt with her. *You big ol' silly,* Kate chastised herself. *You might be a nice lookin' girl for someone like you, but you're not good lookin' enough for a boy like Tommy Jones to give you the time of day.* Even though she was relieved, she also felt a little deflated at this realization. The dividing line between the regular people and people like Kate and her family felt starker than ever. It would always be there. "Yeah, that's her," Kate replied. "But she's older now. You must've seen her when we first came here."

"Oh," he laughed.

She laughed too. The bell rang. "Well, I guess I'd better go," Kate said. "Nice meeting you." She walked away. *That wasn't so bad,* she thought to herself as she headed to her next class. *I can do this whole small talk thing like a normal person.* As an afterthought, as she was entering her classroom, she thought, almost ashamed, regretful for some reason, *he sure was cute though.*

Chapter Twenty-Nine

When it was time to pick Mother up for her appointment later that week, Kate pulled into the dusty driveway, late as usual. The curtain moved. *Crap, she's been waiting on me.* Kate had been forgiven for the time she and Birdie had left Mother waiting in the rain, and now the sweet old lady was all smiles when she climbed into the car. She wasn't getting any better. Dr. Smith had recently discovered the cause of Mother's hands shaking all the time, and it wasn't good news. She had something called Parkinson's Disease, a disease that would progress and get worse, and, eventually, Mother would need constant care. There was no cure for Parkinson's, but Mother was nothing if not strong. She knew that Papaw and her boys were taking the news hard, so she put on a brave face and proclaimed with certainty that God would heal her.

Kate didn't know much about God, except that every time she had ever prayed to him, he had refused to acknowledge her, as far as she knew. But, if it made Mother feel better to believe he would heal her, who was she to say any different? *And, hey*, she thought, *Mother's a good person. Maybe God answers good people's prayers.*

Mother's appointment had been moved to the afternoon that week, so Main street was much busier than usual. Kate had gone in to say hello to Dr. Smith, which was a regular occurrence now since he had asked why she'd stopped escorting Mother to her appointments and had been told that Kate had taken to waiting in the car. "Well, that little girl comin' in here every week was the bright spot a my day!" Dr. Smith had told Mother. After that, Mother always insisted Kate come in the office for a moment to say hello to Dr. Smith. He had been so good to Mother that Kate couldn't decline. She had no idea why Dr.

Smith enjoyed her so much, but she didn't mind seeing him. He truly was a kind man.

Kate enjoyed sitting in the car on such a busy afternoon. It seemed that every resident of their small town was downtown at the same time enjoying the warm, sunny day. Smartly dressed mothers held their equally smartly dressed children's hands, leading them into the drugstore and then back out again. Some of the children skipped out happily with a toy or an ice cream cone. One particularly ornery-looking little boy's mother exited the store abruptly, dragging her little minx behind her. He screamed and fought her all the way back to their car. Kate found this exchange quite entertaining.

Overall-clad farmers, along with their usually younger, more physically fit farm hands, headed, empty handed, into the feed store and emerged loaded down with sacks of food for their animals, then headed back out to their old, overworked farm trucks. The men and their trucks seemed to sag with the weight of the heat of an Indian summer. Kate had asked Papaw one day why he, his sons, and almost every other old farmer she'd ever seen always wore overalls and long-sleeved shirts when they worked out of doors in the heat. He had told her that it was more comfortable to be hot than it was to be sunburned.

Kate was grateful for the distractions. She was supposed to be thinking of something for her and Dean to do when he picked her up Friday night, but how was she supposed to know what people did when they were out on dates together? She should never have agreed to be the one to pick. *Dumbass*, she thought to herself. *Shouldn't have even agreed to go in the first place.*

By the time Mother got in the car and was ready to go home, Kate was no closer to figuring out what she and Dean were going to do. She was grateful Mother was in a talkative mood. It took her mind off her dilemma.

When they pulled into Mother's driveway, she asked Kate to go into the house with her. She had baked a cake and said she wanted Kate to take the rest of it home to Mom and the girls, even though they both knew Mom wouldn't touch it. She never really ate anymore. Just drank. Apparently, Papaw, on the other hand, had quite the sweet tooth, and Mother had decided he'd eaten enough cake for the week. "Can barely even button up his shirts anymore for that big ol' belly," Mother laughed. Kate gladly agreed to take the cake off Mother's hands and went inside.

"You oughta eat a piece here before you take it home to them sisters a yours. They'll have it gobbled up before you can get the plates down outta the cabinet." Kate agreed, and she sat at Mother's old wooden table marveling at this woman who was always so instinctive. Kate couldn't help noticing the tremor in Mother's hand as she handed her a delicate white dessert plate piled high with a perfect slice of bright yellow butter cake. She couldn't imagine this woman, who had raised three children and run a household so skillfully, someday being incapacitated. She couldn't imagine Mother not being able to make a perfect butter cake. The thought made her sad.

She stayed and visited for a little while and was surprised when Mother brought up Tommy Jones from school. "Your uncle John's hired a boy from your school to help 'im out on the dairy. You know 'im?" Mother asked the question innocently enough, but there was a definite twinkle in the old woman's eyes, as well as a devilish grin on her face. "That is one handsome boy." Mother lowered her chin as she said this, looking up at Kate, eyebrows raised with meaning.

Kate laughed, almost choking on her cake. "*Mother!*" she replied, shocked.

"Wha-at?" Mother asked innocently. "I'm old, not blind!"

They both laughed at this.

A half hour later, feeling closer to Mother than ever and vowing to spend more time with her, Kate walked toward the car carrying what was left of what might be one of the last cakes Mother ever made. As she neared the car, Kate was surprised to see, out in front of the main dairy barn, Tommy Jones himself. *Shirtless, of course*, Kate noted. He was loading bales of hay onto the back of a farm truck. She was considering running back into the house to tell Mother that she was missing the show. *She'll get a kick outta this*, thought Kate. *Dirty old woman.* But Tommy caught her eye and waved. She had been smiling, imagining Mother's reaction to shirtless Tommy. She hoped he didn't think she was smiling because he looked so good. Her cheeks reddened. *Mother does have good taste though*, she thought as she waved back.

Then her thoughts were interrupted because he was yelling at her. She couldn't quite make out what he was saying. She shook her head to gesture that she couldn't hear him. To her surprise, he waved again, but this time was gesturing for her to come to him.

So, she did. The closer she got, the cuter Tommy got. He was tanned. And muscled. And sweaty. By the time she reached him, she was red in the cheeks, but not from the brisk walk.

"You brought me cake?" he asked, that sideways grin of his melting her insides.

"What?" she asked, unable to take her eyes off him. *If this boy knew what I was thinking I'd never be able to look him in the eye again,* she was saying to herself. *What is wrong with me?*

"The cake." Tommy gestured toward Kate's hands.

"Oh!" she stumbled over her words. "Cake!" she laughed. "Yeah, sure. You can have it," she said stupidly, unable to take her eyes off his.

He didn't take his eyes off her either. He reached down and picked up a chunk of mother's cake with his bare hand and put the whole thing in his mouth.

He somehow managed to be even more handsome chewing with his mouth open.

An hour later, Kate drove away from the dairy without her idea for Friday night, without her cake, and without her virginity. But she did have a big, goofy smile on her face. *Sometimes less is more,* she thought, as she turned up the radio and headed home.

Chapter Thirty

Kate went on her date with Dean as scheduled Friday night. She hadn't bothered to come up with something for them to do because her plan was for them to just ride around and for her to let him down easy.

"So, what did you come up with for us to do tonight?" Dean asked as he helped Kate into the passenger side of his mother's station wagon.

Kate laughed to herself as she said, "I didn't come up with anything. I was thinkin' we could just ride around and talk, and then if we come up with something we can go do it. If not, we don't have to do anything." *Nothing like getting over the jitters before a date by sleeping with another guy*, she thought to herself. Kate actually felt quite confident about going with Dean. She'd ride around with him, enjoy their evening together, and at the end of the night, she'd tell him she thought of him more as a friend. This seemed like a simple thing to do since she'd been able to do nothing the past few days except think of Tommy.

But their night did not go according to plan. Though Dean wasn't as skilled at literally charming the pants off a girl, he was sweet and sincere. They rode around and talked and got to know each other. Though they didn't go anywhere spectacular or do anything that would have seemed memorable to someone else, Kate had to admit to herself that she had a really good time. She couldn't remember ever speaking to anyone, besides maybe Aunt Bobbie, who genuinely wanted to get to know her as a person the way Dean did.

Before Kate knew it, Dean announced that it was late and that, if he ever hoped to take her out again, he'd better be getting her home. Kate found herself sad their time together was over for the night, and she couldn't quite let herself break things off with Dean. *I'll do it next time*, she told herself.

Birdie and Beverly wanted to know every detail when Kate got home that night.

"He's really sweet," Kate said.

"Did y'all kiss?" asked Beverly.

"No," said Kate. "He walked me to the door and held my hand the whole way, but when we got there, he said, 'I want to kiss you goodnight, but I know nice girls like you don't kiss on the first date, so I won't even ask.'"

Kate didn't say so, but she would have kissed Dean if he'd leaned in. As he walked away, she remembered Tommy and realized she hadn't thought of him even once since she'd ridden away from her house with Dean.

Both Beverly and Birdie fell back on the bed giggling at that. "He's soooo sweet!" Beverly squealed. "Are y'all goin' on another date?"

Kate grinned, suddenly shy in front of her sisters. "Yeah, he's picking me up next Friday night." Kate couldn't help but giggle with her sisters this time. She felt giddy.

I'll just avoid Tommy, Kate told herself. *I just made a mistake. I'm never talking to him again. Yeah, he's handsome and sexy, but he's not my type. He only wants one thing from me. Dean wants a real relationship. Dean is definitely the one for me.*

But Kate saw Tommy again the next time she dropped off Mother, and the same thing happened. It was like she couldn't resist this boy. She wanted to. She knew he was no good for her. He all but ignored her at school. The only time he ever wanted anything to do with her was when he saw her once a week on the farm. Kate brought this up a few months into their "relationship," and she told Tommy it was over. "I can't keep doing this," she said.

"Why not?" asked Tommy, wide eyed, pretending to be clueless.

"Well, because it's wrong," Kate answered, trying to keep herself from looking into those deep blue eyes of his that always weakened her resolve.

"Why is it wrong?" he asked. "Aren't you having fun?" Tommy grinned and sauntered closer to her, then reached out to caress her cheek.

His hands are so soft, Kate thought, feeling herself giving in and hating herself for it. She couldn't help but smile. "Yeah, I'm havin' fun."

"Then why's it wrong?" Tommy asked, his voice turning tender.

She couldn't bring herself to tell him about Dean, but she knew she needed to choose. When she was with Tommy, she wanted nothing more than to be with Tommy, but when she was with Dean, she wanted to be with him. "This is all just so confusing. I mean, what are we doing? You don't even talk to me at school. Are we boyfriend and girlfriend? Are we not? Are we just having sex?"

Tommy looked her deep in the eye. "Kate, it's just complicated. I'm going away to college next year. I have a scholarship, and my parents are depending on me. They're putting all this pressure on me. When I'm with you I can forget all of that stuff for a little while and just have fun."

Kate broke eye contact and turned to finish buttoning up her shirt. "So, this is just fun for you? Nothing else?" She already knew the answer as she turned back around to face him, but she had to ask anyway just to be sure.

"Well, yeah. Isn't that what it is for you? I mean, you didn't think we were gonna get married, did you?"

Kate avoided Tommy's gaze; she had no answer.

Tommy laughed. "Oh, Lord, Kate. What did you think? I was gonna work on your uncle's dairy farm for the rest of my life and you were gonna be my little homemaker wife?" He looked at Kate, expectant.

That was exactly what I was wishing for, she admitted to herself. But even as she thought it, she realized it wouldn't happen, couldn't happen. It was the first time she admitted to herself that she really had been hoping for this ever since the first time they'd been together in the barn. "No," she lied.

"Listen, Kate, I really like you. But I can't let myself fall in love right now. I have a plan. It's my dream to get out of this town and make something of myself. I can't let myself end up like my dad," Tommy said, a pained look in his eyes. The look on his face told Kate there was no changing his mind.

"So, what was I to you? Just some meaningless fling?" Kate had once heard a woman ask a man this question on a soap opera. It had sounded ridiculous and silly to her at the time, but now she understood. She was disappointed and confused. Wait, *wasn't this what I wanted? To end things with Tommy so that I could have a real relationship with Dean?*

"Hey, look at me," Tommy pleaded, gently grabbing Kate's chin and forcing her to face him. "It's not meaningless. Not to me. What we have is special. No, it can't last forever. But that doesn't mean it's not special."

Kate looked away again.

Tommy didn't resist her turning her head and dropped his hand to his side, dejected. "Look, if you want to end it, let's end it. No hard feelings. But I'll never forget you. And I'll miss you."

Kate had the perfect opportunity to make her exit, but, for some reason, she just couldn't do it.

Over the next few months she continued to see both Tommy and Dean, careful to keep the boys from finding out about each other. Tommy never changed his tune about not wanting to have a relationship, but Kate couldn't seem to force herself to give up Tommy. She was grateful when winter set in and he wasn't needed as much at the dairy.

She was able to drop Mother off several weeks in a row without having to be tempted by Tommy.

Her meetings with him, however, had not gone unnoticed.

One day in early January, when Kate was dropping Mother off after a doctor's appointment, she asked Kate to come into the house on the pretense of wanting to give her some sugar cookies to take home to the girls.

"Oh, it'll just take a minute," Mother said when she tried to protest. It was freezing out, but Kate could never resist Mother's requests. She hardly ever asked Kate to come in. And, when she did, she always returned the favor with a homemade treat, which only made Kate feel even more guilty.

"Alright," Kate said.

After they'd lumbered into the house, Kate waiting patiently for Mother, Mother produced an old tin full of homemade cookies. It hadn't escaped Kate's attention that Mother's hands had been shaking more and more lately. Mother always blamed it on the cold, but Kate knew better. She felt guilty for spending so much time with Tommy and then going home and telling Mom and the girls that she'd been visiting with Mother, which was what she should have been doing.

As she sat at Mother's worn, inviting kitchen table, she looked around and realized Mother's usually very well-kept home was starting to look a little shabby. She understood that Mother couldn't do as much as she used to be able to do. This only cemented the guilt she'd felt walking Mother into her house. They'd greeted Papaw in the living room and headed straight for the kitchen.

"So, I noticed you sure spent a lot of time talkin' to Tommy this past fall," Mother stated, getting right to the point.

"Yeah," Kate said, unable to avoid Mother's intent gaze.

"You like 'im?" Mother asked.

Even though she hadn't seen Tommy anywhere except school, where they couldn't really talk, since Uncle John had said he wouldn't need him again until spring, Kate couldn't help but smile at the mention of his name. "He's okay," she responded.

"He's more than okay," said Mother, grinning wickedly.

Kate laughed. "Yeah, he's more than okay."

Kate knew then that Mother knew, but she also knew that she could trust her grandmother.

"Y'know he's goin' off to college somewhere out east this comin' fall, right?" Mother asked knowingly.

"I know," Kate admitted.

"He's a real nice-lookin' boy, Kate, but he ain't stayin' in Oklahoma. That boy's mamma 'n' daddy got big plans for him."

"I know, Mother." Kate looked down at her hands, which rested on Mother's old, wooden kitchen table.

"Alright, sweetheart. I just wanted to make sure you knew," Mother said, not elaborating, but somehow conveying that she knew much more than she was saying.

Abruptly, Mother changed the subject. "That silly ol' Doctor Smith," she said. "He said I oughta start thinkin' about getting a provider this spring to help me out around the house." Mother pretended to laugh this off, but the look on her face said that she knew she was getting worse.

"What's a provider?" Kate asked.

"Oh, you know, somebody who would help around the house."

Kate looked around at what was once Mother's meticulously kept kitchen. "That doesn't sound too bad," Kate commented.

"Well, maybe not to you, but to me it's the beginning of the end," Mother said pointedly. "What it means is that I'm gettin' worse." Mother placed her hands on the table in front of her and looked down at them. She continued to speak. "It's more than just helpin' around the house. A provider is someone who comes to your house and cleans up for you, but they do more than that. They bathe you and make sure you've been takin' your medicine. They cook your meals." Mother looked Kate in the eye. "They do the things you can't do for yourself anymore." She smiled sadly. "What he was sayin' was that it won't be long 'til I can't take care of myself anymore." She studied her kitchen meditatively. "Or this ol' place."

Kate didn't know what to say. She knew enough to know that this conversation was way above her maturity level. She realized she must be the only person Mother felt she could talk to. Bobbie was gone. Mom was useless. And, in these moments, only another woman would do. Mother didn't feel like she could talk to Papaw, or to her sons about this. Though she was young, she was, in Mother's eyes, at least, another woman, one Mother felt she could talk to. Kate decided to try to comfort Mother since she didn't know what else to do. "Mother, Dr. Smith's just bein' safe."

"I know," Mother replied, trying to put on a brave face. "I just wish you were a little older. You already take care of everybody around you. If you were just a little older you could do it. You could be my provider." Mother looked hopefully at Kate.

"Would you really trust me to take care of you?" Kate asked, surprised and flattered.

"Well, sure I would, sweetheart. You've been takin' care of me for a while now."

Kate had never thought of it this way.

Mother continued, "I always feel so bad for you, havin' to miss school every week to take me to the doctor. You're a kid, Kate. You ought not to have that kinda responsibility on your head already. But you never make me feel bad about it. You just do what you have to do to take care of me. And I want you to know I appreciate you. I know it can't be easy."

Kate felt bad. She had always looked forward to taking Mother to the doctor, at first because she got to drive, then because she got to see Tommy without anyone knowing. *When did I become okay with Tommy being a secret? No, that's not what's going on. When did I become okay with me being Tommy's secret?* she asked herself, shamed. "I never minded, Mother. I enjoy getting to spend time with you." She felt selfish for telling this lie, for making it seem like she'd been taking Mother to the doctor for all this time because she wanted to spend time with her. She knew that was why she *should* have been doing it.

"Well, maybe I can hold out 'til you're graduated from school and you can be my provider. If you want to, that is."

"Well, I'll tell ya what, Mother. If you're lookin' for a provider when I've graduated from school, I'd be honored to do it for you."

Mother grinned. "It's a deal."

Kate didn't say anything to Mother, but inside, she knew her grandmother would need help long before Kate graduated from high school.

As Kate drove away from her grandparents' house, she resolved to be a better person, to think of her grandparents more often. They were good people, and they deserved to be cared for. If their daughter wouldn't take care of them, she would.

Chapter Thirty-One

Over the next few months, Kate was extra attentive with Mother. She started going into the waiting room again instead of sitting in the car until her appointments ended. Dr. Smith seemed tickled to see her every week. It was too cold, anyway, for her to sit in the car and listen to the radio.

Dean kept coming around, though Kate wasn't sure why. They still hadn't taken things to the next level, though he had tried a few times. He was always the perfect gentleman, however. They had kissed a few times, but that was as far as she was willing to go. She just couldn't bring herself to have sex with him. She had learned her lesson with Tommy, and she didn't want to get her feelings hurt again.

***

1975

Mom began to insist that she meet Dean. Kate usually waited for him on the front porch and managed to get away from the house before Mom could embarrass her, but it was becoming increasingly difficult to get Joyce to take no for an answer.

Finally, one Friday night in early March, Mom wouldn't let Kate leave the house. She was adamant that Dean come to the door when he picked her up. Kate was a nervous wreck when he knocked.

"Well, *hello*, Dean," Mom greeted him. Her voice sounded sarcastic and Kate was immediately embarrassed. *God, I hope she doesn't run him off*, Kate thought. She had recently admitted to herself that, despite her best efforts, she thought she might be falling in love with Dean. But at the same time, Tommy was always on her mind. *Is it*

possible to be in love with two people at the same time?
She asked herself this question many times.

"Hello," Dean said. Kate could see that his cheeks
were red. She wanted to rescue him. She had told him
months ago about Mom and now she wished she hadn't.
She could see that he was as nervous as she was.

"Have a seat." Sarcasm still dripped from Mom's
voice. She gestured to the old, broken down, brown and
cream-colored couch. Mom had gotten it out of someone's
front yard. Well, that wasn't completely true. Mom had
made Kate and Birdie get it out of someone's front yard.

Dean sat down, and Kate sat next to him, hoping to
calm his nerves.

Dean tried to be cool, but his bouncing foot gave
him away. His knee was bouncing up and down so fast
Kate had to scoot away a little to keep from bouncing with
him.

"How y'all doin'?" Dean asked in a high, squeaky
voice she didn't recognize. He sounded like a schoolgirl.
Kate was mortified. *Mom will rip him to pieces*, she
thought. She could see that Birdie and Beverly were trying
not to laugh. She wanted to punch both of her sisters.

"You sure been seein' a lot of my girl." Mom got
right to the point.

Dean had no reply.

"I hear you play the guitar," Mom said.

This seemed to comfort Dean. "Yes, Ma'am, I do,"
he replied.

"Well, where is it?" Mom asked, expectation in her
voice.

"Well, Ma'am, it's in my mamma's car," Dean said.

"Well, whose car are ye drivin' tonight?" Mom
asked.

Dean grinned. "Only car I got is my mamma's,
Ma'am."

"Well, what are you waitin' for?" Mom asked. "Go git the damn thang."

When Dean returned, his nerves had calmed. He almost seemed excited.

Yes, Mom was drunk, but Kate wanted to hug her. She could tell that Mom was trying, in her own way, to make Dean feel welcome. They didn't go anywhere that night. Mom and Dean played songs they both knew by heart on their guitars, and the girls sang. They hadn't done anything like this with Mom for so long that Kate couldn't help but feel Dean was good for their family. She didn't want to put any pressure on him. After all, he was just a kid like her, but she couldn't help but feel like he belonged.

Surprisingly, Dean, when he was leaving late that night, admitted that he liked Mom. "I mean, I know she's a drinker, but she's fun too. Ya gotta admit it," he said, smiling. He was standing on the front porch holding his guitar. Kate couldn't help but fall a little more in love with him. He was the most handsome boy in the world at that moment.

He even made my drunk mom fall in love with him, she was thinking to herself. *That takes some charm. He could've left with me and maybe even gotten lucky, but instead he spent the whole night with my mom playing old songs on the guitar with her. He must really love me.* The thought made Kate feel like she never wanted to let Dean out of her sight again, but she had to let him go eventually.

For the first time in a long time, she didn't have to make herself not think of Tommy when Dean left that night. Dean was the one who dominated her thoughts. Over the past few months, she had thought of Tommy less and less. She still missed him, but a little less every day. And she fell in love with Dean a little more every day. Not just Dean, but his family. He had five brothers and sisters, some older, some younger.

Kate found Dean's family endearing. Every child had a responsibility they took very seriously. Their mother, Joan, worked two full time jobs and did all that she could do to provide for her children. Things had always been tight for their family, but since Joan's husband, her children's father, had passed away the previous year, things had been extremely difficult for their family.

Kate respected Dean and his older siblings for picking up the slack for their mother by working any odd jobs they could find to help with bills and living expenses, but, more than anything, she respected Joan. Even though times were hard for her, she kept herself together. She kept her family together. She was nothing like Mom; she had refused to let the loss of her husband destroy her.

Instead of giving in, Joan worked harder to make sure her children were okay. Kate couldn't help but admire Joan for the sacrifices she made for her children. She also respected the older siblings, not only for working to help pay the bills, but for making sure their younger siblings were taken care of when Joan was working. Kate loved Dean, but she also loved Dean's family, the way they looked out for each other.

She had gotten so comfortable around Dean that she had shared her struggles over the past few years with him. He had been unbelievably supportive, which only made her love him more.

Chapter Thirty-Two

Kate and Dean's relationship had been solidified in all but one way. The two had spent so much time getting to know each other that sex had been placed on the back burner, especially once Dean had figured out how old Kate was.

They'd been on a date, and Dean had asked out of the blue. "So, how old are you, really? And don't tell me you're sixteen. I've already figured out you're younger than Beverly, and I know she just turned sixteen."

The question caught Kate off guard. "How old are you?" she asked defensively.

"Almost eighteen," Dean said in that honest way he said everything.

"I'm almost fourteen."

Dean sat silently. "Oh, my God," he finally said. "I was afraid of that."

"What?" Kate asked.

"You haven't even gotten a driver's license," Dean said.

"So what?" Kate asked. "Does it make a difference?"

"Of course, it makes a difference, Kate," Dean said. "Why didn't you say something sooner? For God's sakes, I tried to --" his voice trailed off.

"It's not that big of an age difference," Kate tried.

"Yeah, actually it is."

"See, this is exactly why I didn't say anything. I knew you'd make a big deal out of it."

"It is a big deal, Kate!" Dean exclaimed, much more forcefully than she'd ever heard him speak before.

"No, it's really not, Dean. I've told you about my life. You know I had to grow up before I was ready. I've told you before that I haven't ever really felt comfortable around people my age."

"Yeah, exactly! That's why I thought we got along so well! I thought I was maybe two years older than you. But I'm almost five years older than you! Are you even in high school yet?"

"Almost! I will be next year."

"Oh, my God." Dean ran an exasperated hand down his face.

Kate and Dean's relationship became rocky after she told him how old she was. She felt stupid for not thinking about the age difference before. To her, it wasn't even an issue. She had always felt so much older than her peers.

Tommy, on the other hand, knew how old Kate was, and he had no problem with her age. Uncle John needed his services again come spring, which meant that Kate was forced to see him every time she dropped Mother off after her doctor's appointments. At first, when he waved at her, he was easy to resist. She remembered how badly he had hurt her the previous winter, and she wanted nothing more to do with him. But, after a few weeks of Tommy trying to get her attention, she finally gave in.

We're just gonna talk, she told herself, knowing she was in dangerous territory. She and Dean hadn't talked in almost two weeks. This made it easier for her to walk over to Tommy.

"Hey, stranger."

"Hey," she said, trying to play it cool.

"You still mad?" he asked, wearing that dangerous sideways smile.

"Mad about what?" Kate asked, feigning amnesia about the last time they had spoken.

Instead of answering her question, Tommy pretended he hadn't heard it at all. He closed the gap between them.

"Hey!" she yelled. "Has anything changed since the last time we talked?"

"Nope," was all he said, looking her straight in the eye.

Kate could smell the rain in the air. The dark clouds above were heavy, threatening to burst any second and soak them both.

Tommy didn't seem to notice when it started to sprinkle. His intense stare refused to let up, and Kate hated him for it, but she was at his mercy. She wanted to say no, but it wasn't in her to deny him.

This time, as she drove home, she didn't feel elated like she had after the first time. The rain poured down on her mother's windshield, and all she could do was cry. She loved Dean, and she had just betrayed him yet again. What was it about Tommy? No matter how hard she tried, she couldn't say no to him.

***

Kate decided to give up on men altogether. She had realized over the past few days that she was in love with two guys she had no business even speaking to, and she had decided the best thing to do was to cut them both loose. *I'm not even in high school yet*, she told herself. *If I'm gonna do anything with my life, I've got to take school more seriously, like Aunt Bobbie told me.*

Of course, Dean dropped by right after Kate came to this realization. It had been a few weeks since she'd seen Tommy. He'd tried to stop her the next time she'd dropped Mother off, but she'd refused to pay him any attention. *He's going off to school in a few months*, she told herself. *Stop now while it's your decision to make. You don't want to be one of those girls they write songs about who get their hearts broken.*

"I missed you," Dean said, standing on the porch. "I'm sorry."

"I missed you too," Kate answered. And she had. She'd missed him a lot. Since she'd denied Tommy, all she could think about was Dean.

Dean smiled at Kate's confession. The sun wasn't quite down yet. The days had started getting longer, a sure sign spring was finally there to stay. "Wanna go for a drive?" Dean asked.

"Yeah, I do."

After they'd driven all the dirt roads Wewoka had to offer, Dean pulled off on a deserted one. They sat and talked, and they decided their age difference didn't matter very much in the grand scheme of things.

"I tried not to think of you while we were apart," Dean said. "But I just couldn't help myself. Kate, I love you."

And she knew it was true. Her heart skipped a beat. "I love you too, Dean."

"I know you're young, and that's okay," Dean said. "I'm not in any hurry. And I want you to know that sex doesn't mean anything to me compared to what you mean to me.

The realization hit Kate like a ton of bricks: *This whole time he's thought I was afraid to have sex with him. He's not thinking about whether he can afford to fall in love with me. He just is. Whether he likes it or not. He just can't be anything else.*

This realization removed any reservations Kate had. She had no more doubt. She chose Dean.

Chapter Thirty-Three

In early May, Kate's school counselor called her in. "Kate, I called you in because a couple of girls have come to me and told me they've heard you vomiting in the bathroom, and I'm concerned about you."

Kate had learned to hate guidance counselors over the past few years. They always got in the way; they could never mind their own business, and they could never do anything to help her. All they did was make things worse every time they stuck their big noses in her business. "Well, you don't need to be concerned about me. I'm fine," Kate countered.

"Honey, I can help you," the counselor said.

"Oh, really?" Kate asked snidely. She had realized late in April that she must be pregnant when she'd missed her period and started having morning sickness. She made up an excuse to take the car into town and went straight to Dr. Smith's office. It was the only place she could think to go for help.

"I need to see Dr. Smith," Kate had told the secretary.

"Do you have an appointment, hon?"

"No, but if you tell him I'm here he'll see me," Kate said.

"You're Mae Smith's granddaughter, right?" asked the secretary.

"Yeah," Kate responded, relieved that the secretary knew who she was.

Ten minutes later, Dr. Smith entered the waiting room. "Katie Rhea!" he bellowed, happy to see her. "What can I do for my favorite girl?" he asked, all smiles.

"I need a favor," she had said.

***

Dr. Smith, obviously disappointed, but desperately attempting to hide it, took Kate's blood, told her to come back in two weeks, and swore his undying secrecy.

***

"Yes, I can help you," said the school counselor.

"How?" she asked. She already knew she was pregnant. The big question now was who the father was. If she was any more than four weeks along, she was in trouble. If the baby was Dean's, she knew she could count on him. If it was Tommy's, well, she was on her own.

The school counselor cleared her throat. "Well, Kate, I hope I'm not overstepping my boundaries here, but I'm going to assume you're in *trouble*." The counselor's emphasis on the word let Kate know this woman wasn't as stupid as some of the other counselors she'd come across in the past. Before Kate could deny it, the counselor hurriedly continued. "You don't have to answer me either way. Just hear me out."

Kate listened intently.

"Sometimes, when a girl finds herself in trouble, she has options she doesn't know she has." The counselor looked at Kate knowingly, begging with her eyes for Kate to follow her line of thought.

"Okay..."

"Well, there are plenty of couples out there who are willing to adopt. If I were dealing with a young teenage girl who found herself in a situation where she might need a service such as this, I might be able to put her in touch with someone who could help her. The girl would know her baby was being cared for and loved, and she could finish school, have a chance at a real future. No one would ever even have to know if she didn't want them to."

Kate had never considered the possibility of adoption. *This might be a way out*, she thought.

Kate had been watching Beverly, who was, by this time five months pregnant. It did not look enjoyable. All she ever did was sleep and vomit and cry. Mom knew, but she never said anything outright. Kate had tried to ask Beverly about her plans, but she would only say she was fine and that her boyfriend Mark was "making arrangements" for them. Kate did not want some guy, no matter how sweet he was, and some damn kid "making arrangements" for her life. She had plans, or at least she wanted the option to have plans. She had no intention of being tied down by some squalling, helpless kid. Kate had her fill of taking care of other people. She had promised herself before she'd found out about the pregnancy that after Mother didn't need her anymore, she was going away to somewhere she only had to worry about herself. She was sick of putting everyone else's needs before her own. If Dean wanted to come along, great. If not, she had gotten over Tommy, and she could get over him too.

When she returned to see Dr. Smith, he told Kate what she had already known: she was pregnant. By the doctor's best guess, she was between six and eight weeks along.

"Well, honey," Dr. Smith said with a sigh. "I sure am sorry for ya."

"I know. Nothin' I can do about it now," she replied with a shrug, attempting to lighten the mood.

"Well, maybe not nothin'." Dr. Smith's voice trailed off.

Kate looked up, surprised. "What?" she asked, desperation in her voice. "Is there something I can do?"

Dr. Smith looked away. "*No*," he said forcefully. "Nevermind. Forget I even said anything. Even in the worst circumstances, it's not an option.

"But, Dr. Smith, I don't have any options!" Kate pleaded. "Are you saying you could get it outta me?"

Dr. Smith took a step back and sighed, sadness in his eyes. "Honey, I told you I wouldn't say anything about why you came to see me, and I won't. I need to tell you something, but I'm gonna need to ask you for the same thing in return.

Kate nodded.

"Years ago, I had a little gal come in here and ask me the same thing you're askin' of me. She'd got herself in a mess, and she needed my help. She'd took up with some ol' boy who'd been comin' around the farm trying to get her to pay 'im some attention. Well, she fell for 'im hook, line 'n' sinker. Few months later, he wudn't nowhere to be found, and she's in a whole mess a trouble. Said there wudn't no way she could tell her mamma an' daddy. Said they's good, wholesome folks and they'd disown 'er if they found out. She was such a sweet little gal that I couldn't tell 'er no. You remind me a lot of her." Dr. Smith looked Kate in the eye, pensive, pleading for her understanding. He sighed again and continued.

"I done what she asked me to. The procedure was simple enough. Everything seemed like it went fine. A few days later I got a call from her mamma and daddy. They were frantic, beside themselves. Said she'd been in some sorta accident and was unconscious."

Dr. Smith's story sounded somehow familiar to Kate, but she was so wrapped up in her own problems she didn't have the patience to hear about some other stupid girl who had gotten herself into the same mess Kate had gotten into. *God, I wish he'd get on with it*, thought Kate. *Maybe if I just humor the old man, he'll decide to help me to get rid of this problem.* She pretended the best she could to be interested, hoping he would take some mercy on her when he was done with his story.

"Well, when I got to her, I knew she was in distress because of what I'd done. The accident was just a coincidence. But she had sworn me to secrecy; I couldn't say or do anything to help 'er without her mamma 'n' daddy findin' out." Dr. Smith stopped here and looked Kate in the eye. "I was worried sick about that little girl. Didn't know if she'd make it, to be honest, but I'd gotten myself into a pickle. I couldn't do much more than nothin' for 'er without gettin' us both in trouble.

"Well, long story short, she ended up makin' it, thank the Lord, and went on to marry a nice boy and have 'erself some beautiful babies when the time was right. But for those three days, Katie Rhea, I just about went outta my mind thinkin' about what could happen to that little girl. And at my hands. I swore that if she ever woke up, I'd never again play God, and I've kept my promise all these years.

"Only time I've ever wavered was when I saw the results of the pregnancy test on you. You're just so young, kid. And you're not gonna have much help from your mamma, that's for sure." Dr. Smith forced a sympathetic smile and patted Kate on the shoulder. "I thought I might be able to help you, sweetheart, but as soon as you walked in here today I looked at your little face and realized there wudn't no way I could put you at risk like that."

Great, thought Kate as she left Dr. Smith's office. She'd had had sex with Tommy for the last time and with Dean for the first time within two weeks of each other, so Dr. Smith's test told her nothing. *How am I going to know whose baby this is inside me? It doesn't matter anyway*, she told herself. *No matter what, I'm giving it up for adoption.*

***

Kate fell into a deep depression over the next few weeks. When her sisters tried to talk to her she ignored them. When Dean knocked on the door, she told the girls to tell him she wasn't home. She almost completely stopped going to school; every time she went there, she felt like all the kids were staring at her, talking about the pregnant eighth grader. Kate was humiliated, especially the last day she had gone to school.

She had been able to avoid Tommy. He was so much older than her, their classes were nowhere near each other. So, all she had to do to avoid his line of sight was to stay out of the cafeteria. She also realized he must not be looking for her either, and that was perfectly fine with her.

She'd already been having a bad day. She had been nauseous all morning and was having a hard time staying awake in her classes. Just when she was thinking it couldn't get worse, she rounded a corner, heading to her next class and there stood Tommy in the doorway, looking right at her. She turned to go in the opposite direction, but he caught up with her before she got too far.

Tommy walked beside her, but he didn't try to stop her. He looked straight ahead when he spoke. "We gotta talk."

"No, we don't."

Frustrated, Tommy stayed silent for a moment. Then, "Is it true?"

This time it was Kate's turn to stay silent. She marched straight ahead toward the school's main entrance. She was done with school for the day. She had been supposed to meet with the counselor again after lunch, but she'd had enough. She was going home.

"Wait!" Tommy shouted when they were outside. Kate had picked up the pace and was soon running, running away from the school, from Tommy, from her life.

Once he was out of sight she slowed to a leisurely walk. *Despite how shitty it's been, this is a pretty day,* she thought, desperate to think of something other than these problems she had created for herself. *Damn, for once I can't even blame Mom for how shitty things are.*

Kate had been picking up on a slow, steady change in Mom lately. She still drank. She would always drink. None of the girls held out hope anymore that she'd quit someday. But they could all see she was trying. One day she even had a real conversation with Beverly about where they were going to put the baby once it got there. Nothing big had happened, but all the girls could see Mom really was putting forth effort to change in her own way. *It won't last*, Kate told herself. *No way she's foolin' me again with that bullshit act.*

Lost in her own thoughts, Kate didn't notice the old farm truck roaring up beside her until Tommy was coasting at her pace, staring at her.

She sighed, "Whaaat, Tommy? What do you want from me?" She rolled her eyes.

"Just get in the truck." The words were clipped, but his tone was tender, so she got in.

Chapter Thirty-Four

"It's true, idn't it?" Tommy asked as soon as Kate had shut the door of the truck.

"Yeah, it's true." She looked down at her lap, unwilling to make eye contact even though she could feel him staring at her.

"Shit!" Tommy yelled. He hit the steering wheel with the palm of his hand.

Kate snuck a glance at his face. It was red. He was breathing hard.

"Nobody knows about you. I mean, they know about me, but they don't know about *us*."

Tommy looked at Kate. "I don't know what to do, Kate."

Kate couldn't help but laugh at this. "*You* don't know what to do? Well, boo *hoo*. Poor little Tommy doesn't know what to do," she spat. Now she was yelling. "*I'm* the one who's got this - this *thing* growing inside my body! *I'm* the one being made to feel like a piece of *shit* at school! *I'm* the one who'll be left here dealing with this shit while *you're* off at your fancy rich kid college! Oh, yeah, Tommy! You *poor* little feller! What *ever* will you do?" Kate could hear the mean, vile things coming out of her mouth, but she couldn't seem to stop.

"Kate! *Stop* it!" Tommy yelled over her. "You don't understand! My parents, you just don't understand what they're like."

"Oh, *right*. I don't understand. How *could* I understand? That's what you mean, isn't it? Go ahead, Tommy. Say what you really mean. I don't understand what it's like to have parents who care about what happens to me. That's what you want to say, isn't it? Is that why you liked me? Huh? You knew you could do whatever you wanted with me because I didn't have anybody at home who gave a shit about me?"

"Kate, I like you because you're you. I didn't even know anything about your family when I first saw you. God, you're so *stupid*! Why do you think I got that job on your goddamn uncle's farm? One of my friends saw me watching you one day and he knew your family had the dairy." Tommy sighed and looked away. "I asked for a job there because of you. I wanted to have a reason to talk to you." He stopped and looked at her.

"I know you're self-conscious about your mom and your dad and all that, but that's you, Kate, not me. I never even thought about that stuff. I only thought of you. I tried real hard to keep tellin' myself that I was just havin' fun with you before I left for college, but... but..." Here he faltered. His big, blue eyes seemed to be begging her to believe him.

Kate wasn't going to let herself fall for one word of what Tommy was saying. *He's just being nice to me because he doesn't want me to tell anyone about us.* She willed herself to look straight ahead.

She decided to call his bluff (At least, she told herself that was what she was doing.). "Okay then, what should we do? Do you have any suggestions?" Kate knew it was silly and naive, but she desperately wanted Tommy to say he would marry her and work on Uncle John's farm. She could work as a provider for Mother, and they'd raise their baby together and live happily ever after. But that was just a stupid fantasy. She shoved the thought out of her head just as quickly as it had wheedled its way into her brain.

Kate was almost relieved when Tommy suggested he get some money together and take her to see a man he'd heard of who would get rid of it for them. This she could deal with. It was what she was used to. *People will always disappoint you, Kate,* she thought to herself as she opened the passenger side door. *That's all you can ever count on.* "Go to hell, Tommy."

Shit! Kate wanted to kick herself before she was even out of the truck. *If I'd said yes, I could get rid of this thing and get back to my life. But screw him and his money! I'm not some whore he can just throw a little money at and get rid of!* She told herself as she watched Tommy drive away.

Kate's pride was hurt, and when she walked up to the house, she didn't notice the strange car in their steep, gravel driveway. But, as she neared the front porch, she couldn't miss the enormous woman knocking on their front door. Her hair was gray and pulled back into a severe bun. She wore a hideous brown, shapeless dress with white polka dots all over it. Kate stopped. This woman had the look of someone dangerous. A state employee, perhaps?

Mom swung the front door wide open.

"Ha-ay, Joyce. How are you?" Kate immediately disliked this woman. She pronounced Joyce "Joe-us" and she said the word 'you' like she was saying "yew." Kate was relieved after she'd heard the woman talk. *Not a threat, just an uppity bitch,* Kate said to herself. *This oughta be good.* There were not very many things Joyce was good at anymore, but putting a woman like this in her place, well, that was what Mom was born to do.

Maybe it was from years of listening to Mom talk about these kinds of women, but Kate couldn't stand them. She knew their type. They always exaggerated their Midwestern accents. It must have been because they were under the false assumption that it made them seem cute, or quaint. To Kate, it just made them seem ignorant. These types of women attended church religiously, and, yet, they were consistently the meanest people Kate had ever come across. Gossiping for them was a sport. She'd met plenty of them throughout her life, plenty of future ones too. They disgusted her, and they disgusted Joyce. *Huh, something we agree on. Imagine that,* thought Kate as she assessed the drama unfolding in front of her. She could see Beverly and Birdie peeking out the living room window. Nobody wanted to miss this show.

The woman continued after Mom only stared at her in disgust when she'd asked how she was doing. "I ain't seen you in church lately. Everything alright?" She asked nervously.

"We-ll." Mom dragged the word out, openly mocking the woman's practiced accent. "If it ain't Miss Evelyn Johnston, as I live 'n breathe! I guess you just come to check on us outta the goodness a yer heart. That it?"

"Well, Joyce, a lot of us at church been wonderin' about you 'n yer girls. There's been some thangs goin' around about Katie Rhea." She whispered that last part, but still managed to be loud enough for Kate to hear her plainly.

Must've taken her many years of practice to get that stage whisper down pat like that, thought Kate. She wasn't quite sure what she should do. She'd had a bad enough day already. The last thing she wanted was for Mom to go on a rampage when she found out about her.

"Now, I know you don't like people talkin' about you 'n' yer girls, so I come to check on y'all. That way, I could put those nasty rumors to rest for ye." The woman grinned widely, seemingly proud of herself for doing such a good deed.

Evelyn pointed to the brown Oldsmobile sitting in their driveway. "I thought y'all might want some food."

Mom's eyes became slits. "What in the hell would we want with your goddamn food? Mom looked the woman up and down slowly and asked, "You tryin' to lose some weight?"

Evelyn was stunned to silence.

Mom continued. "I got an idea. How 'bout you get your fat gossipin' ass in that jalopy a yours and go on back home to that fat, lazy husband a yers and those fat, ugly, worthless kids and mind yer own goddamn business? How's that sound, Evelyn?"

As Joyce was saying these things to Evelyn, she walked slowly forward, pointing her finger in the woman's face. Joyce was a good four inches taller than Evelyn, and she was an intimidating woman when she wanted to be, which was often. She got so close Kate knew Evelyn could smell Mom's breath. *Cigarettes and stale beer*, thought Kate as she listened, grateful to her mother for not letting this woman get a word in.

"They're sayin' she's pregnant, Joyce!" Evelyn managed as she was trying to navigate the porch stairs backwards, Joyce still advancing on her.

Uh oh, thought Kate. She expected Mom to turn her murderous gaze from Evelyn to her, but Mom surprised her. She just kept right on backing Evelyn toward her car. Evelyn's round face was red and wet with sweat., her eyes round with fear.

Evelyn's words came out in a rush. "There's a couple." She had to pause to catch her breath. "At our church. Young. Sweet." She paused for another breath. "They're wantin' to adopt a baby."

At this, Mom stopped, stood up straight, blinked, and turned her head toward Kate. Then she looked sideways at Evelyn, tilting her chin toward her and squinting those hellish hazel eyes.

Shiiit! thought Kate.

"Oh, I see. You think that because we don't have as much money as this 'rich, successful' couple, they'll be better parents to my grandbaby. Is that what you're sayin', Evelyn? Well, I got news for you, lady! Joyce Bloom's grandbaby ain't for sale!" She screamed it right in Evelyn's face, then gave her another once-over with her eyes and smiled, amusedly for good measure. She turned on her heel, stuck her nose in the air, and strode back into the house slamming the door behind her.

Faced with the decision of whether to remain in the yard with Evelyn, who was still standing staring at the slammed front door with her mouth wide open, or follow Mom into the house, Kate chose the latter.

As soon as she shut the door behind her, she regretted her decision. Beverly and Birdie stood waiting, their arms crossed in front of them. "You're pregnant?" Birdie asked. She seemed more hurt that Kate hadn't told her than surprised.

Beverly said nothing. She only smiled.

"You keepin' it?" Mom asked matter-of-factly. Kate was shocked that Mom didn't seem even the least bit surprised.

"Don't know what else I'd do with it, Mom," Kate replied, not wanting to get into all the other options she was considering.

"Hell! I guess we're just gonna have us house fulla babies runnin' around here come Christmas then, ain't we? Guess there are worse things," Mom said.

She doesn't even seem mad, thought Kate, confused.

"Hand me my cigarettes, Katie Rhea. And run down to the store 'n' gitcher mamma some beer."

"Mom, you don't have any money."

"Well I'm sure you'll figure somethin' out. Now hurry up. I got somewhere to be tonight. And don't get them small cans again. I like the tall-boys." Mom dismissed Kate with a wave of her hand and busied herself by shaking each of the near-empty beer cans on the coffee table to see if she'd missed a sip somewhere.

Hope

Chapter Thirty-Five

Over the next few months, Kate tried to live life as normally as she could. She and Beverly fixed up the house as best as they were able. Kate had never seen her sister so hell-bent on cleaning every corner, every piece of furniture. Mom even got involved. She'd disappear for a few hours and come home with baby clothes, diapers, baby bottles, everything the kids would need, by the looks of it. When the girls asked Mom where she was getting the money for all these things, she'd grin and tell them she had her ways.

School had let out. Kate was grateful there weren't so many prying eyes boring into the back of her head anymore. The hotter the temperature got that summer, the bigger Beverly seemed to get. Kate had barely started to show so she could ignore her situation for a little longer. She found it strange that with all the baby talk around the house, she felt nothing for the thing that was growing inside her, except maybe contempt.

At first, she'd hoped maybe she would have a miscarriage. But she knew the farther along she got, the less likely that was to happen.

Dean never gave up on Kate. He stopped by the house once or twice a week, but she refused to see him. He knew by now she was pregnant, and he assumed the baby was his. Every time he came by the house, he brought some small baby item. Diapers, a rattle, little pink booties. When Kate's fourteenth birthday came in July, he brought the baby a frilly pink dress. She guessed this meant he thought it was a girl. Even though they were sweet gestures, Kate couldn't even bear to look at Dean. He reminded her of all the mistakes she'd made.

Watching Beverly was even worse. Kate could not imagine she was going to look as grotesque as her sister did in only a few months. It made her sick to her stomach. She hated what was happening to her body. When the thing inside her started moving she didn't think she would be able to stay sane. She had no desire to feel it fluttering around inside her, mocking her. She wanted to scream every time she felt it.

The temperatures soared in August. On some days the air was so thick with humidity Kate felt she could barely breathe. Beverly was miserable. Her feet and hands had begun to swell, and she had started craving the strangest foods. By this point, at almost six months along, Kate, too, was obviously pregnant, though not nearly as noticeably as Beverly was.

"Kate, I want something cold," whined Beverly. "I'm dyin' from this heat!"

Birdie wiped sweat from her forehead. "Come on, Kate. Let's take her to the store. A popsicle would be so good right now. I'm not even pregnant, and I feel like *I* might die, it's so damn hot!"

They had been sitting around a fan they'd propped up in an open window, doing their best to stay semi-cool, but the house remained stifling.

"Pleeeease," begged Beverly. "We still have some food stamps left."

"Pleeeeease," echoed Birdie.

"Fine," Kate sighed. She hadn't been out of the house much since she'd started to show, but it was so hot, even she had to admit it was worth going out to get something cold.

In the grocery store, the freezer aisle felt heavenly. The girls lingered for as long as possible discussing their options for frozen treats in depth. It was a happening place on such a hot day. People came and went as the girls stood around soaking up the glorious cold air.

"Kate?"

The familiar male voice caught Kate off guard. *Tommy. Goddammit! I thought he'd have gone off to school by now.* Even as she was thinking these things, her heart leapt at the possibility of seeing him just one more time.

In the months since their last meeting, Kate had counted and recounted until she couldn't deny it anymore. She was not carrying Dean's baby. She was ninety-nine percent sure it was Tommy's.

Beverly and Birdie stood looking at each other, confused. In all the times they had talked about Kate getting pregnant, she had never even hinted she had ever even spoken to Tommy Jones.

"Er, hi," Kate said.

Tommy immediately looked down at her stomach. For weeks, she had been painfully aware of the growing bulge, but, as Tommy stared, she realized the thing was now visible to her in her peripheral vision. She tried to suck it in, but it wouldn't budge. *God, I hate this thing!* Kate thought for the millionth time. She pulled self-consciously at the hem of her shirt.

Tommy was a quick study. He noticed the girls' confusion and came up with an explanation for their knowing each other. "Uh, I work on the dairy for your Uncle John. I'm the one who helps Kate get your grandma back and forth to the car when she goes to the doctor. Well, I used to be. Until I had to quit. I'm leaving for college next week."

Kate's sisters seemed satisfied with this explanation. They appraised Tommy's fine physique, giggled and whispered to each other, stole glances over their shoulders, and then giggled and whispered some more.

Kate and Tommy waited in awkward silence until the girls had had their fill.

Finally, Beverly and Birdie grew bored, and they went back to perusing the ice cream, which called to them from behind the cool, glass freezer doors.

"I'm supposed to be getting my mom and sister stuff for ice cream sundaes. I'm not really sure what all to get. Would you mind helping me? They said something about nuts and cherries. I have no idea where that stuff is." Tommy eyed Kate meaningfully.

"Sure," she replied, catching Tommy's not-so-subtle hint. Looking back at her sisters, she said, "Y'all stay right here. I'll be back in just a minute."

Once they were out of earshot, Tommy asked, "So, how have you been?"

"I've been okay."

"You look good." Tommy smiled, gesturing toward her growing stomach.

Kate looked away embarrassed.

"So, I guess you've decided to keep it?" asked Tommy.

"No. I'm not keeping it, Tommy. I hate this thing inside me. I hate how it's taken over my life. I'm giving it up for adoption."

"Are you sure?" Tommy asked. "I mean, is that really what you want to do?"

Kate tried to stay calm. "What I want to do is go back and do things over again. What I want is to deal with the things normal fourteen-year-old girls deal with. But I don't have much of a choice, do I?" Kate looked at Tommy. There was no malice in her eyes this time, only resignation.

"Kate, I want you to know I'm sorry. I didn't mean for things to turn out the way they did for you. I want you to know that if I could change things, I--"

Kate cut him off here. "Tommy, stop. Just stop. I'm giving it up for adoption. I'm a kid; I can't *raise* a kid. And I don't want you to have to worry about it. I know I was mean to you the last time we talked, but I don't have any hard feelings; I mean, it was fun while it lasted, but neither one of us wanted this to happen. Shoot, we're *both* kids. This thing'll be fine." Kate gestured toward her stomach. "I'm sure somebody'll take it and give it a better life than we ever could've."

Tommy looked at Kate, regret causing him to appear much older than his years. "Y'know, I'll be all the way in Virginia. It's not like I'll get to come back very often and visit. I sure would like to see you though when I do come back."

Kate smiled sadly. "Tommy, I don't think that's a very good idea." She wanted to say yes, but, even though she was young, she was not naive. Kate knew that her sitting around waiting and hoping that Tommy would show up to see her twice a year was no way to live. "You'll have a life there. You'll make friends. You'll meet girls. In a month or two you won't even remember me."

Tommy clenched his jaw and pretended to be checking out the neat rows of colorful pickle jars cleverly displayed in the aisle they had wandered down.

Kate watched the silhouette of his face contort, and she thought he might be on the verge of tears. *Why?* she wondered. She watched his nostrils flare slightly and she could see from her angled view that his brow had wrinkled as well. She looked away so that he could collect himself and maintain his dignity.

"Yeah," he managed, after he'd regained his composure. "You're right." Tommy smiled that brilliant smile of his, the one that always put the people in its vicinity at ease. "You sure are smart for bein' so young."

"I know," Kate joked, relieved the mood had lightened.

But it seemed like the moment the mood was lifted, it fell again when Tommy asked, "Will I get to see you again?"

Kate attempted a smile and said, "Probably not. But, hey, we'll always have the barn, right? I think memories are underrated."

Tommy laughed, and Kate felt a rush of sadness, realizing suddenly this would probably be the last time she ever heard that sound ringing in her ears, the last time she would see this beautiful boy laugh, her final intimate moment with him.

Standing there in the pickle aisle of a grocery store, six months pregnant, Kate realized, too late, and, in a way, too early, that love is never simple, and it's often disappointing in the end.

Chapter Thirty-Six

Kate's grocery store encounter with Tommy spurred her to come up with a plan. The more she watched Mom and Beverly prepare for the arrival of her baby, the more convinced she became there was not one single bone in her body that wanted to keep this baby. But who was she going to give it to? Even though she didn't have any maternal feelings toward it, she didn't want it to suffer. She wanted it to go to a good home.

That's why, as soon as school started, even though she had no intentions of going back in her current state, she got herself dressed and made herself go.

"I'm here to see Mrs. Crenshaw," Kate told the secretary, hoping she looked more confident than she felt.

"Is she expectin' you, sweetheart?" the secretary asked, eyeing Kate's swollen belly.

"No," Kate replied. Then she hurriedly added, "But if she's busy I don't mind waitin'." She did not want to have to go back there again. She was determined to get this taken care of that day.

The secretary smiled sympathetically. "I'll let her know, sweetie."

She didn't have to wait very long. Fifteen minutes later, Mrs. Crenshaw opened her door and called, "Kate?"

Startled, Kate jumped up out of the uncomfortable chair. "Hi," she said lamely as she lumbered into Mrs. Crenshaw's cramped office.

"Look at you!" Mrs. Crenshaw exclaimed as she closed her office door. "How are you feeling?"

Kate was taken aback by her school counselor's frank acknowledgement of her pregnancy. Normally people, especially adults, tried to pretend they didn't notice it. Even Mother refused to mention Kate's growing belly, although they still made their weekly trips to the doctor together. She was noticing that Mother was not big on discussing things that made her uncomfortable.

After Kate's conversation with Dr. Smith when he had explained his refusal to help her with an abortion, she had begun to wonder about the girl in his story. She sounded eerily familiar to Kate. The next time she picked Mother up for her appointment, she asked her to tell the story about Mom falling out of the back of the truck again.

"What do you mean when you say she wasn't the same after the accident?" Kate asked.

"Well." Mother thought for a moment. "Y'know, now that I think about it, she was actin' strange that whole week before the accident. Maybe it was even longer than that. She was just sa cranky. Couldn't even talk to 'er without her throwin' a fit 'n' runnin' off bawlin'."

Kate listened intently, gobbling up the story as she drove the familiar route to the dairy. When Mother paused, Kate looked over, nodding her agreement, encouraging her grandmother to continue.

Mother sighed, her chest visibly rising, then falling. "That was a strange time for yer mamma. It still don't really make any sense to me. After she woke up, it was like everything about 'er had changed. She didn't laugh no more, wouldn't hardly talk ta anybody. She didn't want to go anywhere. Now, of course, as time went on, she seemed like she got a little better. But she never was the same happy, outgoin' girl after that. Like it completely changed 'er whole personality somehow." Mother closed her eyes, shook her head and sighed again. "I never will understand it."

Kate did not immediately respond. She was too busy putting two and two together. The girl in Dr. Smith's story was Mom.

***

"I want to give it up," Kate replied when Mrs. Crenshaw had asked what she could help Kate with.

"Are you sure?"

"I'm positive."

"Well, you're in luck, young lady." Mrs. Crenshaw had brightened. "I happen to know a couple from my church. They're very sweet. Good people. He's actually a teacher here. His wife is an airline stewardess. They've been trying to have a baby for years, but it's just not in the cards for them. I'll bet they'd be tickled to death to adopt your baby and give him or her a good home."

Kate thought about this. She liked the sound of a teacher and an airline stewardess raising it. They would give it a home like the one Bobbie and John had tried to give her and Birdie.

"Sounds good. Let's do it." Kate felt like a weight had been lifted from her shoulders. She could return to her life, and she wouldn't have to worry about feeling guilty. She wouldn't have to wonder if it was being taken care of. She'd be free. "What do I have to do?"

The counselor looked at Kate skeptically. "Well, I guess the first step is for you to meet them."

"Alright," Kate said, relieved. "Set it up. Call him in his classroom right now. See when they can meet." She rose from yet another uncomfortable chair, preparing to leave.

"Wait a minute, Kate," the counselor requested when she saw that Kate was about to leave. "Are you sure you want to do this? These are good people. All they want in the world is a baby. I don't want to get their hopes up if you're just gonna change your mind. This is serious."

Kate locked eyes with Mrs. Crenshaw. "You think I don't know how serious this is?"

***

As Kate left the school, she felt light as a feather. She walked home in the oppressive heat, but not even that could dampen her mood. She had the urge to skip down the road, like she used to do with Birdie when they were younger. She smiled to herself when she thought about how funny it would be to see a pregnant girl skipping down the street. Mr. Knight and his wife, the people who might want to adopt the baby, must have been as desperate as Mrs. Crenshaw said because they set the meeting with Kate for the very next evening.

Chapter Thirty-Seven

Kate slipped out of the house easily. Mom and Beverly had roped Birdie into helping them set up the baby's crib, which Beverly's boyfriend Mark had brought over that day. He had been working double shifts at a local garage to save up enough money for them to get their own place before the baby came, but, just in case, they were going to set everything up at Mom's house. Beverly and Mark seemed proud and happy. Even though Kate did not envy them, she could see they were in love and genuinely looking forward to starting their life together.

Their good vibes must have been contagious because Mom was all a-flutter, excited a baby was on its way. She wasn't even drinking that much that evening. She could almost pass for sober. *Who knew?* Kate reflected. *All this time, all we had to do to get her to straighten up was get ourselves knocked up. Hmm.*

Charlie and Ann Knight were everything Mrs. Crenshaw had said they were. Kate, once she'd arrived at the restaurant downtown that was to be their meeting spot, was surprised to find she recognized Charlie. Not as Charlie, of course, but as Mr. Knight. He was the cool high school science teacher, the one all the kids liked. Kate had never thought of teachers as real people. They were just the voice at the front of the classroom. It had never occurred to her they had real lives, real problems.

Charlie and Ann were clean, bright-eyed professionals. They both looked to be in their thirties. They were all smiles and very attentive. She liked them immediately. She could imagine them being the kind of parents a kid would feel proud to call their own.

After the initial pleasantries, Ann got right down to business, which made Kate like her even more.

"So, Kate, how far along are you?"

"I'd say around six months," Kate responded.

"Oh, wow. So, you're due in late December? Early January?"

"Probably."

Ann and Charlie seemed confused for a second. "You don't know when you're due?" asked Ann, concern wrinkling her otherwise smooth brow.

"Well, I've added it up," Kate said, not wanting this hip young couple to think she was stupid. "If it's Tommy's, it's due in December. If it's Dean's, it'll come in January."

"Oh," Ann laughed nervously. "So, you haven't been to the doctor? And you're not sure who the baby's father is?"

"Well, yeah, I went to the doctor," Kate answered, offended that these people thought otherwise. "I went as soon as I thought I might be pregnant." Kate had promised herself she would be frank and upfront with these people. She had felt confident going into the meeting. She had something they wanted, and she wouldn't let them make her feel ashamed.

But, now, with all these questions, her confidence was beginning to falter. *What if they decide they don't want it?* she asked herself. *What will I do then?*

"But you haven't gone in for regular checkups? Have you been taking vitamins, at least? Taking care of yourself?" Ann asked, worry plain on her pretty, carefully made-up face.

Why do I feel like I'm in trouble all of a sudden? Kate asked herself.

Charlie must have sensed Kate was not happy about the direction their conversation had taken because he jumped in then. "I'm sorry, Kate. Ann's just nervous." He gave his wife a knowing look, and she put her hands in her lap and leaned back against the soft faux-leather booth, staring down at them, admonished.

Charlie continued, "It's just that we've wanted a baby for so long that we've sorta become neurotic about it." He laughed gingerly. He seemed like he was afraid they might scare Kate off. And he was right. "Ann doesn't mean to offend you. She's just nervous." Charlie smiled in a kind, paternal way that helped to disarm Kate.

I bet he'll be a good dad, she thought. Despite herself, she smiled.

"I take my grandma to the doctor every week. The doctor, he knows about me, and he tries to check on me without her knowing about me, uh… my situation," Kate said, attempting to placate Ann.

"Oh, so your family doesn't know?" asked Ann, no judgement detectable in her voice this time.

"Well, my mom knows, but my grandma's kind of old fashioned. She's sick," Kate added hurriedly. "I just don't want to make things worse for her." Saying this helped Kate to realize why Mom never said anything about being pregnant when she was a kid. Mother was a good lady. No person in her right mind would want to disappoint Mother.

"Well, that makes sense." Charlie's voice was sympathetic.

They talked for over an hour. When Kate left the restaurant, she felt better. Charlie and Ann didn't like not being able to contact her, but she had patiently explained to them that Mom wouldn't understand. Kate had decided that she wasn't going to tell her about the decision she'd made until it was over. If the Knights started coming around the house, her plan would be ruined. After the way Joyce had acted when Fat Evelyn brought up adoption, Kate wasn't taking any chances. She silently thanked Mrs. Crenshaw for filling her in on how these things worked. Even though Kate was underage, it was her decision to give the thing away if that was what she thought was best. Mom had no say-so whatsoever.

Chapter Thirty-Eight

Over the next few months, Kate's plan fell into place. She'd met with Charlie and Ann several times since their first meeting, and, as she'd gotten more comfortable with them, she'd told them about Mom - how she could make a scene and how she always managed to get her way - and they seemed to understand.

As Kate sat on the porch wrapped in her Mother Theresa blanket, smoking cigarettes, ruminating on the events that had led up to her current situation, she could hear Beverly's baby boy inside the house, crying. She had thought that maybe once Beverly had her baby, she would be tempted to change her mind about the adoption, but, if anything, it only helped to solidify Kate's decision.

Beverly had complained one day in early October that her stomach hurt. At first, Mom just shamed her and told her to stop whining. But, throughout the day, instead of the pain in her stomach subsiding, it only got worse. Finally, annoyed with her complaining, Mom had told Kate to run Beverly up to Dr. Smith's office to have her checked out. Beverly didn't think she was due for at least another three weeks, so no one considered the possibility of her being in labor.

Dr. Smith squeezed in Beverly almost immediately, being partial to Joyce's girls. Kate opted to sit outside in the waiting room. She hadn't been sitting there for very long when Dr. Smith appeared in his office doorway, harried, motioning for Kate to join him. And Beverly. And her *baby*.

"Kate, you girls are the strangest kids I've ever seen," Dr. Smith said as he swaddled Beverly's newborn baby. "I'll be darned if this gal didn't hop up on that table and push this baby out not thirty seconds after I walked in the room. I'm surprised she was able to get into a gown and get up on the table! Lucky I got here when I did to catch this little feller!" Dr. Smith laughed and shook his head as he handed Beverly her baby. "Never even heard a squeak out of 'er. In all my days I've never seen anything like it."

Beverly, flushed, but smiling, took her baby and gazed down at him tenderly.

Kate was disgusted.

***

After a short stay in the hospital, Beverly was now home with her baby, which was why Kate was sitting outside on the porch smoking cigarettes. She didn't want anything to do with that kid. And she sure didn't want to see Beverly. Every time she looked at her, all she thought of was giving birth.

As Kate was trying not to think of what was waiting for her, a car slowed in front of their house and turned to pull into the driveway.

Dean, thought Kate, panicking. *Shit*! She hurried to put out her cigarette and tried to get to her feet as quickly as she possibly could, but she was encumbered by her now large, rounded belly. So, resignedly, she gave in to the reality that there was no way she could make it inside before he could get out of the car. *Goddammit*! Kate thought. *Guess it's time to face the music whether I want to or not.* She'd been thinking about what she was going to tell Dean and settled on the truth, minus Tommy. She knew it would hurt him to find out she was giving it up for adoption, but she also knew it would hurt him more to find out it wasn't even his. As the car door opened, she steeled herself for what was sure to be an unexpectedly rough night.

Kate, however, had no idea just how unexpected this night would be.

Chapter Thirty-Nine

Even though it was dark, Kate knew immediately that the man who got out of the car wasn't Dean. For one thing, he had the gait of an older, tired man, not the spring in his step that a younger man always seemed to possess.

"Is that my Katie Rhea?"

As soon as she heard his voice, tears sprang to Kate's eyes. "*Dad?*" she asked, incredulous. "Dad?" Kate jumped to her feet in an instant, despite her cumbersome state. That voice was the best sound she had ever heard in her whole, entire life. She ran to him. He opened his arms wide and embraced her. She felt like a five-year-old again. Wrapped in his arms after so long, it was the best feeling she had ever had.

It had been years since she had even allowed herself to think about him. "Dad, where did you come from? How did you find us?" Kate sobbed into her father's chest. She hadn't felt that kind of safety in so long, it was like she had been starving to death her whole life and, for the first time, tasted food.

"Oh, my baby, my Katie Rhea!" To Kate's surprise, her father was sobbing just as hard as she was. Even though he was squeezing the life out of her, she never wanted this moment to end. *He's here. He's really here. Everything will be okay now,* she told herself. *Everything will be okay.*

Finally, Kate pulled away. She had to see her father's face, make sure he was real.

"You think there's anybody in there who'd want to see their ol' dad?" he asked, nodding his head in the direction of the house as he wiped away happy tears.

Kate immediately thought of Birdie. Though she was reluctant to share Dad with anyone, she knew Birdie would be beside herself with joy. Arm in arm, they made their way to the house.

***

Dad stayed with them for two weeks. Kate had never been happier. Mom, on the other hand, seemed extremely agitated the whole time Dad was there. She seemed skeptical of the reason they'd let him go.

"It's called pancreatic cancer," Dad had told them. "They say it's bad, but I've never felt so good in my life," Dad smiled. "I'm not too worried about it. I'm going back to Arizona to stay with your grandma and grandpa, and once I'm better, we can get on with our lives."

The illness sounded ominous, but Kate refused to let herself think about it. If Dad said he could beat it, then he could. She had complete faith in her father. He had said that, if she wanted to, she could meet him in Arizona once she got things settled, and she could live with him and Grandma and Grandpa Bloom. Birdie could go too if she wanted. They all could.

Beverly said that she would never leave Oklahoma because the father of her child lived there, and they were going to make a life together.

"Well, I can understand that," Dad replied patiently. "Maybe we can visit each other."

Beverly, appreciative of Dad's respect for her authority as a new mother, said that would be nice.

Mom never outright refused Dad's offer, but she never accepted it either. She had been on edge ever since he had come back to them. Kate figured she was ashamed of herself and how she had raised her husband's children, or, rather, failed to raise them.

Birdie and Kate, on the other hand, would have gone back to Arizona with Dad as soon as possible if it wasn't for the minor inconvenience of the thing that was holding up Kate's life, her happiness. Kate encouraged

Birdie to go ahead and go back with Dad, but, loyal to a fault, Birdie refused to leave her sister. "I'll go when you can go," she said.

Kate knew there was no use trying to change her stubborn little sister's mind. But, to herself, she thought about what a bad person she was. *I'd leave her without even looking back*, she thought guiltily.

Kate and Dad had a lot of private discussions while he was in Oklahoma.

As they sat on the porch one evening, enjoying the change of the season, Dad finally brought it up. "I see a lot of things have changed since I've been gone."

She had been dreading this conversation. Taking one last, long pull from the cigarette she'd been smoking, she crushed it beneath her foot and steadied herself. "Dad, I know you're disappointed." She sighed. There really wasn't much for her to say. She had no excuse for getting herself into such a mess. "I'm sorry. I'm not keeping it though. I promise I'm gonna make something of myself. I'll make you proud someday." Tears gathered in the corners of her hazel eyes.

To Kate's surprise, Dad laughed. "I was talkin' about you smoking cigarettes in front of your mom."

Caught off guard, Kate laughed too. But the laugh quickly turned to tears. She hugged Dad. "I'm sorry."

Dad hugged Kate back, hard, and whispered, "Oh, Katie Rhea, listen to me. You don't have a single thing to be sorry for. You've been surviving, kid. Don't think I don't see that."

"I know. I'm just so ashamed."

Dad pulled away from their embrace. "Look at me, Katie Rhea."

Kate leaned back so she could see the twinkle in her father's blue eyes. *He always has a smile for me*, she thought to herself.

"I love you. No matter what you decide to do, that won't change. And, y'know, sometimes the mistakes we *think* we make end up being the best things that ever happen to us. Some of our *mistakes* are what we end up treasuring most in life."

Chapter Forty

Beverly's baby cried nonstop the day Dad left. Kate didn't even mind it. She felt so melancholy as she watched him pull out of the driveway, the baby crying in the background seemed fitting.

She went into labor a little over a month after Dad had returned to Arizona. She'd been hurting all day and had gone to bed early that night. When the pain woke her, Kate knew it was time.

She'd packed a bag weeks ago. In the small zippered pocket within, there was a handful of change. Surprisingly, she wasn't scared at all. She was giddy with excitement. Finally, she was going to be able to put this nightmare behind her. She silently slipped on her shoes, grabbed her bag, and tiptoed out of the house.

The plan was for Kate to walk to the payphone a block away from her house and call Charlie and Ann. They would pick her up and take her to the hospital where she would give birth and then get rid of the thing before Mom and the girls even knew she was gone. When they finally figured it out, it would be too late for Mom to throw a fit or for the girls to talk Kate out of her decision. The papers would be signed, and there would be nothing any of them could do about it but accept it.

Then Kate and Birdie would be free to board a bus for Arizona and be reunited with Dad and Grandma and Grandpa Bloom. Birdie would forgive her soon enough, and Kate would be able to start over again in Arizona. *Maybe I'll go back to school*, she thought.

Kate's plans were altered when she stepped outside. There was snow everywhere. It was several inches thick on the ground, and Kate could barely see for all the fat white flakes swirling around in the air. She had to be careful stepping down off the porch. The steps felt like solid sheets of ice under her feet. *I should go back in and get a coat*, she thought, as she made her way carefully down the steps, shivering from the cold. But she knew she couldn't go back in. Normally, Mom, Beverly and Birdie slept like the dead, but with the baby waking up every few hours to eat, everyone in the house slept much lighter than usual. *I can't risk it*, she told herself. *If one of them wakes up, my plan will be ruined.*

Kate felt sure that if she was very careful she could make it to the payphone. She was barely out of the front yard when a wave of searing pain ripped from one side of her belly to the other. It hurt so badly, she had to stop. Despite the freezing night air, Kate was suddenly sweating. *Oh, God*, she thought. *What the hell was that?* This pain was much more intense than the uncomfortable cramping sensations she had been experiencing earlier.

After two or three more of these intense spasms, she found that if she doubled over and stood very still for a few minutes, the pain would subside.

For the first time, Kate found herself scared of the pain. *If it hurts this bad now, what's it gonna feel like when I'm at the end?* Kate was suddenly jealous of Beverly and the easy time she'd had giving birth.

Though it was only a little over three blocks to the payphone, it took Kate over thirty minutes to make her way there. Between the pains and the slick ground, she was starting to think she might never make it.

When she finally saw the light from the payphone, she wanted to jump for joy. She could see the thick snow blowing in little cyclones above the booth. She had to pause one more time to wait for the gripping pain to ease, but then she was there. *I made it*, she thought, triumphant. Despite another wave, she was grinning when she stepped into the phone booth and closed the sliding glass door behind her.

Kate picked up the receiver and dialed the number she had memorized for the occasion. She waited breathlessly. Nothing happened. "What?" Kate said out loud. She hung up the phone, reached back into her bag, and pulled out some more change. She dialed again. Still nothing.

Suddenly, without warning, Kate felt a warm gush of liquid between her legs. *Did I just piss my pants?* She asked herself. *I didn't even know I had to pee.*

What should I do? Kate asked herself. Her hands shook. Her whole body was shivering, and now her pants were wet. *I have three options*, Kate told herself. *One - I go back home and wake up Mom. But, if I do that, she will throw a fit for me to keep it. Two - I try to call them again and wait here like we planned. But what if I can't get ahold of them?* Kate pictured herself when the sun came up, naked from the waist down, covered in blood, and holding the thing in her arms to stay warm. *Three - I walk to the hospital. Surely, it's no more than five blocks.*

Kate immediately eliminated option one. She wasn't going back to wake up Mom. That left options two and three. After doubling over again from the pain, Kate counted her change. She had enough left for one last phone call. *If I can't get ahold of them, I'll walk*, she told herself.

Kate dialed carefully. Halfway through the process, she felt another wave of pain coming on. *I can do this*, she told herself, finding it ever more difficult to push down the panic that was rising in her throat. She tried to ignore the tightening of her belly, but it was so intense, that just as she dialed the last number, she dropped the receiver and fell to the ground.

Faces and voices faded in and out of Kate's consciousness. First it was Mom: "You big ol' silly," she was saying as she threw her head back to laugh. Then it was Beverly's baby, screaming, red in the face. Next it was

Birdie. "You should have told me, Kate. I could have helped you. What are you gonna do now all by yourself?"

Kate was dimly aware the pains were still coming, only faster now, more intense, roiling, angry, like a summer thunderstorm. But there was nothing she could do.

Still, the faces and voices faded in and out. "You should have let me help you take care of this a long time ago." It was Tommy. Kate watched as his face morphed into Dean's. "I would have loved you, Kate. I would have stood by you."

The voices faded, finally, but the faces still appeared and disappeared, floating above her in the phone booth. Kate was aware the glass walls were now covered in condensation. *My breath*, she thought, panicked. *That's my air. I'll die without it. I can't let it escape.* She tried to suck it back into her body, panting in and out. But her concentration faded when Dad's face appeared. He looked disheartened. He was shaking his head. Kate knew she had disappointed him, and it hurt even more than the hot knife cutting through her middle. *He's gonna die,* she thought. *I'm never gonna see him again.* But before she had time to dwell on this, Aunt Bobbie's face appeared in front of her. She was smiling, as usual. Kate couldn't hear Bobbie's voice, though she desperately needed to. Somehow, Aunt Bobbie spoke to her anyway. Her lips weren't moving, but Kate could hear her as clearly as if she was standing back in Bobbie's kitchen, talking to her in person. "You have to wake up, Kate," Bobbie said. "I know yer scared, honey, butchu have to wake up now. It's scary, I know, but everything'll be okay, sweet pea. I promise. Do you trust me?"

"Yes," Kate replied, hanging on her aunt's every word.

Aunt Bobbie gazed kindly down at Kate. "Take my hand, baby girl."

Kate tried to move. "I can't, Aunt Bobbie."

"Yes, you can, baby." Aunt Bobbie held her hand out in front of Kate.

"Come on," she coaxed. "Remember how strong I said you are? You remember that talk we had?"

"I remember," answered Kate breathlessly. "But I don't feel strong."

"Oh, honey, none of us feels strong. Didn' you know that? We're *all* lost. We jist go through life doin' the best we can, hopin' that every now and then we get somethin' right. Come on now. Take Aunt Bobbie's hand. You can do it."

With every bit of strength she possessed, Kate, not wanting to disappoint her aunt, held up a weak, shaking hand.

Bobbie grasped it and squatted down, getting her face as close to Kate's as she could. "I want you to remember somethin', little girl. You always gotta hold out hope. No matter what. You hear me? At the end of the day that's why we don't quit, little girl. Because we always have hope." Bobbie stood and yanked Kate to her feet with more force than Kate would have ever imagined her aunt possessed.

Kate felt herself floating. Then she heard a loud noise, like a car door slamming. She woke to find she was in the backseat of a car. She tried to lean forward to see Aunt Bobbie, but she didn't have the strength. She let her head fall back, and as she lost consciousness, she tried to recall what Aunt Bobbie had said.

Chapter Forty-One

"Kate! Kate, can ye hear me? It's Dr. Smith. Can ye hear me, Kate?"

Somebody lightly slapped her face in soft, repetitive patting motions. Kate was positive she could not open her eyes, but, if it would make Dr. Smith stop, she would try. Gingerly, she tested her eyelids. They fluttered. *I guess I'll try to open them then*, she thought, surprised she wasn't dead.

"There she is," Dr. Smith crooned, grinning like a proud father. "Thought we'd lost ya there for a minute. You ready to have a baby?" he asked.

The question brought Kate back to reality. Everything from the past few hours came rushing back. Kate looked around, taking in her surroundings. She was confused when she saw Charlie and Ann standing near her bed, worried looks on both their faces.

"It's alright," said Dr. Smith. "She's got a few minutes. Y'all can talk to 'er."

Kate, still assessing her situation, realized she lay in a hospital bed in a hallway. Dr. Smith was dressed in a green surgery gown and a strange looking cap. Another pain zoomed through her body, and she grimaced, bracing herself for the squeezing sensation that would feel like it was slicing her in half.

Charlie and Ann exchanged worried glances.

"It's alright, folks." Dr. Smith reassured everyone. "Hold on, Kate. Breathe. Look at me," he coached. "We're just waitin' on a room to be cleared out. This ice storm is not keepin' the stork away tonight! You're the third mamma we got in here tonight, Miss Katie Rhea." Doctor

Smith went on talking until he could see the contraction had loosened its hold.

Charlie, seemingly seized by an overwhelming urge, rushed to Kate's bedside. "Kate, we're here for you. No matter what happens, we'll be here for you."

Kate didn't know what to say. She was still very confused. "What happened? How did I get here?" she asked, breathless from laboring, but desperate to know what happened.

"You don't remember?" asked Charlie.

Kate shook her head. Another contraction overtook her, and she had to wait for it to subside before she continued. "I tried to call y'all."

Ann stepped forward then. "You did call us, honey. At least, we suspected it was you. No one would say anything on the other end of the line, so we decided to drive to the payphone and make sure you were okay." Ann broke off then, holding back tears. "There you were," she sobbed. "In that phone booth. Poor little helpless thing. I thought you were--" Here, Ann broke off, unable to continue.

Charlie picked up his wife's thought and continued it for her. "Kate, you are one brave young lady. We promise. We promise we will give your baby the best home we possibly can. We are honored you chose us." Charlie took Kate's hand and smiled down at her, obviously holding back tears of his own.

Kate wasn't sure what they expected her to say. She was the grateful one. These people were giving her another chance at life. They were taking on her burden. She wanted to tell them how thankful she was. She wanted them to know that she appreciated them, but just then Dr. Smith announced it was time.

Man, I'm glad I'm getting a room, she thought to herself as she was wheeled away. *I think I need to poop.*

Kate was surprised to find that she was not taken into a hospital room like the ones she had seen on television. This room was stark white. There were silver utensils on a table. And bright lights shone overhead.

Before Kate had a chance to comment on the fact that they had taken her to the wrong room, an urge overtook her. *Oh, my God, I think I'm gonna shit my pants in front of all these people*! Kate thought, panic snatching reasonable thought from her mind. "I have to go to the bathroom right now!" she shouted to anyone who would listen.

She started to try to get down off the bed and realized that sometime between the phone booth and the hospital, someone had changed her clothes. She now wore a hospital gown. Before the thought could completely register though, a sensation like nothing she had ever felt before erupted from her pelvis. She screamed. Dr. Smith rushed to her side.

"Hey now, sister! You're all right! I'll take care of you."

"This thing is ripping me open from the inside," Kate panted, sweat breaking out on her forehead. She looked up at Dr. Smith, pleading. "Please help me." By this time, Kate was crying. She was terrified. *I'm going to die*, she thought. *This thing's gonna kill me.*

"Kate, look at me, honey," Dr. Smith said. "You're already almost done. I bet you don't even have to push but two or three times and this'll all be over. Can you do that? Can you push real big for me two or three times?"

Kate shook her head. She was sweating profusely now. Unlike before, the pain wasn't coming in waves anymore. It was there. To stay.

Dr. Smith went down to the foot of her bed and looked between her legs. "Oh, yeah. You're there, Katie Rhea. You ready for this to be over?"

Kate shook her head up and down vigorously. *Yes, I'm ready for this to be over*! she thought.

"Alright, Kate. Listen to me. I want you to bear down and push as hard as you can! Push as hard as you can! Can you do that?"

Kate's mind wasn't even working at this point. She was like a robot. She did everything Dr. Smith asked her to do, no matter how much it hurt. She had one thing in mind: the finish line.

Dr. Smith was right. On the third push he told her to stop. Then he said the words she thought she'd never hear: "Head's out!"

Another push, and, simultaneously, Kate felt herself emptied, and she heard a sharp cry. *It's over*, she thought to herself, relief washing over her.

Kate had thought they would take it away as soon as it was born so she wouldn't have to see it. That was how Mrs. Crenshaw had explained the process to her. She'd said it made things easier for the "birth mother." So, Kate was speechless when Dr. Smith, smiling like an old goat, plopped the thing down on her chest. "It's a girl."

"That's against procedure, Dr. Smith," the young nurse who had been assisting him commented in a low voice, eyes wide.

Dr. Smith was looking right at Kate, the devil in his mischievous eyes, but he was speaking to the nurse. "What are you gonna do?" he asked. "Fire me? Hell, I'm ready to retire anyway."

The Front Porch

2016

He placed the last page upside down on top of the neat pile he'd been building. He sat silently clasping his hands between his knees and staring at the wooden porch planks beneath his feet.

"That bad, huh?" she asked.

"Does she keep the baby?" he asked.

"Yes."

The man looked up at her. The corners of his mouth turned up in a poignant smile. "I know."

Confused, she asked, "How did you know? Was I too obvious? I didn't think I gave away any hints."

"I know because I'm the man you're supposed to meet today. I'm your father."

She stared at him open-mouthed. She wanted to speak, but she was too stunned. She was afraid if she tried to talk she'd start crying and not be able to stop.

"I know I wasn't supposed to be here 'til four, but I was so nervous about meeting you that I got in my car at four o'clock this morning and just started driving. I found a little park around the corner and sat there for almost two hours trying to figure out what I'd say to you when I finally met you.

"It all sounded so - I don't know - so - *inadequate*, I guess. I couldn't sit at that park any longer, so I thought I'd take a walk and go by your house to make sure I had the right place and maybe get a peek at you. When I saw you out on your porch, I froze. I couldn't decide whether I should go ahead and show up or go back to my car and wait 'til four. But, when I saw you, I knew I couldn't wait. It had already been too long.

"I knew I'd be nervous to meet you, but I had no idea just how nervous until I started walking to your door. The closer I got, the more I started sweating and shaking and losing my nerve. I forgot everything I had planned to say to you by the time I got to the top step and saw your little face."

She tried to interject here, but the man, her father, couldn't seem to stop talking. She guessed he had been holding in what he was saying for many years, so she let him continue.

"Before I got here, I had some serious doubts you were even the right person. But when I saw you sitting there, lost in your own thoughts, I knew. I knew you were my daughter. Yeah, you look a lot like your mom, but I see a lot of my mom and my sister in you too. You're so beautiful. I know I have no right to be, but I'm just so proud of you."

Still in shock, she listened to every word, amazed. *How could I not have known?* She asked herself. The whole time he was talking, she studied his face, trying to find a piece of herself in his features, his mannerisms, anything. But she was so overwhelmed with emotion that she was unable to concentrate on any one thing long enough to find any resemblance. "I'm glad we met like that. I think," she laughed.

He laughed too, relieved.

After the tension lessened a bit, it was easier for them to talk. "I want you to know," he said, "I thought your mom was giving you up for adoption. The last time we spoke, that was what she had decided to do. I had that scholarship waiting for me in Virginia, and school was about to start. I thought it would be better, easier on her and me, if I left. I thought it'd be easier for her if I just made a clean break.

"I went back home during Christmas break of my freshman year, so I was in Wewoka when you were born."

Her father looked away for a moment. She knew that look. He was trying not to cry.

"Here's somethin' I bet you didn't know. Your aunt Beverly knew a lot more than she ever said. She woke up that night when your mom left to go to the hospital. Out of the blue, I got a phone call in the middle of the night. She said your mom had gone to the hospital. Well, I rushed down there, thinkin' I was gonna tell her I loved her, and I wanted us to make a go of it. But when I got there, those people who wanted to adopt you were standing in the hallway with your mom talking about how they were gonna give you a good life. Your mom seemed happy they were there. So, I turned around and left. I cried all the way home." Here he paused, took a moment to collect himself.

"I left after Christmas and did my best not to think about you. But, no matter how hard I tried, I thought about you every day. I wondered what you looked like, how you were doing...if you were okay.

"After I graduated from school, I came back for a while. You wouldn't remember it; you were still so young. But I went to your house and knocked on the door. Well, first I went to see your Uncle John. He told me where you two lived. What he didn't tell me was that your mom was married. And her husband did *not* want me anywhere near you or her. He made such a scene, yelling, calling me names, trying to fight me. We ended up in the front yard, and you and your mom were standing at the front door watching all the commotion. I only got to see you for a few seconds, just a glimpse of you. And, as soon as I saw you, I knew I'd made a mistake I could never put right." He sighed. "I don't know what I was expectin'. I guess I thought you'd instinctively know I was your dad and come runnin' to me. But I could see it in your eyes. I was a stranger to you."

She didn't say anything, but she had a vague memory of the day her father was referring to. She and her sister had discussed it at length. They had tried many times to investigate and figure out who the strange man was, but to no avail. Their mother refused to talk about it. The only thing she remembered about that day was that the man kept repeating over and over, "I just want to see her."

Her father shook his head, and a single tear rolled down his cheek. "I want you to know that I have no illusions. I realize we won't be spending holidays together or anything like that, but I thought you deserved to know. I wanted to give you the chance to confront me, to say all the things you've probably been thinking about me. I deserve it. All of it. And a helluva lot more. I just want you to know I'm truly sorry."

She smiled. "I appreciate you coming here. You didn't have to do that. A lot of men wouldn't have."

"Well, it took me long enough, so don't be too appreciative. I'm just so happy you turned out to be such a lovely woman," he said, almost inaudibly. "I'm glad I wasn't around to mess that up for you."

"Well, I'm not gonna lie and tell you it was a bed of roses," she replied, shaking her head back and forth, busying her hands by picking at her cuticles. "We had it rough. And the man at our door - my step-dad - he was not a good man. I coulda used you, y'know."

"I am so sorry. I didn't realize it was bad for you. But, you're right. If I'd have stuck around and done what I knew was right, I would've realized."

"Yeah, that's very true. But who knows? If I'd had a perfect childhood, I might not have turned out to be the person I am today. And, even though it wasn't perfect, I'm honestly happy with the person I am today. I'm glad I'm so close to my sister. I can't say for sure we would've ended up so close if we hadn't been through so much together. And I wouldn't risk the relationship I have with my sister for anything in this world.

"Also, you have to give yourself a little credit. You didn't know she was gonna keep me. She told you she was putting me up for adoption. I'm sure you thought I was going to a good home."

"Well, either way, you were my child. And I should have fought harder for you."

"Hindsight's twenty-twenty, right?"

"Right."

"It's not too late, y'know. For us to have something to do with each other, I mean. I have a million questions. We might not ever have the typical father-daughter relationship, but it'd still be nice to maybe get together every now and then. Maybe meet the rest of the family? Do they even know about me?"

"They do. I told my father about you years ago. Man, he would love to meet you. Of course, my wife knows about you. And I think my sister's always known. She's said things here and there throughout the years. She was never the type to stick her nose in other people's business, but I think she knew. I have a sneaking suspicion that my sister is the one who told your aunt Beverly about your mom and me.

"I'd be happy to have any kind of relationship you were comfortable with, young lady. I figured you wouldn't want to have anything to do with me. I'd be honored to stay in touch with you." He sounded sincerely pleased.

"Well, okay then." She nodded, delighted that her father wanted to get to know her, happy that they'd met the way they had.

"It's getting late, and you still need to write the ending to that book. And I don't want to wear out my welcome," he said, standing, preparing to say goodbye. "Did meeting me help at all?"

"You know," she said, puzzled, "I'm not sure if it helped with the ending to the book or *not*. But it sure helped me. As she stood to walk him to the edge of the porch, it was as if a dark cloud had lifted from her life.

"I know it doesn't matter what I think." He stepped down the porch steps. "But, even though I'm proud to have a schoolteacher in the family, I'm even more proud that you're goin' for it. Working toward your dreams, your real dreams. That takes guts. It's not for the faint of heart, that I know. You're a talented woman. You really are. You sure can spin a yarn." He winked. "Don't give up on that," he said.

She smiled. "Oh, don't worry. I won't. I don't think I could if I tried."

And then the man, a little less of a stranger now, turned to go. But, as he reached the last porch step, he turned. "It was nice to meet you, Hope."

"Nice to meet you too, Tommy."

Hope reseated herself, watching her father walk toward the road, marveling at what had just happened. *I cannot wait to call Hannah. She'll never believe me.*

As she sat, trying to digest all that had happened, it occurred to Hope that her visit with Tommy had helped her to remember what her little sister really meant to her. As she'd said the words to her father, she'd known they were true. Hope wouldn't risk her relationship with Hannah, her little sister, for anything in the world, not even a life that included a father.

A rush of clarity hit her, and she realized how lucky she was, how fortunate she had been all along. She realized that sometimes the happy ending has been there all along. All that's left is for us to see it.

Hope wiped a tear from her eye, smiled, and turned back to the waiting laptop to finish her novel.

Chapter Forty-Two

It was December 23, 1975. Kate looked out the window. *Still snowing.* She wasn't in too much pain, physically, anyway, but she was in agony, emotionally. She finally had to admit to herself that he wasn't coming back for her. She'd had this childish fantasy throughout her entire pregnancy that Tommy would give up his scholarship, come running back to her and tell her he wanted to marry her and raise their baby together. But nothing slaps a person in the face with the hard, stinging hand of reality like giving birth at fourteen. *What should I do? I can't take care of a baby. I'm fourteen years old. My mother is a raging alcoholic. We have no money. I will have exactly zero people to help me. Well, not zero. There's Beverly. She has a baby. She can help me to figure things out. And there's Birdie. And Dean... I know he loves me. And he was so excited when he thought we were gonna have a baby together.*

Of course, I should do what's right and give this baby a good home. That's what makes sense. Charlie and Anne are good people. They would give this baby a life that I could never give her. I can't believe I'm even thinking about keeping her. But, then again, wouldn't her life with them, no matter how easy it was, be a lie, sort of? Yeah, Charlie and Anne are good people, but they're not her people.

Kate wished for a moment she had never even seen the baby. But as soon as she was born and they made eye contact and she held her in her arms, she knew deep inside she could never give her up. She counted the tiny baby toes. Ten. She counted her tiny fingers. Ten again. She listened to her soft, even breathing, felt the weight of her warm little body snuggled next to hers. There was an instant, unexplainable connection. Kate was powerless against this tiny little thief who had stolen her heart.

It would have been easier if she'd never held her, never smelled the top of her head, never looked into those sleepy blue eyes, but she had. *Oh, Kate*, she thought finally, *be honest with yourself for once. You already knew what you were gonna do the second you saw that baby's face.*

I just can't give her up. The poor little thing's already got two strikes against her. But I know I can give her a good life. I already love her. I'll love her forever. That's all that's important. Isn't it? Everything else, we'll figure out as we go.

She had never even let herself think about giving her child a name; she'd never even let herself think of this baby as anything but an "it," a "thing." It had always just been too hard. She had made up her mind a long time ago that she was giving it up. *What should I name her? I should take this seriously. It's got to be a good name. I mean, it's the only thing I really have that I can give her: a good, solid name.*

She thought about all the people in her life. Who had had the biggest influence on her life? That was easy: *Aunt Bobbie. Nah, I can't name her after my aunt. She wouldn't like that. It's got to be a strong name. Aunt Bobbie would want me to pick a name that makes her feel like she has some sort of say in who she becomes and how her life turns out.* She continued to think.

What was the best time in my life? When did I feel good about things? Again, Aunt Bobbie came to mind immediately. The time she had spent with Aunt Bobbie and Uncle John had truly been the best time in her life. She remembered feeling loved, feeling important when she was with them, feeling wanted. *Hey,* Kate suddenly realized, *I'm naming this baby. I'm really doing this. I'm keeping her.* For the first time in a long time, Kate felt right. She knew keeping this baby was what she was meant to do. It wouldn't be easy. She'd been watching Beverly over the past few months. Taking care of a baby was not a simple job. But she couldn't deny that this was the right decision. She couldn't explain it. It didn't make any sense at all. Yet, she knew. She just knew. *I'm gonna be a mom.* The thought both exhilarated her and terrified her at the same time.

Kate let her mind wander back even farther to the time right before they left Arizona to head to Oklahoma. That car ride had always been such a good memory for Kate. There was a feeling in the air, a feeling that started the day they left, the day Kate and her sisters sat in the car outside their old school waiting for Mom to come out so they could start their journey home. She remembered watching Mom walk out of the school with a spring in her step. She remembered feeling happy. *No, not happy,* she thought.

Suddenly, she remembered everything about that day and the way it had made her feel. She remembered the heat of the day, the anticipation she felt waiting on Mom to come back to the car. She remembered her thoughts, the way she had felt right before they pulled out of the grocery store parking lot. She hadn't recognized the feeling that had stuck in her throat. But then it had come to her: *Hope maybe?* she had asked herself.

***

A few minutes later, a nurse walked in. She wore her white uniform too snugly and the front collar dangerously low. Her hair was a brassy red, and her make-up had been applied with a liberal hand. As she bustled around the room, neatening this and tidying that, she asked, "How ya feelin, sweetheart?"

"I feel really good," Kate answered. "Really good."

"Well, that's good to hear!" smiled the nurse, a little too sweetly. "That nice couple's out in the waitin' room, y'know. They're ready to see the baby." She waited expectantly, then said, "I think you are so brave. You're doin' the right thing, hon."

"They're not seeing the baby," Kate asserted.

Surprised, the nurse stopped pumping the blood pressure cuff she'd placed around Kate's arm and craned her neck so that she could look Kate in the face. "Honey, what are you talkin' about?" she asked, confused. "They're ready to take their baby home. You can't do those nice people that way. And besides, don't you want that little ol' thing to have a better life than what you've had? You don't want her to end up in the same predicament as you when she's your age, now do you? You're a fourteen-year-old girl. Don'tcha wanna get on with your life and get back to doin' the things other girls your age are doin'?"

Lord, thought Kate. *Where's Mom when you need her?*

If she'd ever learned anything from Joyce Bloom about dealing with people like the woman perched beside her on the bed, now was the time to use it. Kate sat up straight, looked the nurse squarely in the eye, and channeled her inner Joyce. "I'm not giving her up. Do you hear me? She's *my* baby. And her *name's* Hope Bloom."

***

Mom came in to visit later that evening carrying a bouquet of familiar-looking yellow flowers. She didn't seem one bit surprised when Kate told her she had decided to keep the baby.

"Oh, Katie Rhea, I knew that's what you were gonna do the whole time," she claimed, a smile threatening the corners of her mouth. "I brought cha somethin'. These look familiar?" she asked as she held up the flowers.

Kate looked closely at the flowers. When the nurse had come in earlier, she had given Kate some pain medication, which had blurred her senses. She tried to concentrate. The flowers looked very familiar, but she couldn't place them.

"Golden Lantana," Mom said. We used to plant 'em in Arizona when you were little, remember?"

She did remember now that Mom had said the name. They were the flowers Mom always insisted on planting because they were tough. They held up in the Arizona heat.

"I figured you'd get more from seein' these than from some big speech from your mamma about how hard this is gonna be," Mom said sheepishly. "But we're all here for ya. I know that's not sayin' much, but I bet between the four of us we can get that little girl raised."

Kate smiled. "Thanks, Mom."

"You're welcome, Katie Rhea." Mom bent to hug her daughter. Though Mom seemed sober, Kate sniffed the air around her as they hugged. *Phew! Only beer*, thought Kate, relieved. *She's gonna behave herself while she's here.*

"I saw Dean out in the hallway," Mom commented too casually as she straightened back up. "We stickin' to that story?"

"What story?" asked Kate, feigning ignorance.

Mom flashed that sideways, knowing look at Kate that always seemed to say *don't bullshit a bullshitter* and said, "That baby's too pretty to be Dean's."

Mother and daughter held eye contact for a moment, and Kate answered, "That's the story we're stickin' to."

Without batting an eye, Joyce replied, "All right. I'll go get Dean."

As Kate watched Mom make her way to the hospital room's heavy, white door, she realized she was exhausted. Her eyelids had just started to droop when she was startled back into wakefulness. Mom had stopped short of leaving the room, turned and said her name.

"Yeah?" Kate managed, stifling a yawn.

"I never worry about you." Mom smiled. "You'll always make sure you're okay, and I know you'll always make sure that little girl's okay. You're strong, Kate. Yer just like yer mamma."

The End

About Kari Joyner

Kari Joyner's debut novel, *Bloom Where You're Planted*, is her first attempt at novel writing, but she has been teaching high school students to sharpen their writing skills for over fifteen years. She's also been sharing her love of reading with young people for as long as she can remember. She has estimated that she's read over 100 novels aloud to her students throughout the years because she believes hearing a good story when you're young can start a lifelong love affair with reading. Kari resides in Newcastle, Oklahoma with her husband and children.

Social Media

Facebook: https://m.facebook.com/Kari-Joyner-106062587632114

Twitter: https://twitter.com/kari_joyner @kari_joyner

Instagram: https://www.instagram.com/karijoyner/ @karijoyner5

Acknowledgements

First and foremost, I have to thank my family for passing down the love of a good story and the talent to spin a yarn. Without being brought up surrounded by exaggerators, gossips and tall tale tellers, I'd never have had the gumption to sit down and write this story.

I also have to say how grateful I am to my husband Mike and my kiddos, especially the two still living at home. There were a lot of "fend-for-yourself" meals eaten while I was writing this book - and not a lot of complaints. I love you guys! Mike, thank you for ever so gently pointing out to me the times I went on for too long or made the characters explain too much! I still can't believe you read my whole "girl book" - and liked it! And gave me some fantastic feedback! I am blessed to be married to someone who supports my dreams and encourages me to go for it.

And who could forget the girls? You guys are the best. I am so lucky to have such strong, supportive, empowering women in my life! Shari and Sharee, I was shocked when you showed up at my house right after I finished the book and stayed for the entire day and late into the night reading every word aloud with me so I could hear and fix my mistakes! Who does that?! Y'all are seriously the best. And Adrienne, I can always trust that you will give me your honest opinion. And thanks for telling me about your dream! I honestly don't know if I would have kept trying to publish the book if you hadn't told me! Jenna, thanks for pointing out the things I needed to fix about the church! I never would have remembered all those details!

Thank you to my kiddos: Masi, Luka, Owen, Katie, Kyle. I am so honored to be a part of your lives! You provide daily inspiration in all of my endeavors. Always remember that all I want for you is everything! Anything is possible, as long as you're willing to work for it.

Thank you to my school kiddos: your enthusiasm and wide-eyed advice were so refreshing!
Rich Shifman, you have helped me so, so, so much. Not only were you the best beta reader ever, but you *taught* me what a beta reader is! You taught me how to write a decent query, how to navigate the overwhelming world of submissions. I am in your debt, sir.

Solstice Publishing, I can't believe you're taking a chance on me! I am unendingly grateful for this phenomenal opportunity. I hope I don't let you down!

Made in the USA
Coppell, TX
24 May 2020

26003959R00157